Virgil Kills

Virgil Kills

Stories

Ronaldo V. Wilson

Nightboat Books

New York

ISBN: 978-1-64362-118-0

Design and typesetting by Rissa Hochberger
Typeset in Untitled Serif and Akkurat

Cover artworks by Ronaldo V. Wilson as follows:

Top Center and Bottom Right: *SBucks, January 21, 2020, Sacramento, CA*. 2020. Digital Collage.
Top Right: *VerveHeart, January 19, 2020, Santa Cruz, CA*. 2020. Digital Collage.
Bottom Left: *LPacific Heights, February 2, 2020, San Francisco, CA*. 2020. Digital Collage.
Top Left: *After MommaSpine, February 25, 2020, Santa Cruz, CA*. 2020. Digital Collage.
Center: *Come and Take It, March 7, 2020, San Antonio, TX*. 2020. Digital Collage.

Cataloging-in-publication data is available from the Library of Congress

Nightboat Books
New York
www.nightboat.org

CONTENTS

Virgil

Critique

Vestibule

Sacra

Line

FOR VERGELIO, THEN, AND NOW.

Virgil

Before they were both more famous than they are now, CeeR sent Virgil's collection of poems to Madge, another famous writer and editor, a person with whom Virgil would never talk to by telephone, but a person, nevertheless, whose comments by e-mail revealed her feeling that his collection was too weighed down by his dreams. Madge was unable to see the fun in the characters beyond a pressing trauma she observed in the writing, that the black father was an alcoholic—and, ultimately, that a drive couldn't be *fun* for these "abused" children. But the little brown kids, rolling around in the back of their Mom and Dad's station wagon, swerved around by their drunk driving father, were thrilled. In fact, they'd have been equally happy being jostled around in a total stranger's trunk.

Virgil realizes that dreams matter to him most because, in them, he feels somewhat sure he is present. This isn't epiphany. In the "novel," out of which he would model his own first major work, a little brown girl stares into both a crowded bus and a cage folded into a dream and, simultaneously, out of this dream into a "world," where she recognizes a caged gorilla, King Kong, an Ape? It didn't matter what it was. What mattered was that that big, black animal was, curiously, eating buttons.

Material Objects. Material Bodies. This is what often codes Virgil's dreams, and, in his world, anything can slip into any form, in and out of dreams, in and out of life: birds that rivet space, crickets that saw into the beating of the night. In the end, his world is not and is like the city where he just arrives by train, an ongoing slick of movement in which he can recall, riding along its surface. And when he awakes out of sleep into writing, blurrily seeing, Virgil enlarges the letters on his screen, and enters into what he thinks of fondly, as a return.

Malcolm meets Virgil in Penn Station, upstairs on the Amtrak level. In Virgil's unconscious, as in life, the station is long, a white stretch of tan-flecked floors, softly muted beneath Malcolm's feet. Malcolm is black, too, and, like Virgil, is split into what looks like a walking kaleidoscope for a second, a series of limbs with stuffed yet elegant bags shifting around her body, a moving antipode to the self, a slight explosion of her forming, and maybe this explosion of what she becomes is tied to the surety in her walk.

In the booth at Teaser's, Virgil discovers a monster. His face is tiny, and his hair is like corn silk. Does Virgil touch it? If only for a second, Virgil does, and the corn silk head moves, but its face is still, and below Corn-Silk's legs are black shoes that look like Merrells, but he can't quite tell if this brand is actual. Virgil gets down to it. The dick, itself, is not remarkable—that it is there is what actually matters. And he is asked, maybe by Corn-Silk, or another, maybe by Guapo: "Do you like the bush?"

Exploration is what he tries to explain to WinTrueLiar of his expectations, as a poet and critic, his need to know, to plot, to understand the source-work emerging from the object of exploration, but it is all so futile. In the end, Virgil doesn't even understand how to discern between the pronunciation of the word, *fu-tile*, to sound more like, *feudal*. The word's start hangs on his teeth and lower lip, the "f" like extra sulfur, packed at the tip of a matchstick, and no matter what, it pushes him closer to an understanding of the self that he may shore up, or release at will, *to light*.

Virgil is, for certain, in the city. Clean is there, too, and so is Butch. And one or all three of them are in the shower. Virgil slips Butch the white bar of Dove that Tallina, in Bikram, says makes him smell *so gentle*. What if Virgil said this back to Tallina? "You smell like, *whatever.*" Virgil sometimes feels his world is being held hostage and that, concomitantly, he is giving everyone what they want to hear, but in the end, he is not getting what he wants, though he does have everything he needs.

This is what happens: D_C asks Virgil, "That's all you have?" D_C looks down at the bag that contains a belt, maybe some wingtips, nothing really excessive, one pair of jeans, socks, undies, loosely laid in the small duffle. The sensation of his self is often split in these filled and half-filled bags, Virgil broken into realizations of scenes he carries around.

Sometimes it's simple. A black leather bag of varying size fades in and out of the dream. It shifts. It becomes both lost artifact, figure and anchor. Sometimes its unfurled release is more complicated. Like once, Virgil held his sister in the dream, all healed up from surgery, and he held her as he only did when she was a girl, and he, a boy. Or he is a thief, running about in a neighborhood, a white towel around his waist, fresh from stealing a newspaper from one stranger, only to return it to another, under a walkway, covered by an awning, stones on the roof, desert plants between pillars as he wakes.

For Virgil, dreams are not only telling in the sense that they reveal how much he is pulled from one field of anxiety into the next. They somehow keep him pointed in directions that echo his critical concerns. For instance, in one movie scene, a slave, of course, in a chain gang, is taunted by his master. As he is attempting to tie his shoe, he stumbles, and at the moment of his rebellion, or the thought of rebelling, he looks up and pushes the shotgun tip into the overseer's head, an act akin to a mistake, but the overseer's head, in any case, is blown to smithereens.

In another scene from a different movie, one slave tells another not to look at someone, a woman, a sheep, a hammer tie. Virgil does not remember exactly what it looks like, but a knife comes out. It's soon lost in the dirt, maybe behind a tree, and the Master, drunk, cannot retrieve it because he is too high, and a long string of spit comes out of his mouth as his slave, all at once, both runs away and tries to explain himself. For Virgil, these slave visages, hovering so adroitly in his sightline, never dislodge.

Perhaps it is out of this realization that Virgil tells himself he won't feel threatened through the rest of the day. No Explosions. No being Blown Away. How much does he want to reveal, and how much does he want to understand? All he wanted that morning, while watching the news with Butch, was to know from President Curious that the terrorists would be bombed by the U.S., "nuked" he gut-sung the word to Butch.

Virgil would, in fact, accurately forecast the event. "Basically, he'll say, *You tried it, and now we will destroy you.*" It's close to what WinTrueLiar told him over the telephone to describe his own self-assured nature—that, in the end, because he equated his art and academic productivity with B-Balling, that he would win at any cost, like Michael Jordan and like Kobe Bryant, that both of them, like him, were not interested in being liked, but only in being the best. And near the end of the conversation WinTrueLiar, a very established poet, said to Virgil, still mid-career, *"I will beat you."* But he wasn't talking directly to Virgil, more around him.

Virgil asks himself in the echoing of this, *What can I map?* In the city, the ground below him in the terminal contains a few bags shifting, some of them shared, all of them in various permutations of being filled, or not, all parts moving. Virgil does realize that the sound around him, a clap on a thigh, a gull sweeping, a brief coast below a forever sky, the mountains less a tug than a constant pull back into a source, an urgency he needs to return to, like the nightly ritual of putting in his mouth guard, his top teeth slipped over by hard plastic to keep him from grinding, and cracking apart.

Virgil, of course, is not like DerPrincipal, who is broad of back and so hairy, as if a human carpet, someone he would have fantasized about, in bed, as a child, a man he would want, at least, to touch for once in his life. But why does he feel that he needs to get so close to one body after the next, bodies that repeat his wanting to be so close to his absence in relation to their abundance?

One, who clearly smells like shit, has a walrus mustache, wispy white hair that splits into bangs above two eyes that leer forward into the elevated screens. He features a vitiligo cock, marbled up from the base, so that in the theater, his white dick looks black. And, another, The Army Ape, is tight but small, and soon will be on his knees. His butt is hard, rocked, and his body is "sick," is what Virgil wants to tell him, but he cannot say anything, not because he has nothing to say, but because he feels resigned to being silent in acting out this small advancement of desire.

However, DerPrincipal fucks up, makes a fatal error that reveals his most searing flaw. After begging Virgil to leave the Sugar Hole with him, he vanishes into another booth. Come join us. Come with me. Come into my Zombie Minefield. "I'm not good at being good," is what DerPrincipal confesses to Virgil, but Virgil cannot bear the statement, because it is a familiar one.

Virgil doesn't remember the name of his first boyfriend, but he does remember the "book" this "Analyst" wrote, and the section he was so proud of, the one in which he described a psychic breakthrough, when he pissed into the water, his aim to meet the bowl's center. For him, the loud splashing was magical, a revelation, a mark of his own freedom, no porcelain sides to silence his release, only the pot's water meeting his urine, a first music.

Maybe in "The Analyst's" self-involvement, Virgil would discover his own. Maybe in this reclamation of sound, celebration of a solitary, sonic stream, Virgil would recognize a path to his lurking towards being happy, and alone, ripped away from scrutiny.

In the Sugar Hole, The Canadian's body is like a golf tee, or in close-up, a Weeble (Wobble), or the wooden top inverted and not spinning, not stuck but left motionless on its side. Virgil hates the wideness between his eyes. "I think I fucked you before," is what The Canadian says to Virgil in the little booth, the place where Virgil, he seriously feels, is doing research where he belongs, the place where he is learning how to read again.

The rubber smells like rubber, but Virgil thinks of the walruses on the beach, the way they battle for supremacy, a pounding of tusks into the leathery face of the other. On the beach, the Old Veteran Walrus pounds the young punk, who obviously wants to rule, take the harem for his own, but the Vet lifts up and smacks its tusks into the punk's neck, six inches slashing in, then ripping, to open the face of the young challenger, leaving its split cheek flapping.

Virgil learns from the bull how to use his scarred hide and fat to his advantage, though he is mainly smooth. He is splayed on his back on a leather couch, his tits are out and they are being eaten, one by DerPrincipal whom he thinks he loves, and the other by Thick-Cock-White-Ghost, who is like an aged anchor for Virgil.

Will Virgil return to the Sugar Hole to find DerPrincipal? Seeking love—its activities? Virgil is, he thinks, like a saint of the booths, or in another way, a predator.

Virgil looks for the nervous, the ones confused by their shifting desires, exactly those who've not shut their brains off to possibility, those lost in the wrack of an endless want to get one more suck, all the same. Fuck that. Virgil realizes he is not lost either. He mines loss. There is a difference. Wondering, there is something that does confuse him, something that he cannot at first register, as it marks its presence, wings clacking against glass, the cicada in the chandelier he cups to release, though it flashes outside, back to him, crashing into the sliding glass door, dead, it was so shocked.

Before the elevator comes, Virgil is suspended on the top flight of the historical building. Dogs growl behind an apartment door. But all he is doing is waiting, and all Virgil recalls is taking up too much of the lane on East 39th, driving up to Harlem to see a poet and novelist he'd never read before, and to eat, though he had already eaten, doing so sitting at a table up against a wall with Love who was wearing a body-shaped black dress with a white line for a belt, and because Virgil is, indeed, a narcissist, his memory of the poet and novelist's story unveiling, which concerned him less than Love's desire, as immediate as the sightline against the building in which Virgil and Soft-Fat finally did it.

Behind one wall, above Bryant Park, is the apartment Soft-Fat owned, the place in which Virgil recalled being one night several years before. And sure enough, that night before he got laid, Virgil ordered a chicken cutlet, fried and red-sauced, served massive on a plate. Virgil may have saved most of it for later, but what he recalls is being abandoned by Soft-Fat after being fucked by him. Soft-Fat's cool skin, and the calamari that Virgil shared with Love, next to Bryant Park, gives to the pressure of his fork, as he recalls Soft-Fat's unbound belly, and Love's glasses tinting in the sun, and streaked with her tears from all night and all day crying.

Virgil is not sweating, nor is he hot, but Love thinks he is sweating and hot. Virgil seeks the shade, not the building's shadow, not what's unlit temporarily, but what's blocked in a discrete moment. And it is for this very reason that the wall he finds is not a wall, but a black gap revealed between two boards. Virgil understands something about space and simultaneity, in how the dogs's growling behind the door opens up into his ears, then, and floods in, even later, as he dreams of meat and waste, pulled out, and casually drained away in the shower. When he rinses his fingers clean, is he dropping them out of the way from the mirror to spare himself his own vileness? What is Virgil hiding? Like the resin left on the sheets of Clean's hotel bed, as one in stains, one in a nasty mark—this is what they share.

"This is what sold me," Virgil hears as he enters the Grand Courtyard, his temporary oasis from Adam Clayton Powell Boulevard. In some unique approximation to gentrification and his own exclusion from belonging, anywhere, any longer in this city, he cannot find a way to interpret his feeling in seeing, in understanding the space between his body and theirs, or his very expensive shades, and maybe theirs, too.

When Virgil escapes the reading by the poet and novelist, bored by every minute, and expelled by some inane audience question to which he did not await the answer—he couldn't drive away fast enough. To escape from the city, or the memory of the whites with their dogs, one tall red-headed massive muscle-bound Harlem Gentrifier with a Doberman on leash. This Doberman owner in Jean-Cut-Offs made Virgil feel both sickened and safe, his white calf muscles and pet's sharp brown dog-jaw confusing any threat, every local assault, simultaneously, teased and tamed.

What about that reading made Virgil fall into a bored stupor? Is it that the readers were so proud and happy to be seen, to be recognized, to tie everyone implicated in that room to a history that certainly Virgil is a part of, Black, but all Virgil cares about is their black shoes? One, a white woman's, featured a series of buttons at the ankles, and the backs, leather flags openings, elfin. Another, a suede boot with a gummed rubber wedge soul, flat along the bottom, another, a black boot with a zipper that wound diagonally around the boot, itself, but then the surprise, a clasp for a single button that peeked from the top.

In these corners, Virgil should feel at home. Perhaps this is the discomfort that he renders, a discomfort he can't place; but Virgil, instead of behaving, pretending to care, chatting, leaves, slips away, moves far from the site of what he can't let in. Blackness is stuck to him, and he can't quite shake it off enough for him to see it clearly from any distance.

What does he understand, and where does he figure his own relationship to that from which he drove away? He wore no bomb. He was real. Virgil's own Blackness, he is realizing, is found, not in the opacity of its realizations, but in something different, a series of notes that find themselves captured in his disdain for stable fictions, not the fictive characters that he wants to feel alive with, breached histories, ripped memories, no such seen in the prizes gained from the sodden mourning, or resounding, knowing applause. This makes Virgil such an always reading somebody bitch, he can't quite control, so much so that he barely notices, like the gouge on the bottom of his car, there, but he does not see it— though still, it annoys.

One body blends into the next for Virgil, the absence of any hair on one chest, the frock on another, the rounding saliva in one mouth, the sharpness of the grassy Sauvignon Blanc in the next. Virgil only thinks about his own story, the deepest tug of it bringing him back to his own face. For the take, he dances holding a mirror in a grass field, next to the San Francisco Bay, on the rocks, where his left foot is bent in a black boot. The boot is ripped on the left front, close to the middle of this foot, and he feels fat, but kicks out anyhow, his leg stretching for the camera that lays flat on the rock.

No one else's story matters to him as he is making his, but in some way, his story is something that he understands only in relation to how others see him. That morning, Virgil sunk to the floor of his bathroom, his back settling against the tub and the shower's sliding door, just after CeeR informed him of the impression he left on the search committee. One told her they thought Virgil was *a Narcissist*. He knew, no matter what he did, no matter how hard he tried, in his suit, and his luxurious brown boots, and matching bag, that he wouldn't get that job. But still, he was flown out, and helped the name-caller move a desk, and the same name-caller helped Virgil to set up the projector, so during the first talk on his campus visit, he could show his images to the faculty.

How many correctives can he somehow offer to leave the impression that he is nice enough, or at least "declawed," to borrow a term from GGP; and, ultimately, how much would Virgil need to learn to settle by internalizing such an obvious attempt at shaming? And consequently, at what point must this contract break, the cracking of it, like an echo released in his stomach, a reverberation deep up in there, a feeling that some-how he will never quite abort? Maybe this is the well in the infinitely breaking sadness that Virgil will carry in him forever, something that gloms onto his lower back, stuck, no matter what he says in his own defense.

A run recorded on a run, and this run played on the detachable speaker capsule packed in a case, the case on the ground, then the detached speakers Virgil sets on the flat bait catch on the long arm of the pier. So too he sets the camera up to capture himself walking, then sashaying, then jogging toward it, but none of this before his mirror comes out, seemingly from his pocket, spun to flash the sunlight directly into the lens.

Like the episode where Sasquatch fights the Six Million Dollar man in and out of a tunnel, the sun-light after the battle, blasts the camera to produce a reminder of its self, the flash, a blip-star of orange light, but white in the distance, far along the pier, where Virgil dances and signals to himself how present he is, how spectacular his distance, how accurate the line of his leg as he points.

This is how it started, how it all began. Clean real-izes that Virgil cannot see him, because he is so deeply self-involved, and somehow this reality that Virgil understands to be accurate transports him, again and again, far away from that self whom he thought he might become if he could fit back, loosely, into the slim-cut J.Crew shirts he has had to shelve, too recently, for the standard, medium fit.

In his growing fatness, he will never connect with Clean as he once did, as that part of Virgil that did love Clean has gone up some hill, one step in front of the next, away, into the realization that Clean is, forever, bound to a world in which they will never join: an actual castle, two lake houses, hunting dogs, hunting, yacht-rich vacations, a company, a life far into the hills away from the ocean near where Virgil lives. But the real deal is that Virgil will never be his wife, never be her worrying about the dogs stealing the remote and hiding it in the garden, never her laughing in a pub as a glowing young girl, never the woman told she would be the one he would return to marry, never, so full, never so round with hope, waiting, *and* receiving.

"I Could Die." This is what Clean says to Virgil, and Virgil would be lost without knowing when or where Clean died, upon which the existence of their love would dematerialize as quickly as it arose. No start to return to, but between them. This is the risk of their love. And the reward is the retreat into this fact.

The Pig Bar where they first met smells like mold, and the men that sit there are gross and feel dead on arrival, and the one, Gaunt-Face, that Clean said he fucked, and has a big dick, looks, to Virgil, already gone, and stupid, as caught up in a nothing life as the two dancing next to the bar stools. But maybe Virgil's a hater. This is easy to be, and to do, there.

Gaunt-Face is like a corpse that's been knocked around, so that the shape of his dome is flat on top, and his skin, though he is clearly Latino, is peaked, and his hair is gel plastered into wide fork-splits on his barrel-side looking forehead. Clean tells him that when he wasn't there at the hotel, in hospital, his co-workers did not know why. But Clean did. With his marriage on the horizon, Gaunt-Face's ass was being sewn back together, tightened, after it was blown open over time, and failed to close enough for real tight fucking.

The Zombie Zone is what the sticker says on the car next to Virgil as he is driving to Stick's condo, which is nestled into what is not a corner apartment, not much light, in what was formerly a high school. Here is the thing about everything in Virgil's old Western Mass. It can never be beautiful. The grass in the cement, however perfectly mowed in the courtyard, the smattering of people in the Cold Stone, the Basketball Hall of Fame globe, the river stripped of trees from the tornado, never replanted, and the grey and blank light help to remind Virgil of what he was ejected from for his "New California Life," as Clean names it.

Stick has shaved his shit. It isn't what Virgil recalled him doing before. Everything that Virgil wanted when he cruised him in the Starbucks reveals Virgil's delusions, but still, he goes pussy up to get that thin white dick. Stick doesn't even look American, his long body is in almost slim-cut denim jeans, but still somehow wide-legged, faded from the machine wash and dry, and his played out white Pumas, muddled suede stripe, camel or slate. What Virgil said was elegant about him is not elegant in any other world but this one. This is the bait, the charm he holds out to Stick, a sliver of it, and maybe for Virgil it is real, or in the least, a good technique, game, a way that he, as long as he can, continues to find some reason for following Stick home from the Basketball Hall of Fame parking lot.

Inside Stick's condo, there is much more space than Virgil would need if he lived there. There is one window in the living room. Somehow, the beauty in that space is washed over, hidden in the new backsplash, lost in the old, white walls that, no matter how updated, speak of the institution from which they will never be divorced.

Even as Virgil's cock is slobbered on, even as his hole is sucked, even as he is stuck like a cow, even in the graveled feel of a rough fungi-finger nail inside, the thumb almost cutting his pussy-asshole. Nothing stuns Virgil from the weight of how vile, including Stick's missing back teeth, the rest of them yellow. But in this fucking, there is something sweet. Maybe it is in the Irish Spring smell that fills the room, or in how much Stick appreciates Virgil, so much that this gets Virgil off in a way he could not with Clean. He does not know why.

Who knows why? Maybe it is in the picture on Virgil's Photo Stream, the one of Virgil cross-legged in the hotel, in the ergonomic chair, his legs lithe and ripped, lines for days Virgil thinks, his upper body folded, so that the fat is not captured in his stone Nike Dri-FIT, only his arms crossed in front of him, his hands, bent so that one wrist holds up his face, chin resting there, thin, another V, another angle. "You are so Pretty," is what Clean says. Maybe this is from the same unrelenting adoration, but is it enough to get him off? This alarms Virgil, but the absence that he feels in the rush brings him to ask, *How might this be love?*

Late at night, before the porn, some old white man seeding a black boy, or any old man fucking a "teeny," Virgil has taken to watching *The Brady Bunch*, all reruns of his old life. In *The Brady Bunch*, he gathers some first sense of desire he wants to capture. In one episode, where Peter is being an asshole, recording his siblings' secrets by hidden tape deck, he captures Marsha talking to Jan about love. Marsha confesses she feels sick and also happy, odd and equally neat, broken though similarly sutured. All of these contradictions, Virgil knows, somehow point back to his body in love.

He is them, they are all him, and, Virgil realizes, they not only mark his desire, but they train him to give himself up in a way that he could never figure out on his own. Maybe he doesn't need to.

Butch's throat will not clear. Butch feels wet through the night. Butch is thinning, and at the Dinner House, Virgil kicks him. Virgil taps Butch with his toe, fake punches him in that kitchen. The light is open, and the house is cool. The fish is grilled and black on one side, and on the other it's still moist. Here, Virgil feels love, but still every moment of what he eats is outside of itself, and he is, so often, barely there. Not the banging of Bobby's drums in another episode, Bobby looking to find something that marks his musical talent because, unlike his siblings, he cannot "sing." Not the blaring of his bugle into the morning. Not his insane rage-drumming in the garage. But, still, Bobby's family supports him until he exhausts, and confesses that he did not want to play the drums anyway. He chose drums because, he says, he thought this is what *they* wanted.

The father, Mike, in his flat-front, fitted poly-trousers, Carol's dirty-blonde flip at the nape of her neck, the kiss Butch gives Virgil on the forehead while he writes and remembers. What voice does Virgil want to hear? What words does he need to hold? What fear does he hoist around, waiting for some dumb approval, some long weight that he cannot grasp, some irretrievable self cast, caught, in his own no place of being loved? Is this what that search committee had known all about?

The car is a low one, and red, and does 100 as if float-ing, and their name is Manitoba, which is Agender but twinned, and the BMW 328i Coupe xDrive is who Virgil can afford, and hopes to even more easily, as he pro-duces more and more language that creates a balm in his gut. After all the killings, open season, and in a season in which King K says they should fear our resignation, Virgil, too, is resigned.

Virgil is driving, racing after another car. Her name he feels is Angelica, and she's an even march. Virgil, in this dream, is a boy, chasing after something he does not understand, rushed by what others want, what others wish to make of him, marred and constructed, mallea-ble and shocked, wrangled into throws, breathing by the choke of waste-neck-baton.

He speeds along a dark road hoping to keep up with the boys he doesn't even know. They are at a dance he wouldn't even care about, were he awake. Those boys are where the car becomes—a bicycle, frame on the cement, yet chained to the rack, wheel gone, quick release left clutching the air.

The drive from Capitola to "Midtown" Santa Cruz is fast, and there isn't any view of the ocean in the tran-sition from the "1" onramp to Morrissey Avenue when Virgil hears a knock. *Sounds like a rock*, he thinks, but is unable to discern if the noise came from inside or outside of Manitoba. He hopes that the noise came from inside— something he could manage, something that would not ruin his day like a chip on Manitoba's left window door frame, just below the roof, or one on the handle, a scar, tat over an entry wound, or a strip of them: THUG LIFE.

MommaSpine set Virgil's black yoga shorts out on Manitoba, and even though Virgil realizes these would not leave a stain on their red surface, he still removed the shorts from the hood, and hung them on one of the clotheslines she set up in the garage. Resignation is MommaSpine saying her sisters in the Philippines are too far away to ever see again. And even though one of her sisters has just died, she does not answer her husband who asks about his long ago visit to her home, Leon, Iloilo, which he doesn't remember, and MommaSpine tries to forget. Virgil, though, knows some of the story, but he doesn't say anything, about the roll of cash his father wanted to give his then new family, the money, gone the next morning, stolen during the night from his shoe.

Virgil, the boy, on the refrigerator is fat, and smooth; in fact he is striped and brown, and all innocent looking, and as he looks up, dimples, in the studio light of the photographer's bulb. Who knows if that fat, curly brown face would have ever been hit by a bullet? Though, once, he did stare down the barrel of a handgun. Van pulled it on him in a living room. Van on top of the sofa, and Virgil looking at that regular black boy gun pointing dead at Virgil, laughing. And Virgil, not so regular, looking back, or maybe to the side, resigned in the reality that he, at the moment, could be killed. Maybe he was scared, or maybe he recalls out of being scared, a calm when Van opened the chamber to show that the gun wasn't loaded.

When the boys get to the *Party, Party*, there is an open clearing of geriatrics, all of them like little boxes of grey, or white, black and barely moving, but still dancing on the floor around them. The boys want *to get the party started*. But Virgil is thinking of the white-yellow light saturating the pic on the newsfeed. It looks like a warm night, but it is not. What are fireworks are described as "small bombs" that disperse the crowd. *Move the crowd*. The boys want to make the party a success, even though it does not appear they were invited, nor does it feel like the party was productive. This, in a sense, is a riot of no consequence. FloPaT says, "This is not a race riot, but it is riotous."

"Imagine feeling this all day," reports JohnWhite-Funny. Imagine feeling the actual thing, instead of being sick of hearing about it? And the screen is split, and Jon-JonK says JohnWhiteFunny is an ally in his FB post, and Virgil wonders about this binary, the way that feeling is split, not splitting into many selves, but a self who, even at its most luxurious, feels ultimately sad, but looks good, pushes his thighs to touch the mat, and attempts to make something in the connection.

Are you not entertained? Is this what we are doing, Virgil thinks. Is this what CeeR is doing? What are any of us doing, as we wait, well, in our finest of bags and shoes? In the end, he feels he has the ear of the white avant-garde, but, Virgil thinks, as in an illusion, what will he do, exactly? Such sorrow bleeds in the pleasure of his smooth acceleration. And all the warning lights continue to alert: *DSC, ABS, 4×4!* And Manitoba, too, continues to go on, broken. Sorrow, grief—these are impossible to let in, and also impossible to let go, a realization that cannot be marked, let alone, shared.

As the boys sit near their bikes a few feet from one another, Virgil pulls out a pair of stone-washed denim jeans that everyone in the group, including Virgil himself, realizes he cannot fit. Virgil knows this is not because the denim is too small. Perhaps it was the cut that foreclosed the jeans from fitting; but still, in the dream, he explains to these boys that it was only because they shrunk from the dryer's heat.

They are not the jeans on the rack in the HelloKitty Room. Jeans that Virgil lit into the WhackDRYCleaner's about, the jeans they ruined, and even though Virgil told the workers they could do nothing to repair them, that they would have to pay, they did not. Virgil is preserved, and has never returned, a boycott on their stupid business, a pox on their Black Friday, a riot in their cheap hearts.

What is curious about this moment, maybe in his understanding of the jeans being forever too small, is that Virgil recalls wanting to prove himself to the other boys, and maybe to the entire world, at the same time: *We want to be able to walk in peace. We want to eat. We want to be cared for. We want to be knowing, and moving, and being beings.* Is this why Virgil writes?

Virgil is cuffed. Virgil is folded. Those stiff jeans, those hard denim legs that had one day stretched, had once fit both of his legs, and his waist wasn't strangled by the button, but his pumps, as they clipped at the bottom of his feet on the pier, made him feel like he was like a little, thin steed.

Virgil plays like a boy, searches: there is a lion somewhere on YouTube with its jaw torn apart, and his tongue sags, and he cannot drink, but still he goes to the edge of the watering hole to try. The lion drops part of his fallen jaw in, in where Virgil can no longer see it, nor can anyone, but this dip, where part of the face is submerged, broken off, is presumed to be the sign that the Hippo attacked him, and won.

Virgil feels sad. Virgil is alone. Virgil has not touched anyone for so very long, and in this site of not feeling anyone, he is moving around a wide circle, a circle he can't understand, something he does not want to encounter alone, but he is alone, so he walks down a dreamed street, though into a familiar, real house. The dream world he enters is made up of rides he imagined so long ago, dreams he felt as he rode on his bike as an actual boy.

Alone on the bike, it was like he was floating. And in his dreams, Virgil is not ever free, but his movements feel close to it. He floats above the street, wearing only a towel around his waist. He tries to pretend he is super-fit. He pimp walks with his towel in a neighborhood, which is much like the grid he is driving around on with the boys in the car, but this time he is walking, and not driving.

Once in a parking lot, Virgil is tried by a Mutual Black who asks for money, and Virgil says he's preparing for an interview, and he walks away, maybe pimp walking again, a little, to enter the Panera. The Mutual Black is ready to fight. So is Virgil, but for different reasons. In the end, he does not fight because he does not want to scuff his $400 boots in the parking lot, and he shuts the heavy door of MommaSpine's Porsche 928 and keeps it moving.

He walks quickly, because he has a purpose, headed to a familiar place, a house that is white, and has pillars that greet him. Giant squares of walls drop down, and he finds himself walking quickly up to the front porch. Virgil hears the whites having breakfast inside, and sees the square plates that match the square block pillars that guard the house from precisely someone like Virgil. And Virgil, in the dream, though he has only stolen a pack of gum and a single balloon in his life, carries the fear of being caught less than he does the fact of his being deemed a thief on sight.

It feels easy enough though, in this seeing, and in a way, his body allows him to shift and to move, and to wait, and then to eventually *steal* the copy of the *Sacramento Bee*, wrapped in plastic, still flat. He has only seen the *New York Times* wrapped like this, so it can be pretty certain that this comes from Virgil taking the morning paper to Butch. But as quickly as he grabs the newspaper from the porch, he returns it to the first old white lady he sees, walking up to join the other old whites for lunch. From inside the house of stucco squares, he hears chatter of the news of the missing newspaper. He hears them calling the police, describing what they see. "Yes, but is he Black or White?" is being asked, not in the dream, but the question plays from the tiny black volume bar at the bottom of the laptop screen.

As Virgil speed walks away from dropping the newspaper into the old lady's hand, he notices neither she nor her friend look particularly rich. He notes one's long stringy dyed hair, the fallen face, not as jacked up as the lion's he found ripped off by a hippo, but still, he sees it falling, lying there, and sagging, held on by some miraculous tendon. Not dying, or dying less quickly than the lion, the old white lady in the dream takes the paper, "I was supposed to be on Water Duty." "Why are you giving me the newspaper?"

Or maybe it is a skill. Once, when Virgil was an intern in public relations in an office overlooking the Avenue of the Americas, he received coaching by the speech coach of PresidentGipTrick! She taught Virgil, and the rest of the interns, old white lady that she was, how she downturns her mouth into a slight, but hard pursed frown to model her being both attentive and filled with disdain at exactly the same moment.

Virgil, in this instant, realizes that he will be safe, because he knows the difference in the truth and faking it, and that he can wake up from the reality of being caught, but what remains is how exposed he feels with the towel around his waist in the dreamed morning, his fat out, or on a morning well after the dream when it will fit around him easily, and in this fit, this will explain it all, forming to give Virgil back some measure of his life.

No consummation of desire is what Virgil ponders in the bed, his back almost ready to blow out at the base, for even thinking it. It started out after school, when Teacher M would sit, legs stretched out at the front of his empty classroom. Teacher M drove an old red Toyota Truck, left parked in front of the high school well after it was closed, waiting like a beacon for Virgil; for no matter how far away he was from Teacher M, Virgil would figure out a way to return.

After graduation, what did he imagine he would hold onto as he came back so many years in a row, to that class, first, to where Teacher M usually parked, then to the front lot, and then to the empty classroom, again, Teacher M waiting behind his classroom's wall-sized front windows, in full-view, not waiting for Virgil at all, but rather, for traffic on U.S. 50 to clear?

And now, Virgil pays the price for this habit, this need, stalking before it was stalking, lured by the tug of only his desire. The perch he pulled out of the bay was almost flat. Before he caught it, Virgil did not imagine it from the top of the pier. It felt easy to catch, but once it flailed on the end of his hook, dancing the "dance of death," which Fat Alan called it, Virgil held tight the fishing line, barely feeling it rub into his finger, its last useless struggle bound to his longing.

When Virgil comes by Teacher M's classroom again, there is someone new inside, someone grey and old, with glasses, someone whose legs are similarly sticking out, as they were when Virgil and Lil'Daft would sit like two little bitches in heat at Teacher M's feet. Who knew that while Teacher M was describing his relationship to the Lord, his ranking of his love of family ahead of anyone, including Virgil, or his future plans to finish up a master's on Chaucer, Teacher M was actually seeding another woman, would get her pregnant, and leave his then wife, the woman who had all the money, the kids, and kept that house so safe in El Dorado Hills.

Virgil was, then, like all the other lost girls. He was like Lil'Daft, and like Tomato Worm Face Steel Wool Hair, all wanting Teacher M. All of them ready to give up their childhoods to enter Teacher M's imaginary, his orbit of desire, which by proxy included, at least they hoped, theirs. But what did Virgil wish to gain from finding himself caught in the trap of this uneven exchange?

Virgil would confess his desire for Teacher M in the ways Virgil knew would not ruin everything, staring at Teacher M with pig-puppy eyes, feigning confusion about how to keep his growing-away school friends, when Teacher M was the friend Virgil really wanted. Lil'Daft was correct. Virgil *like-liked* Teacher M. His need was something he could not identify, then, but still, never getting into Teacher M's actual world haunted him. Still does. Maybe Madge was correct? Maybe his reliance on the dream world holds him hostage in ways his real life will never overcome.

Consummation is tricky, Virgil feels, and it is so ugly in the dream. Teacher M is wounded. His head is enlarged, and sewn up across his forehead, the stitch is bulky, and he can barely stand. "Did you have a stroke?" is what Virgil asks. But moments before, Teacher M was fine enough, looked the same, feathery thin hair, a dark mustache, big brown eyes, like a toddler's, lashes flowing out around them, as light as the air they moved. He nodded. They walked inside. But the person that Virgil would see there was not him.

Virgil thinks of Frankenstein's monster on the table, the yellow ochre skin, the veins, the forever loss that that monster would carry in his travels, his return, and perhaps even his penultimate escape across the ice. Maybe this is why his encounter with the other version of Teacher M is so difficult to decipher.

Teacher M is seated next to him, describing what happened. While he is naked, his body is thinner than Virgil imagined it could ever be, long and less hairy, and in the reconstruction of this body in this dream, his head is healed. But as Teacher M reveals his story, he releases a perfect dollop of green vomit, the consistency of mashed peas, and the color the very same.

Upon the release of this vomit, Virgil rubs Teacher M's back, and though he would have wanted to grab a bag, fake concern, then go all the way, he does not. He lets it go, the very idea, and fixates on the vomit. Why can't Virgil and Teacher M remain in their respective positions within the dream forever? But Virgil, like Teacher M (according to Tomato Worm Face Steel Wool Hair) has lost his family from fucking around, and Virgil realizes he, too, has a price to pay. He has to contend with the desire that leaves them both broken and wandering within Virgil's unconscious.

Teacher M transforms again. There are no wounds left on his body. It's as though Virgil healed him, allowed him to come back as a mirror of himself. It feels appropriate, really, this body of theirs, hovering, and his wanting Teacher M, a figure that does not evolve from its original representation, but reveals instead someone to hold and to love.

Teacher M is intact. His nipples sport rings, and he is in the tub waiting for Virgil. Finally, *this is how it started, how it all began*, and Virgil is right there, hungry for everything. "Spend the night." Teacher M says this before the tub, before they do it, and Virgil is even encouraged by Teacher M's brother, a sort of cheerleader shadowing in the dream, even though Virgil only met him once, Teacher M's brother, rounder, and with amber hair glowing in the back of the class.

The living room, fabricated in Virgil's imaginary, leads to the site of desire that will hold them all, but what does Virgil do but waddle in the tub, like the electric eel that vibrates just enough to kill the fish it will quickly eat in the water. Or like the fish caught by the bird that "fishes," by dropping a piece of bread into the brown water until the fish surfaces to feed, only to be snatched into the bird's beak, and shaken down its billowing throat.

The weight of the rain coming down on the house, its clicks and shifts, pulls Virgil from this world into the present. How will he understand the features of his body to be unstuck from events that are real, or dreamt? The plot becomes this, a theory—Virgil's feeling generated across discovery. So the plot is also constructed in the fact that he, too, returns to how desire can never be broken, particularly inside of events that would never happen.

The vantage point was clear, the shot an easy one through the apricot tree, between the branches where the hummingbird stood. At least this is what Virgil thought it was doing—standing—but after telling KennebunkActor the story, he would realize that the bird was not. What Virgil could not know then was that the bird, as KennebunkActor described, hovered.

Before Virgil shot the hummingbird, he remembers the sweep of the many of them flying in the trees. In one photo from this time, Virgil has a bucket on his head, his hair curling out, and he is wearing white shorts with an athletic stripe down the side, opening to a small gap— his face, a permanent smile, he holds a hose out in his hands, spraying water into an arc.

But as Virgil took aim, he was not playing. He was, instead, sitting on a card table's padded collapsible chair, alert, the hollow steel legs's rubber grips fixed on the cement patio. Secure, he lined the bird up just under the sight's tip, the snap of the gun, blasting through the leaves, putting a hole in the "standing" bird's neck.

"You were a good aim," is what KennebunkActor said, which exists in contradiction to Virgil's waiting for the struck-dead animal to come back to life, even though it was clear—the hummingbird was dead. When KennebunkActor revealed to Virgil that that hummingbird was not, in all likelihood, ever standing on that branch, Virgil understands this not to be contradiction, but recognition of a different kind, something that would undo him more deeply than the killing itself:

Dheh

Dheh-Dheh-Dheh

Dheh-Dheh-Dheh

Dheh-Dheh-Dhehhhhhhhhhhhh

When "The Eye of the Tiger" came on, Virgil performed his dance of life, not choreographed but felt. However submerged, shooting that bird stretches out in front of him like the "catwalk" that was his backyard's narrow center, the runway, his stage.

GHerm is in a dream, on a bus, and Virgil is peering in at her. They are traveling somewhere, but he cannot recall where they are going, or if they are even traveling together. He remembers GHerm insulting him when they were friends at L.B.H.S. When Virgil recalled his backyard, GHerm said, "Please, you make it seem like it's a grove."

But it was a grove, to him, tomatoes around the entire perimeter, and grape vines in a small trellis at its center, apricots dropping from the tree that shaded the patio. Out of Virgil's mom and dad's bedroom, he would revel in the "grove," even though the window was tinted dark, and it was always cool in there, and must have smelled like smoke. Out of the window, he could see the wide world in which he propelled himself, his tumbling runs, his cartwheels, round-offs:

Dheh

Dheh-Dheh-Dheh

Dheh-Dheh-Dheh

Dheh-Dheh-Dhehhhhhhhhhhhh

After he shot the hummingbird, Virgil watched it hang upside down by its feet, clasped to the top branch, the blood dripping, then bouncing in the grass in front of his still eyes. His response? To toss it over the fence, after shoveling it up with a plank, but not before he stared into its blown-open neck, open so much so that he could not see the wound. Instead, what he saw was a pool of dark green and blue-pink, a seeming oil and water slick, feathers around the exit wound, the bird's loose, broken neck, bent at the color burst.

Virgil is a pig, for at least that day. Are there other Pigs as insatiable as Virgil?—Lost is Grey. In Lost's bedroom there is a rusted bin that was outside, and now it is indoors, and it holds three potted plants. The bin serves as a basin, a flat surface, rusted, and in the center of the surface is a small catch that Lost says was for the animal's blood, not for the living plants it holds now, but for animals it would hold, dead, then.

Virgil is, as Butch describes him, *sick*, for when he was riding Lost, he thought of slaughtering him like a pig. More directly, he thought Lost looked like a pig-cow, a hairy hybrid animal that Virgil rode up and down bouncing on his stiff cock, as Virgil's mostly stayed hard.

Virgil is *sick,* but he could never kill, because the guilt would ruin his life, though at night, most of his recent nights, the last moments spent drifting in YouTube, he looks at those kids who do. Girl Gangbangers who've turned it around for now, but at one time, before they "changed," would make others "meet their maker."

Anger, perhaps, spills from him, too, a feature he can't quite pinpoint, but something comes from within, a memory, perhaps, longer than his very life. When CharcoalBuilder taught a workshop in a middle floor, bundled in "The Mission," just above the street, she took her students into a field of her imagination to a place beyond composition, a place where what happened was animated by failing to grasp it. *She wore polyp shoes.* This is the sentence that Virgil constructed that day.

Virgil watches with MommaSpine the unveiling of two murders on T.V., one that results in capture, the other in elongation, and dissatisfaction, a feeling that Virgil and his mother shared. One, Dad&Killer, remains in Mexico. He eats better than the rest of the prisoners, because his parents send him money. He says being in prison is like living in a small village, and it does look like a small village, at least the way it's captured on T.V.

Virgil brings down a blanket and forces himself to stay, to watch the crime result in the other murderer's conviction, after which Virgil and MommaSpine are satisfied. His getaway bag, hidden in the desert, the cash inside, his Google searches for how to kill and how to get away with it, the Big Bertha sleeve for a left handed club are enough evidence to put that murderer away for life plus 25.

Though the defense attorneys pointed out there was no way that the prosecution or the jury could say the murder weapon was, indeed, a golf club, or that the killer was ever inside of that room, the jury sentenced him, while Dad&Killer still fries up bacon in his Acapulco prison. Somewhere there is a body that Virgil buries in his dream, and he wants to figure out some way to return to hide it, even deeper. DonDon, his brother and accomplice, is in that dream and they conspire to go on living as though they are not killers. Virgil cannot.

Grass grows over the mound, but the fact of the killing remains. His most lazy self doubles—filled with such hate, it holds him between sleep and writing. Virgil thinks that maybe the reason some do not write is because they have nothing to say, and if you have nothing to say, he thinks, maybe the writer should do something else, like snatch out what's inside, to observe, awake, not as the point of production, but in the pull of finding.

"Sorry," is what he heard just before Dr.T pulled the mass out to show him. When Virgil saw it clutched at the end of Dr.T's instrument, the polyp looked smaller than he imagined it would. Though just before, in his Fentanyl and Versed sedated state, he saw on the screen the moment it was snagged then cut out from his hot little hole, and now it popped out at him, an angry red eye. And though he would miss all the calls about the results, he called back, panicked, but to learn it was benign. Still, he reveals this red warning to his lovers, letting them know how he's turned the corner, gotten to be closer to their age, a fellow traveler, sharing issues along the way.

In Manhattan, Dr.S, when he pulled a cyst out, cut from a tendon, a translucent schwannoma from deep in his armpit, Virgil was much more clear, and awake enough to feel the pain as it was being removed. "We have a slam dunk!" is what Dr.S announced as he was carving it out, yanking across a nerve's surface. Virgil jolted, fought and had to be held down, yelling to Dr.G for more anaesthesia, from which he would be rendered unable to move much, his arm, useless, an entire day, but Malcolm would be there to take him back to his long apartment in Brooklyn to sleep off the drugs.

It was snowing then, and wet, but this was all he had to worry about. This and the watercolors of lynched black bodies he made, and of green trees, all on the red table whose metal legs he would detach in order to make it fit as cargo in his first "new" car, an affordable blue Subaru Forester named Desiré he would ship by semi from Long Island to Sacramento.

But this is what's happening now: Virgil feels like the grilled crust on the shrimp is keeping him alive, and so too is the polenta, stuffed in his mouth at the same time, or the bread soaked in the crab that exploded around his plate. Eating Porker, how does Virgil return to the language of all the bodies, the taste lasting so briefly in his mouth?

Virgil's feeling is particular about them, particularly now that he is as smooth inside as he is outside, he thinks, when he is being fucked by Clean, Butch, Lost, BigLashMexDad (who uses a rubber), or The RailMan (though The RailMan is in all likelihood dead of pancreatic cancer). Still, he will not lacerate their dicks during the action from the steel staple Dr.T left inside to seal the hole where there was once a polyp.

Virgil thinks of this for one second, then the tip of Clean's cock, pricked by the staple left in the wall of Virgil's insides after the "defect" was removed. Three to eight weeks to fall out, but, thank God, it fell out in one.

Virgil does not recall a time when he was perfect, because, at the time he was closest to perfection, his BMI did not reflect his muscle mass, or his full head of curly, shiny black hair, his unshaven teeth, or his dimples, settled into the jaw of his skin, as shiny as his hair, clean and free of the worry he must genuflect, now, but still, he tries his best to stay as free of as many blems as possible.

It is out of this desire that he holds onto the tiny steel clip that braced together the gap of his "inner-hoe" wall where the polyp once grew. *Candy*, he thinks, but the staple looks like a miniature spaceship, one he places in a corner of the pressed-wood cabinet sealed behind a mirror.

In another outcome, Virgil may have had to have some of his intestines cut out, been left to sport a colostomy bag, sung a song to others that he's had sung to him by at least one daddy cornered in the Townhouse: "Nothing is going on down there."

This song never bothers Virgil; in fact, the phrasing is like the start of a manifesto, a right of entry into a life, a way to figure out who this old lover will be. Variety in intention. In the mirror, Virgil looks hideous, he thinks, and is tired. Like a meteor crashing into the earth's atmosphere, he is less the rock upon entry, less its burning back into the atmosphere, less able to dissipate. Virgil's glasses are smudged, and worn, and he is old now. Virgil is fat. Virgil is ugly. Virgil is not. Virgil layered together by broad framing devices known as projection, something apparent at the surface of Virgil and the operation's healing wound.

What is called white-hot "nickel" is the metal not the coin. Dropped, by tongs, onto the top of a Styrofoam block, the trick on YouTube is that the glowing ball of metal sinks in, and as the block's exterior cracks, the Styrofoam morphs into a charred black box contracting then cracking. The close-ups are then of the tongs, grabbing, then holding up the nickel ball that was resting on the black surface, its transferred heat still doing damage. The ball is then dropped in a bowl of water to hiss steam. The last shot is a close-up of the insides of the Styrofoam, revealing how it transformed, tongs scraping away the black crust, fissures reveal its glowing insides, warm and red-orange, held—this too, is the money shot.

Kyle from Korea wanted to order a Long Island Iced Tea. He wears braces, little bolts between his tiny top teeth, and he works in New Jersey but lives in Queens. His face, that night, was like a small moon with shiny black hair around it. His smile, pink, and his English moved around his need to make others touch, lifting a stranger's hand onto the arm of another, wanting to force together those he'd never have. "People only hate or like me," and he thinks all Americans are friendly, "They're always smiling."

Virgil soon realized that Kyle understands "American" to be "White," and Virgil thinks Kyle also understands this fact to be confirmed by knowing he would have to walk toward the train into the dark morning, alone, out of the bar, with his big grey backpack over his shoulder. Kyle's hand? Did it slip, along the outside of Virgil's ass, lightly, and how could Virgil recall this as he worried about what was caught in Butch's eye, an irritant Butch would wash out with Artificial Tears? But as Virgil worried, he knew that Kris was being clocked by Scales-for-Flesh.

Scales-for-Flesh's skin, Kris pointed out, was the "Only thing," as in, it was what separated him from the rest of the men Kris slept with, those defining scales Virgil imagined scalloped down Scales-for-Flesh's back, and, like an asshole, Virgil injects into Kris's description, "Psoriasis." Kris, too, knew it was why Scales-for-Flesh wore so many layers of clothing, a full-on suit in the humid city, and even in the bar, buttressed up to his thick neck. It's as if his whole head was wrapped in a cocoon. Virgil caresses Scales-for-Flesh's black Banana Republic button-down stomach, fat and stretched, and not because Kyle pulls his hand into it, but to cockblock Scales-for-Flesh's attempt to get again with Kris, who wears a beard, white and round, yellowing at the base of his stache, stained with smoke, above the rim of his mouth.

When Virgil first tongues Kris, Virgil tastes blood, and thinks it came from somewhere behind Kris's lips, maybe it was his gums. Just inside Virgil's mouth, Virgil wants to forget the taste of blood with his own tongue, but Kris's is short and flat—the surface, raised bumps. However, Virgil is less interested in the feel of the tongue than he is taken by the beard, a cloud hanging from a sky, or cut, almost rounded like a perfectly pruned Hampton's hedge, out of which breath and spit drips into Virgil's mouth. Virgil loves to be kissed like this, and to be wholly stuck underneath Kris's body, or a body like his, to be slowly filled.

Under Clean, it feels like Virgil is entirely lost beneath Clean's body, which is smooth and unmarked. With Clean, Virgil's back straightens along the sheets—flat is the spine from the coccyx to the base of his neck, from which his head leans back, his bald spot digging into the sheet. Virgil takes in all of Clean. The sensation reveals a warm shift in Virgil, an amplification of his need.

Virgil looks up below the feeling, as in moving under the wide rails of the bridge on a three-person Jet Ski, as he looks through the rails to the sky, holding his now-grown-up-baby-niece Avon close to his body, or his hands gripping the small strap on the seat behind her, as he zeroes in on the wires beneath the bridge, the houseboats, his foot dragging in the brown river, cutting as would a rudder, resisting, guiding, just below the surface.

Kris fucks up the shoulder of the brown, raised fabric couch in the Junior Suite of the Park Lane Hotel, because his open ass smells faintly of shit. Or maybe Virgil and Kris fuck up the couch because Virgil blew Kris on it, though Virgil did try to ease Kris down from the couch's shoulder, so that his crack wouldn't ease open, ruining the fabric. "Gamey," is how Virgil describes Kris's smell to Malcolm, over the rice-flour fried calamari they share at lunch, or maybe it is the smell of not shit, but Kris's ass pores releasing the rest of the American Spirit smoke's resin into the sofa, a smell that Virgil will later try to scrub clean with one of the hotel's face cloths.

This is the same scrubbing that he practices in Butch's truck in the basement level of the garage, where the back seat has been leaked on with salsa from Table & Vine. This is the same scrubbing that he will do in the bed of the Sheraton, the morning he leaves, while Clean gets ready to go into the office. Virgil's own soap-soaked puddle, like a soft horizon, spot edged with red, a warm stain from his stomach that promises some animal was once there, ambling into the forest, vanished.

Virgil carries a small ice bag from the Sheraton, filled with hot water and honey-colored shampoo to draw the acidic red from the car seat. The hot bag looks like it should hold a goldfish. It looks like the bellies on the beach above the black sand of the Sacramento River, where the air stinks of beer and weed. The dumb look on the face of the father that lets his little boy jump on the Jet Ski with a total stranger, who, when not holding a child, shows out—the Jet Skier racing up and down the river, preening from the shore, speeding while sitting backwards, and, once, even sitting, balancing on top of the handle bars.

The morning is pouring into his Central Park suite. And in the night's black turning to blue, Virgil looks up and recalls the events that might be painted up on the rust-color walls of the sugar factory he visited with Butch just three days before. How might this tableau, a horizon of language, be caught in another form other than scrubbing, standing on couch-seat cushions, hoping to draw out the stain, now only once there?

Virgil is hopeful that he will not be charged for Kris's stink, that it will dissipate enough for it to go un-smelled. But all morning, the suite still reeks of Kris's ass, something that Virgil has smelled only once, and will probably only smell once. Out of this reality, he eats Clean's pristine ass, and this is exactly why Kris eats Virgil's: "What's wrong with him?" is what Kris asks, when Virgil tells Kris that Butch never eats him out. Maybe this is what helps Virgil decide to kill that black, thick-headed figure in the dream that represents, according to Sshape, Virgil's most damaged self.

Clean is clean. Clean slides into Virgil, thick and slow, and it hurts, and he is tight for Clean, and he will taste his own ass on Clean's uncut dick. Virgil is shocked to taste his own light blood. Clean is above him like a soft plank, his armpit just above Virgil's face, their skin surfacing into one another, like a yacht resting into the water, the bowed hull of a white steamer, and he thinks of the Love Boat cutting across the T.V. screen, or the shot above the island that contains the land and the boat.

Clean's skin is soft and old, and his hair is a golden retriever's but black-grey, loose curls soft in Virgil's hands. Virgil can feel the space at the base of the back of Clean's head, where there is now a sealed hole, where beneath, a tumor was plucked out. The skin now dimples, but is taut over where the skull was drilled, and below this is a metal plate that can't be felt by touch. Virgil feels that he can take all of Clean in, but wonders if he has lost the ability to cum, or gives up this ability, to give his walls up, to be filled, to catch everything Clean has.

Virgil came three times—not then, of course, because he had six Blue Point Oysters to attend to before he was straddled and face-fed by Clean, and before he submitted, and before he would see the morning over-looking the city, as daylight came in the form of the burnt, orange sun. The streak of it lit the steel looking glass along the building, and it radiated across one side of Central Park to the other: "There's nothing like hav-ing your ass eaten while looking at this," is what Kris tells Virgil, and Virgil realizes this is something that he will have to remember, because the view will not be captured by camera, even though he could take the shot with his iPhone.

Virgil orders Kyle an Old Fashioned, not the Long Island Iced Tea that Kyle said he wants, and it is strong, and Kyle's hands are long and thick like a woman's would be thick if that woman were a man, and Virgil and Kris agree that Kyle is lovely, and Virgil points out that Kyle understands nuance, and is skilled in his English because he not only understands who will end up leaving with whom, but that he seems content to leave alone, and this is what Kyle communicates in his loose light plaid cargo shorts, bulky unmemorable tee, and shoes that will forever go unremarked.

Before the after party, Buzz thinks, at first, that Virgil is an accountant, and he thinks this because of Virgil's white, striped grey linen shirt that says, "Made in New England" on the inside collar's tag. Virgil wears this shirt with crisp Diesel jeans, and almost new caramel wingtips, topped off with a John Varvatos navy blue, two-button, barely striped blazer. Buzz wants to open Virgil's shirt, even more than it is already forced open by Virgil's thickening chest. Of course, Virgil is the most beautiful of them all, and he has barely eaten, so he feels skinny, as if a line, and he understands this at the time he is gathering in the exact attention he wants.

Virgil is why they were flanked together in that bar cul-de-sac of sofas and mirrors that could have been a bay window. To the left, Kyle smiles, and breaks into what Buzz and Virgil say to one another in the adjacent couch. What does Kyle hear? Does what he hears matter as much as how Buzz and Virgil connect? Buzz's short white fingers unfastening the classic pull of the buttons in the linen, Buzz's smooth head prone on Virgil's chest, the quick kisses between them. Buzz turns up his head and looks into Virgil's eyes: "You're someone I'd marry." "When I listen to your words..." In the exchange, for Virgil, there is nothing said that's truly urgent. Buzz is a prop. Buzz is a source. Buzz is another anchor.

Virgil as spectacle. Virgil as gift. Virgil as catalyst and exploit, as corner man for no one but himself. Virgil is alone, detaching from Buzz. Buzz snaps at Kyle who looks into the fish bowl, staring at the darting inside, whatever, floating to the bottom. Buzz says "Thank you," or "Have a good night," which means get lost, and Kyle understands this, exactly, but continues to press in. Because Kyle is magnetic, his lips around a stirring straw, his backpack wedged into the corner between sofas, his cell phone plugged into the nearby outlet, Kyle remains, no matter what, always right there.

But Kris is fine. His body is hard. Virgil is relieved at the slightly pushed-out gut, strong, and the jeans are soft, and the belly is soft enough, and the beard is like a teeny mountain, his washed linen shirt, cornflower blue. Virgil knows that what he and Buzz share is a bubble that Kris will penetrate. Virgil helps. He looks directly at Kris, Kris's eyes, then his chest, between his legs spread open wide on the barstool.

So when Kris hears Virgil suggest how Buzz should actually attend to his students around questions of finance and ethics, or maybe when Kris hears Virgil's interpretation of Buzz's own understanding of finance and ethics, this may be what prompts Kris to finally speak: "I'm just sitting here."

As the sun came up from below the city, emerging to illuminate it, on the other side of the window, Kris was eating Virgil out. His beard pushed into the tongue of Virgil's little asshole in which is tucked away what the general doctor could not feel, even though he had his index "pretty deep up in there," even turning it inside, as if on a clock's face, "from six to three." The park featured a brown lake close to the bottom of what Virgil could make out from the 36th floor, and, in him, he attempted to fashion a moat around everything in his sight.

In the bar lounge, three thin white boys pile around one another, ricochet dancing, their bodies in white denim, and in this denim they feel invincible. No one can stop them in what they will do through the night. The waitress in the bar is Black, and she wears braids like a little girl's plaits woven into a ponytail, and baby-girl beads at her tips. She hunches down, skirting along the floor with a steak knife jutting out of her hands, holding it sideways, moving like a crab along the floor, near the table's legs. She latches onto someone's thigh, and as she's moving, she tells us she, herself, has been stabbed. And she is not trying to stab anyone back.

Virgil's dream is a nightmare. It also features another black figure, a shadow, an un-human that writhes half alive on the floor. It can't be placed, but still, it's there. Does it have a head? It does, because Virgil is the one who will aim for it. What does this say about Virgil? What does it say that he finds a white granite rock, lifts it up and smashes the head of this black creature that, he thinks, has stabbed the Black waitress? Black on black crime? Killing, Virgil realizes, is criminal. He tries to even burn what, or who, has been smashed, this, perhaps out of a feeling with which he can't identify.

Scales-for-Flesh spits out "Excuse me," fast and rude to Virgil, as he hugs Kris goodbye, and says into Kris's eyes: "Je Adore you." "I Love You." "I Love You." Scales-for-Flesh does not know Virgil has the dream of a black figure that can't be killed, fully, and certainly can't be erased with a single white rock, but the boys dance in their whiteness, and the waitress, too, though black, too, wants it killed. Or is it Virgil's want? So continuous, Virgil who cannot sleep through any single night without such a battle?

Clean says he does not want to see Virgil screwed over by anyone; or to clarify, that Clean should be the only one who should screw him, and this screwing makes Virgil feel secure, locked in, like the hum of the fan that fills the morning, sure in the ways his body gives over to where the Discovery River meets the Sacramento, the zone where the their currents mix, the push of the warming water around his leg dragging in the river.

Virgil and Avon jet upstream, one holds the other, and they cruise on the surface of the chopping, leaping up the wakes, almost flying, moving as if going home to a sky, and there are hawks that position above them, still in the sky, ready to pounce on the white, small birds that shake the hawks off, drifting away from the threat of their advance.

Virgil wants to paint this memory as large as his mind can encompass, rendered on a bigger wall than he can yet imagine, but when he tries to imagine it, "The Tribes Of Morocco," spoken in Virgil's ear, turns out to be not the "secret" that he thought Rahan was passing on, but rather a small, crowded import store downtown that Virgil will never visit. This place is far from Butch's body, which is shaped like a Hershey's kiss in the early evening before they'll both drift into TV, Butch a stretch of muscle attached by long, thinning limbs, and his shoulders cut, now, dropped above the L-shaped sofas in the sunroom.

Just outside of the sunroom is a full bag of leaves in an ACE bag that will end up on the curb, and the image of the bag set out there is doubled with the sound that it made as Butch filled it. From inside, Virgil saw Butch multiply reflected in the open window through the bushes in front of the house. He can't tell, however, where Butch was in relation to the plants, nor could he make out the sound, whether it was Butch walking away and talking at the same time, or whether Butch was still and pushing leaves into the bag.

But in the morning, the fabric of Butch's shirt looks almost tweed, the infused pattern embedded lightly into the weave. Virgil calls this shirt "old," and Butch wonders why. It's because of its camel-khaki tint, its boxy cut, from circa sometime in the '90s, maybe Tony Lambert, its two darts opening up in the back, the shadows gathering in the dart's creases as Butch turns to leave for work.

And Virgil, later that day, will walk around the park, drafting on the asphalt paths, or running up the grassy hills, Virgil cutting into what he remembers, Virgil, jogging, bitten by a summer horsefly. The wound will mound, only to later sink back into his neck. Virgil watches the rock on their desk. The rock is the color of Butch's shirt, heavy, a dull axe, grooved, "a Native American tool," Butch calls it. Lying on its shadow, it is sloped to reveal its pocked surface on one edge, before the sun totally erases this, two white shiny marks, caught like a drawn eye.

Virgil understands that when he runs through the humid morning mist of the summer trees, near the Connecticut River—on this trail—he realizes his vision. It has taken so many months, but finally, he has abandoned the force of the Being-Yelled-at-Yoga to become involved in his own quiet practice. And in this shift, Virgil learns to slow down. He doesn't even mind the two chatter-joggers that slip by him, symmetrical whites in symmetrical (grey, black) sweats, caps, headphones, discussing the travails of some shared friend.

Virgil thinks of filming the field of crops as back-drop, the empty bike trail, but sadness? He does understand that the Connecticut River is too shallow to dive into, and there is a difference between the currents of one section of the river (one looks plastic, flat, the other like a moving wound, rust) and the next, that each of the textures of the river reflect his mood, so much so that this jettisons his perception from the river to the realization of how long a drop it is to the yellow moss on the steel struts he looks down into while crossing the bridge.

To have a unique relationship with his body in space is how he "opens up" on the run. It's how he theorizes the space between what's close and what's distant. This manifests in the "stunned" feeling one confessed getting after reading Virgil's work. Butch says, "Everyone wants to talk to you." Narcissist, Virgil knows it might be because of his new glasses, Oliver Peoples, the brown and grey custom staggered frames, matte, brushed, contouring his cheek bones. Blurred horizontal layers of colors in thin, composite sections, they make him look "warm and approachable." Love told him this, and it makes him feel nice, though he is not really nice, like when he asks Butch, "Should I steal her wallet?" Or maybe he is nice, because he would not actually steal from the OldCurlyWhiteLadyGlancer who edges her eyes into his sketch-pad, as she also does so into the seat next to him on the Ferry. She tells her husband, CaneWalkingBaldSplotch, to "...be careful honey." OldCurlyWhiteLadyGlancer, Virgil, and Butch watch him, barely balancing in the ticket line, sticking out his tongue in strain. Virgil sees OldCurlyWhiteLadyGlancer's butterscotch wallet in her bag, whose design he does not recall, this and CaneWalkingBaldSplotch's mahogany cane, and the brace surrounding his calf like a white vase.

Before breakfast at Jake's, on the benches outside, a little blue boy sees Virgil sketching, and asks him if he can look in his book. Virgil is generous, and opens his sketch pad, leafing through the pages for the boy and his Mom/Aunt/or Guardian to see. The little blue boy listens to his advice, nods his head when Virgil tells him that it's okay to "mess up." The Mom/Aunt/or Guardian cosigns Virgil's recommendation, and they both follow along as Virgil slowly turns his pages, describing how, in one, he scraped all of the paint off with his Costco card to reveal the original marks, a flat black figure in magenta, a white man's face, caught by pink water-soluble oil pastels.

Virgil, as ever, is invested in the capture of depth. Though he isn't a lone wolf, he understands that "performing" as one who is alone garners his unique relationship to being isolated among others. For Virgil, this is a kind of first source, and from this source, he tries to explain to Music that Western Mass has never looked so beautiful to him before now. The trees are so wet and present, no monolithic vastness that can simply be read as "field." But still, they appear as full, thick and singular, like one green corridor through which he jogs.

But in looking up during his run, Virgil realizes any sense of actual height is too tall to track. When he lived there, closer to these trees, he was only familiar with existing above them by car looking down from the highway into the valley, driving Desiré on US 90—like Manitoba, but much more affordable, and "Knowledge" Blue not "Passion" Red—through the winding mountain view, sometimes looking out at them, so that the trees would appear as only texture.

For now, they are still only color, but that morning, staring into them, he felt that he was attached to the trees as corollary object, his body existing in relation to their wetness, the sound of their dripping around him. This is not the sensation Virgil's and Butch's neighbors reveal in Long Island when one complains after a wind storm about the fallen limbs on their street: "I hate coming home to a forest." "Take a drive through Belle Terre," is how Butch wants to answer, revealing the class understanding he would like to give his neighbors, directing them, over the tracks, up the hill, to the tree-ensconced homes overlooking the L.I. Sound. But the White Fats next door are loud and stupid enough in the heat of summer to cut and clear the trees—they fear the small cracks they see in the tree trunks, imagine their strains leading to the big branches above, saying "they'll crash on our houses...and on our cars."

What they want to destroy is precisely what gives Virgil his energy and privacy at dusk, his "popping" on the synthetic "wooden" deck to Pandora (Egyptian Lover), not afraid of a single splinter in his foot. No need for cover, save the trees, but in the dream, there is a woman who is covered, half-formed under a white tarp. Is she alive? Is she mourning?

Virgil finds himself in a panic. He doesn't know how to let in this half-formed being under the blanket, and he is still between sleep and the place in which the dream becomes an imagined black gay club in New Orleans. The patrons inside are wearing steel-woven masks, the tips shaped into silver horns for eyes. The club is dark and, like the green trail, also wet and dripping, and the room, too, is a corridor. Clearly, this is the inverse of the world of his morning run—so, too, the trees, and the world in retrospect is suddenly dark.

As in, Virgil, that morning, runs by Black Lives Matter lawn signs in the whitest, greenest place where he actually once lived, and since this is his first time actually running where he recalls only driving, he finds it difficult to find his way. Though he is reminded of the possibility of the beauty in life when he receives a text video that shows "Little T" running, counting her own steps: 1—2, 3, 4, 5, 6/7/8/9—10, the last little foot step hitting the launch pad to release the neon-foam rocket in the air, then its slow-mo gliding horizontally into the shady afternoon.

On the trail, another brown runner floats by, and though Virgil is clearly a fatter version of him (he thinks that, though Virgil is only slightly "flabby"), Virgil keeps on his shirt. Virgil is happy that his body does not shake much as he runs. Who would ever know that Virgil's dreams were so wet and black? Too, he is drinking something in the dream, but he can't recall what, only writing it down, quickly, but not knowing how to get back to the dream directly enough to know what it was that he took in. Moving from table to table in the large club, Virgil recalls, instead, an endless set of tables, and around these tables he moves and waits in line after line of people that he knows, poets mostly, and most of them Black, M, K, S, etc.

Of course, in his freedom, he tracks a related sequence: a bobcat on a trail that enters the bush, a house cat peeking behind a glass door, a bird washing itself in a hand. Once, in the city, so long ago, Virgil met a member of the press, the paparazzi lurker who did not fuck him, but laid his long cock along his back, above his crack, and shot cum on him. He was with the paparazzi lurker twice, and both times caught crabs, but this was not as important as his advice to the very young Virgil. Member of the press, this paparazzi lurker said, "If you want to write, write."

What is the difference between the outside and the inside of the dream can only be explained in the pitch darkness that fills the room in the vision of blue and black. Menacing, this threat manifests as black, nylon luggage, and in it, power cords, flash drives, and speakers that shake as he looks at them. These things are not permanent, yet they are there. What in this material is his? What surfaces does he own? Virgil remembers, he was not reading on the stage but he was on it, an intervening MC, who said something like, "How can you play a set during the middle of someone else's performance?"

It's true, a band began to play in the middle of the reading, and there Virgil was, helping out KamQuietDJ, the two of them greeting one another on the stage, heads touching together, black hair above the middle of the floor, Virgil trying, in a way, so desperately, to get KamQuietDJ to see what he needed to do, but this was not possible, because the speaker, even held up against the mic, did not amplify KamQuietDJ's voice above the band's antics.

In the end, what chance did KamQuiet DJ (the only other black performer) have at sharing his work, to read to the (as usual) largely all white audience? Virgil thinking of the video of K and P—how they revealed how funny the two Blacks getting adoration from the white acapella campus group was, the way each Black said "Niggha" right in each other's faces—is what, in the dream, as in life, brings him together in solidarity with KamQuietDJ.

In retrospect of these divergent yet intersecting "stories," Virgil writes the opening lines to a fellowship application, describing where and how he would like to go:

Dear Committee Members, I of traumatized mind and body, seek the time and space to sleep, to not travel to any exotic locale, to travel inwards, a journey through the trauma of my own existence to find others. In fact, what I am hoping to do is to not work on a recognizable project, but to move the material inside to create bridges from one non-existent plane to barely another. Hence for the sake of im/possibility, I need to think of a direction (albeit routed through vectors of the unconscious) to return to the site of abjection— just to see, or "seek" is all. Thus, I submit the space of my body and mind as a site of inquiry, and, at the same time, the tacit understanding is that this might all lead down the path that leads to my own heart, however injured, however inured.

An unknown white woman from a circle of those crying enters the dream nightclub, and she like all of the rest are waiting to "use" the bathroom, which turns out to be an impossibly small stall. There is a plunger visible in the "bathroom" that is actually a music box, or a cabinet, and as Virgil opens it, he realizes that he can't go in, and why? It's too small, but beyond this: a woman slides her foot in the toilet, kicking in the backed up waste, and Virgil is disgusted by seeing her camel, suede, knee-length tasseled boot, no sole, working as a makeshift plunger.

Virgil, suddenly caught up with his entourage, ditches the line. A few people who surround him congratulate him for saying what he said on the stage, that is, "How dare they play the music when the only other black (besides him) in the room is rocking his work?" Is this the subject of his dream? Is this the penultimate plot, its actions or activities emitting from this center?

Virgil isn't sure, but somehow, he knows that if he is to understand the relationship of dreaming to content, he must, like he told that little blue boy, not worry "if you mess up." But what he does not intuit is that the worry of messing up will return, the unfinished business of intention pulling him into the void, breaking him apart, so he'll exist, a wandering subject. The little boy demonstrates this himself, at Jake's, as he walks back and bangs on the closed bathroom-stall door behind which is Butch.

When he decided to scrape away what was once there on his sketchpad, Virgil rid himself of the expected surface to reveal what came up by accident. Only the single cricket realizes it, singing. This is the sound before the symphony of them begins to play, and as the song en masse comes, the ugly, silent cave crickets have no idea what is coming. Before Virgil attacks one, he plots his approach from the stairs that lead to the basement. Despite by evolution to leaping at their predator—a scare tactic—this one is smashed by the Swiffer's naked, rubber bottom, flat, quick. The small broken fragment of the insect corpse reveals no blood, leaving only a small shadow, a trace where half of its body was. Virgil, upon this rendered absence, builds.

Virgil wasn't always so fair; in fact, he was a towering brown body, lording over that LittleDandelion, who still haunts him, or signifies his coming into consciousness around how he was held back by LittleDandelion's power, which happens to so many, *Like us*, Virgil thinks, all the time. *What we need*, he also realizes, wandering in his own Venice, is a bag (it doesn't matter the cost, *You know some are 3500 Euros, some are 590 Euros* whatever), that flesh in the drop of the field of soft, perforated leather will, in fact, fill his need, his conspiratorial kin with something that was, after all, once out of his pocket's reach, but never his heart's, a longing, a drift to return—but to where will he return? If it were so easy, and it sometimes is so easy, Virgil would settle into the fight of his life, or the fight of his mother's MommaSpine's who is held together by pins, and steel, valves shut, stunted—she says, "It was too much candy."

They say we can put her back together, her spine, the root gone, compounding in on itself, fused vertebrae, killing the nerves. There was a prayer. There was an attendant. Virgil does not have a God of his own, like she does. But he has never so long walked on back-to-back double shifts, on any such hard hospital floors, caring after the left-behind, and not caring after that back of hers that is no longer able to turn them over in their beds, nor to lift them further away from their dying.

Once S-olds, Virgil's very important poetry teacher, noticed something, that something was missing, that something in the poem wasn't right. It wasn't ekphrastic (nor did Virgil think of that encounter between objects as a possibility in language and being, as in: what one thing could be made without the other) but, still, to her wise eyes, he left so much of the poem out. Why? It was, he felt, somewhere else, something out of his reach in a room, a gym, a community center, where he saw another black body dancing.

Virgil could see into the arc and point of the dance, wanted to make the connection between his poem and that body, but felt lost in the cross-wiring, an incomplete link, which, to S-olds, was so obvious. The solution—remove the poem. But what Virgil knows now is that this connection is impossible to solve, two planes whirling apart into the ever distance of the not knowing, there, only traces of a past lined into the present.

For instance, Virgil does not know the name of where he first went to school, but he can see a day there unfold before him in a home movie shot by MommaSpine. He does not need to make this life, nor does he need another entry to make the whole, whole. It is a special day: "International Day," Virgil recalls, at least that is what it was called on that base in Millington, or was it Guam, or does it matter? Further, does he know that the Super 8 clip cannot be optimized, that even after four hours, there will still, in the end, be the same error message and no upload?

It is unalterable, but somehow, what Virgil wants is exactly what Virgil gets. He slows that blue boy version of himself and asks in realization:

"Why would I ask you to wipe under the table, on this wet, wooded deck?"

It has, indeed, rained, and Virgil, after all, has gone off on the waitress at Aldo's—and when she says to The Musician, "I like your necklace," which is a big black/brown seed on a gorgeous African-American woman,

Virgil, the violent, has a Kara Walker moment. The seed should go where it goes, plunged into the seeker. *Ponderous is so far from pondering*, Virgil realizes within a few clicks, but this does not change his anger, or his tone, nor his need to plant the seed somewhere else, somewhere far from the neck, somewhere away from The Musician, somewhere into the drift of pulling the pieces of his protracted anger into this recounted point:

"I went off on her, and she still smiling."

There isn't a song as he tries to hold onto what he remembers. The silent movies would get stuck, and suddenly a burn, the black boiling opening up into the shot, and then Virgil's dad and Naldo would stop and splice, find the wound in the film, and close it. And then they would all watch, and eat popcorn popped in a pot.

MommaSpine sewed. Patterns to make her sons, not fit in but stand out, covering them in costumes of origins, of other countries, lederhosen, or silver rivets in black slacks, hi-boots for a little brown boy as a blue matador in whose head? Anything to make, to represent the country in which they were imagined to live, anything to figure out a way to be, to find a way, not back, but into where they landed.

And suddenly, Virgil is compelled to cut, to paste, to build. Little white boy on a Sit 'n' Spin. Little white boy in a brown field. Little white boy in a fact. Little white boy who has it all, who, surely, given his tiny body, still contains the force to say:

You know, you don't want this. I don't want you to have anything I want to have, and to steal it is for you

*to be the toy itself, which is after all mine, and because
it is not yours, we in fact have you, Virgil, surrounded,
if even by me.*

Virgil, the man, could not give a care. Virgil, the man, is
old. He oscillates. He cuts to salve the patch. Understands
opposition, not as tension, but as drift, though Virgil, the
boy, is lost when trying to recall his mother, not dead, but
so alive, a kind of constant return to that which evades
him, to that which is like a bolo that kills, or like a skip on
a street, or like a bolero, or like a summer hat, or like that
which MommaSpine has sewn together in the form of a
weapon to save his imagination.

Virgil's dad understands baggage to be like things
one should carry, like the poet DKBlaster explained how
like in a video game, one picks up weapons along the
way, as if by chance, as if by accrual; and if one does not,
and if one, simultaneously, cannot let things go along
the way, one dies. But hit, reset. *What will Virgil carry
along the way?* he realizes, shifts. He will not take a side,
nor have a take. *Leave Virgil Alone. Leave Virgil Alone.*

The little white boy is not the Blu Boy, who is the
little brown boy who got that bully back. Who waited
with a set of heavy keys on a chain with other keys, to
move into smack his assailant's freshly haircut head in
the nape of his neck:

"SALLY BOW!!!"

The little Blu Boy had been, after all, sewn together
by silence. Two fingers spit on would clip a neck back,
but keys? A revenge so quick, not caught—Virgil knew
that when he leapt, and struck that older white boy,

it would crack into his enemy's soul to know he could never retaliate. The fact was that the little brown boy he would want to fuck up for fucking him up, bad, had slipped into the safety of his class.

In the memory of that furious sentry pacing, wanting to kill Virgil, Virgil thinks some about LittleDandelion, his little wish, blown into his face, and in the sun, the sun that Virgil makes his arms move around above his head, forming into the shape of another eye, elbows out, and then he arches his back, torso up into the sky, back against his chair, like he must have done, so long ago, then in relief, relief in getting his most hated back, then walking home, and leaving the next day, (Blu Boy) forever.

Critique

Squat is bearded, shorter than Virgil, and more com-pact. Squat's face, in every instance—in the kitchen, or in the brown living room, near the collage art (of shells, of wires, or in spirals, or glued artifacts), near the bag of Wavy Lays, or near Virgil's coughing from the gym chlorine—is also near the heavy door on the corner of the hard-to-find house below the street sign, in front of it, covered by leaves.

What defines Squat's prettiness? Nothing too far beyond the breath, which is short, because Squat is fat, his dick a nub, and his hair is thin and soft. Squat asks Virgil to feel it, and his balls, equally soft, the latter big, the former, silk, each guiding Virgil's touch. In a sense, Virgil can take it or leave it, but really, even though he won't recall exactly where he was that night, he wants to hold onto the tenderness of Squat's body.

Of Cyndee, not Sin-Dee, Virgil tells Squat in his kitchen: "He takes the air out of the room." Over the expensive salami and hard cheese that Virgil brought and the very decent Figge Pinot Noir (Carmel-by-the-Sea), Virgil makes this assessment about Cyndee, not Sin-Dee, the sous chef who came to Squat's house "dressed." Cyndee, not Sin-Dee's "real" name is Will, who Virgil saw as soon as he walked through the door. Will, on his knees sucking cock, out of dress, is bet-ter looking than Cyndee, not Sin-Dee, because this bitch in a latex corset, hot pink, with some black, long sleeve fishnet top, and "natural" hose. And Virgil, upon seeing this hoe in the living room, retreats back to the kitchen, washes out the cloudy wine glasses, trying to not make it obvi he wants to flee, despite Squat's softness and the promise of a gangbang, how-ever unrealized.

Still, the promise of a gangbang is a feeling he holds in his chest, something that does not stay, but instead, is maintained. There's no equivalent metaphor, because all he sees of Cyndee, not Sin-Dee is the fishnet pattern showing off his white arms, and his chunky cheap boots, off-pink wig, and his face, busted, so much so that Virgil cannot even look at it, straight on. But he feels its heat. "Ugly" is what Virgil thinks, dented perhaps, dark lips, but more than that—they're wide.

Face like the wide smiling sun graphic on CBS Sunday Morning is what Virgil conjures next to this hate, his own self, wider than he can ever imagine, wider than the surface of that smiling, winking sun he recalls before he walked the several blocks to bus tables and wash dishes at Rice Bowl, which was an important walk, because it was attached to that sun and the show's anchor, Charles Kuralt, a real dream for Virgil.

Virgil realizes he is obsessed with embedded desire, skipping all the steps that lead to it, to what he wants, now, now that he is stable—which only means he has the time and resources to end up at a sex party on a weekend evening with little else to do. This is not cruising. It is examining an early memory, triggered by the present, a memory collaged against another party he wants to remember.

Virgil remains nice, as he cuts through the salami, and leaves the hard cheese in small chunks. Later, at Stream's place in Frisco, he cuts a new piece off, and in doing so, the block has fallen to the floor. The cut wedge could be a doorstop. But like on a good river cruise, one has time, and freedom to take—it stops—and so goes, memory.

Below the collage art, there are toys, a laundry basket—objects that echo Squat's description of what usually happens here when there isn't a sex party.

"My daughter stays home, but sometimes travels. Her husband works. My kids let me live here. They don't know."

"Did you feel alone? I mean when you went?" Virgil wants to ask himself, but Stream asks, and sings through the night what Virgil tries to offer, quiet, and for them to be safe, but Virgil is wandering.

I gazed—and gazed—but little thought
What wealth the show to me had brought:

In Wordsworth's "Daffodils," the pull for Virgil, is in its privation—more exactly, to discern that the scene of privation is what Virgil experienced: in that home, lying fallow, waiting for something to evolve, like a cruise but not quite.

What does is SkinBagFucker, a top, who looks like he lost all the weight but is left a tall, gaunt, loose bag of skin. He fucks Virgil for a sec, but Virgil is otherwise unmoved. The Other sits there lost, his pants open as he talks about his ex-wife, how he hates her, and the kid they share.

SkinBagFucker pulls out, as Virgil is removed, because Virgil wanted to get to know The Other, tortured divorcee, horned up on Squat's family couch, pants a half crown around the ankles, belt flopped open, Virgil just barely remembers, but forgets Squat, who sent a follow up email, never to be answered.

The floor of the Gold House is dotted with chipped paint, and shavings from the color pencils, the skins black and curved, edges tipped with copper and silver flake. In his collages, Virgil wants to create something direct, something that stuns him from the dream in which he sees himself from behind, seated in a class where he's never been in real life, a dream in which his hair is shaved from the back to his bare scalp, two flaps spreading like blonde-red wings puffed up on both sides.

In a sense, there is hope in the dream, despite his rachet do—a hope that, ultimately, there is a way back into sense-making, a gesture captured in the drift away from the body, a drift in which Virgil sees himself, strong as the curve of trees revealed in the distance since the neighbors across the street have removed even more trees. Close-up, two drops hang from the arms of a small branch that reaches to either side of Virgil's sight-line. Far away, a birdbath is chopped into a tree stump. From its center, a black rod extends to its tip, a hook, from which a glass feeder hangs.

Editors want work. Not that Virgil isn't grateful—he is producing, sure, but rarely ever from the deep quiet he needs. He imagines his work to be children he will never have, legacies left to claim. Though Virgil cannot recall any single child that constitutes this fantasy, he does remember a yearning he's after, a mode of escape: an art-making schedule, a slow race against teaching and more meetings.

So far removed is Virgil from his painting, the tip of his finger, the brush, this "brush," the ballast—maybe this is what Stream heard as maturity in the speaker's voice? In it, glue and tape adhere: these constitute the elements of the line. The secret to Virgil's narrative ability, however, is that Virgil's voice is severed, leaving no direct connection to the self.

In fact, Virgil is of every consequence at several removes from his own work, not because he doesn't understand it, but because he has a constant need to attend to work outside of writing. And so often, he feels impatient, not like when he's writing—in writing this does matter, but in art it matters less. There, he can go back into the dirty page, push his pastels into the shape of a scorpion's claw, capture its serrations with either empty pen tip, or fingernail.

There is so much that Virgil wants to do, so much he wants to fulfill in the silence he now has, lost in the collapse of surfaces—the homemade press of the broken lead into paper where Virgil imagines and seeks. If the writing is like the baby he will never have, the human baby that is, then the fictive grows thick and in dots on the ankle, and they scratch off. This is a mirror, too.

After yoga—his home practice—Virgil scrubs and then applies the lotion, then the Lotrimin, and Virgil, who has never spent his day "getting high," does recall, while feeling "high," visiting the Agnes Martin paintings in the Guggenheim, and the small video room, where Martin, between strokes, says, "You have to perfect," or "You can never make a mistake," and in the moment of thinking this, Virgil wants to think of the relationship between freedom and absence.

Virgil promises that he will take a walk around the block, but he does not—and the memory of the promise recesses into both a past, and into a day that has only just started. In this start, there is no *fresh scent*. Instead, there is a quieting yellow that fills the room, light penetrating the impossibility of seeing anything, but inside of this glow, a feeling. Virgil will walk alone in the soft grass, follow to where Butch says, "Come, look at the flowers."

Butch provides the real: the fat oranges, the stuff left in the cracks, the removed carpets, the sound of the flute that fills Virgil's ears, the violin, the mustard yellow leaves that coat the low hedges, and the harsh turning tea, Emperor's Clouds & Mist. Sometimes, in these mornings, there is a weight that throbs in his imagination, surging down his arms.

MommaSpine's neck will not turn all the way, no matter how hard Virgil massages it. How hard it is to move away from remembering running with her as a boy in the Navy Housing yards, fields, no matter how wide, in which they kicked the soccer ball in a tight, yet syncopated circle, with one another. Virgil, in this circling, with his mom, moves between zones of memory and place, too often sinking inside the bodies of the men that he has wanted forever, and now it is his time to move around them, and to collect.

Archetypes: these start with their eyes, blue and grey, to want to remove them, to keep them in jars. In the Tupperware is a mix of seared tuna with the first olive then blackening avocados, cut in chunks that transfix and hold. Is this the way collage works, the mix of fragments, the source work of the self, suspended?

Peter Brady is bladed, in a dream, which is as recent as the drift of the knife in the dish rack slitting into the finger, and soon after recalling this, how the wrist was almost broken between the refrigerator and the light switch. After these occurrences, Virgil realizes he has to slow down to see, or else he would have been hospitalized, too, moments after MommaSpine (Heart), and soon before Butch (Knees).

Dreamed Peter Brady is "trans," but in this version, TransPeter is wearing a white dildo. Does it come out of his hood, a vent? Is he, too, a Cuck, like the Orange Buffoon, who is on his knees, reconciled to his own white race in front of the brown Sheiks, and, too, where the shipmen have tricked TransPeter into going to the pier, where they've trapped him? He stares into a floodlight, a President, Real or Fake.

But too, Virgil feels the lights against his face. In the still painting, Virgil wants to work on, even in the midst of writing, from the security cameras that still the actual view outside of his windows: Virgil is adrift, and looking to be loved. For Virgil, too, this is a constant constraint: five pink flowers and a green smudge.

They stone now-non-trans Peter Brady without hurling stones. He falls into a black lake, where his head is hit by a propeller, noggin' cut open, death-bled, and his corpse floats to the surface. Virgil is watching him rise, for in Virgil's foot is the smallest piece of their Long Island home, a sliver of wood embedded, a splinter that does some damage over the days, the days after he flies his wounded foot back to Santa Cruz.

Virgil was afraid to run on it, but he did anyhow, the forward momentum edging him into a state of being out of time. Surely it is a hate crime when the white fueled by a white site stabs a black through the chest? What would MIA say, Ariana Grande? Nails/Ballbearings/An enlarged perimeter—everything, for Virgil, is chaotic, except for the line.

Surely, there is no way that Virgil will be charged for Peter Brady's propeller-death, but Virgil does not die along their travels. Nor Terrorist—Is this Virgil, the Narcissist? Sure, but who cares? The collage demands this construction, and so too, fiction does the breath, the breath of the line, and the feeling, too, especially as it hovers into the succinct Peter trying to hold onto the edge of the boat, ruddered away, pulled not to safety but to the place holding his body up for views and likes.

"Take off your clothes," as if suddenly they know who he is, and at the same time, they realize he is still alive. Virgil, vis-à-vis, or *in* Peter Brady, or TransPeter, *is* ripped apart. Therefore, Virgil boils water for his tea—it is always after the water is hot, and while he is pouring it into his cup, that he is reminded of the two young black gay men who were scalded to near death in their morning still asleep embrace.

Whilst in one another's arms, one of the men's mother's boyfriends, black long-haul trucker, who slept over from time to time, caught the sight of "...all that gay," wanted them unsealed, like stuck fucking dogs. He burned them apart, and in doing so, maimed, scarred, and fused them together forever to Virgil's imaginary, each morning bound with Virgil's simple, hot green tea.

A small girl, white, captains the boat in which Peter Brady finds his demise.

Something else happens below the water. Virgil realizes that writing, the act of the body in the turns of its written emissions is, too, is like a dance: *What is it that one needs to render in that water? What does one need to face?*

Perhaps for Virgil, it is when he waves, energy ticking from his fingers through the elbow, across his shoulders, to the other side, surfacing into the collage of anything Virgil constitutes as his fantasy, the arm's translation, into his daily swim.

Conclusion: *If the music in the freestyle is the language, then too, the keyboard is the instrument, a sonic place, typing, where the body is fixed against the current of sorrow.* Virgil's strikes and pulls, and every scene that he renders is the same scene in which he locks and looks: This is where Virgil finds himself propelled, moving around.

On the subway platform, Virgil shows off to the two blacks. One, he notices much more than the other, because that one is making a sound. This sound manifests somewhere between beat box squeak and crow, or between a scream from a girl (or boy) being pounded out by a Chubold, or the actual Daddy Mugs—certainly into a boy—or the dryer which strains at an internal hinge, leaking its song, or the steel pulsing subway tracks, sound widening towards the waiting passengers.

The dream, itself, is suspended, so much so that he believes that Butch, upstairs, has died sometime in the night, or is actually dying at the moment Virgil hears these noises. But of course, Butch is alive, and the sound he makes in the night is not at all melodic, yet it's something Virgil wants to hear.

What was that?

A bird crashing into the window.

Or maybe the sound is not a sound at all, but The Defeated's mouth, which is like an octopus' opening, the teeth separating. The jaws emit a beak, first, over Virgil's eyes, jutting out to cover his face with its cutting. Virgil's tongue is short and wide in his mouth.

Virgil's teeth, though yellow, are symmetrical, and they keep him attuned to what he needs to make. When he tries to pull away, he is drawn back into the arms of The Defeated, dragging him from what he wants to be.

The puffy black bird—it snatches a blueberry from the bush and gorges it in the windowsill in Virgil's vision, but the birdbath is empty. How does this absence attach itself to the fear he feels when he moves away from the blacks on the platform?

Nothing to stare at, no window, no anticipatory longing.

Virgil under attack by blacks is a racist constant—

"Let me see what you're writing," and Virgil, like a punk-azz bitch, says, "You mean my term paper?" and this relinquishment, forces him awake. In retrospect, Virgil cannot adequately reconstruct the dream, but he does recall the arrangement of power, a power over him, daring him to stand up from his desk by the boy, all black, while Virgil saw himself, as half, settled, even then, in the tension.

The encounter remains with him, but the dream, by the time he gets to its construction, is so far away; in fact, only the most racist remnants remain in his dream, the boy's hair a minor fro, a muscle shirt, the ash on his jaw, his body thin, arm curvy and strong. Virgil's body, flows, his hair, wet with Ultra Sheen, reading *Tennis* magazine, yellow Dee Cee's with thin white piping down the side, all from Kmart, even then, Virgil was fattish.

It is less being between dream and memory that reveals the saliency of the experience, but something else, it's what manifests between waking and carrying that drives Virgil's critique. The morning (or post-nap) is the space where Virgil examines what just happened. The plot is pulling out of his own unconscious, and the plot is also pulling up something from a past he has tucked away. It is not accidental. It is, after all, a way of seeing into the questions of who that little brown boy was, and who this black man is, all in the space of saying:

I will not chase the consumptive.
I will, instead, involve myself in the productive.
All against the threat of whiteness—

The sale on the Oliver Peoples frames. The artist who "redacts" language from the *NYT*—Blackness, or us, or all: In there, too, exists, plot.

Or the plot is in the fact that he cannot recall a single isolated idea, once it is written on the page. Perhaps it is the sea of argument he is after. CandidateOrangutan sports a red cap and wants to build a giant, *beautiful* wall between us and them, brown and white, and in the movie *The Boy in the Striped Pajamas*, there is a fence, and one boy (Bruno) goes under it, to look for his friend's (Shmuel's) father only to be caught up in a gang sweep and gassed to death.

He, the little white boy with brown hair and blue eyes is gassed along with him, the boy without hair and rotted out teeth. White/White. This happened, *but bitch so did Slavery*. So, the confusion is in the plot that divides the reality of what Virgil is into what he hopes to be, the submerged self, caught in the fantasy of becoming one wall, or the other—In other words, what sense might this scene make, and what's the urgency of its return in the face of what Virgil chooses to watch, what's real, and how might he sleep to disgorge these considerations?

Queen M says that the structure of the project that Virgil will carry as he moves across the fictive is bound by his dissertation, in what she names an "invisible scaffold,"—Virgil, attentive to dreams and memory, is also attuned to form. This is to say that he is interested in the ways that form works in collusion with vision, not content. Though this is crucial, Virgil knows that he's liquid across such thoughts.

He understands this by way of walks—even in a Port Jefferson Station strip mall parking lot, he attempts to figure it out. This time, he is talking to Stream, who is interviewing to elevate into another strata, from now being out of work, to the prospect of being in charge of directing cruises for the rich, those who can charter yachts to freedom, any single booking, a business expense.

Battle into whiteness, a city by the sea—

To work in prose, for Virgil, is not like working in collage, or in poetry. It is closer to being free. The freedom to pursue a line remains the source of the possible, to remain nimble in order to engage in the present, so any one encounter is only a set of coordinates as artificial relations between the subject and the scene, or the scene as the encounter becoming palpable within the scope of the dream—or chance—Virgil's notations, life, etc.

By the gassing, Virgil is not devastated, but he wants amends, amends that cannot be made outside of what he renders or recalls. In the second part of the dream, Virgil looks at the unveiling of a boring party. There are Asians in that dream. The party, unveiled in stages, is a picture, opened up in sequences. The dream is staggered against this. A sequence is formed. Wind chimes, birds garble, and bark, too.

Some go on vacations to get away, but Virgil understands he must remain in one place even if Virgil goes. On vacation, Virgil likes to stay in the hotel, or he goes nowhere, or he goes back home to understand the limitations of who he is.

When Virgil returns to Sacra, to his childhood home, his father, Forgetting, To Live says, "You look just like Daddy....When you came into the house, you looked just like Daddy." Virgil reasons it is only because of his baldness, but he realizes it is not only because of this, because Forgetting, To Live says, "Isn't it funny how heredity works?" And he looks at Virgil closely to see something in his face, a long-remembered glance between a father and son from a past in which Virgil and Forgetting, To Live, connect.

On the other side of the green wall is a poster where DaddyJoliet is depicted running for an elected position. Virgil will read the poster, but before he does, he thinks *Gubernatorial,* a tangle in his head, and tongue, too, so he looks up the spelling before he writes it, but not after lifting himself out of bed into the home office to greet the old black and white poster that reads: *Assistant Supervisor.*

Knowing that DaddyJoliet was invested in a political life guides Virgil in the complexities of the conversation he has on the telephone with an editor. He tells the editor that he has written a play about his engagement with diaspora and mixed-race identity, things that Virgil negotiates, but are never spoken by MommaSpine, though Forgetting, To Live is the one that often recounts her past, in stories, to their children.

They hold memory, in secrets, in just out of sleep conversations behind their bedroom door, in the quiet early morning, and Virgil, as he can, listens and records. What to carry forward, and what slips out in the process? Virgil imagines himself a mobile site of identity, a wire trick in which he is: a gesture, a resin, through which to communicate, a way in—

Virgil: I see the rationale for the POV of the main character, from the buzz of the military biplane, and the water below its belly returning to the sea.

Editor: I don't understand—it seems so abstract, though I suspect dense enough for unpacking.

Virgil: Look closely, you will see in me, a story of my mother's fear, the fear in leaving behind who MommaSpine loves, her yellow family, for the black man she also loves, but the trouble is there is a radical fracture in this leaving, in the resultant family, a family with severed histories, a family heard in sing song voices submerged in a Skype call between CeSis, MommaSpine and those still alive. The main character cannot engage—right now—and so suspends in this refrain:

If they did not leave the Philippines, they'd be caught, and hung by their toes.

In the Skype call when MommaSpine returns from the hospital, she learns another brother has died. Her sister has died. She knows it. Her family has stolen, money, again, and things.

We wanted to send for them, to go to school, here.

Editor: But do you understand these parts? Are they retrievable? Do you understand how they may figure into a cohesive unit?

Virgil: Lots of questions, but I think so—Perhaps there's a connection that has to do with me being the conduit for the very desire of their love, and its separation—to think through all the parts left in that Subic Bay Grey shot from inside the plane, out—this is the difference between memory and what's on the Super 8 reels, what's left behind "at the bottom of the sea," as Forgetting, To Live sometimes says.

Editor: I don't understand how it imports, but I do understand that it has to do with being mixed between incomplete, yet received and worn histories—this is something I do hear in your echoing so often, maybe even subliminally, the haunting phrase: WHO DOES HE THINK HE IS?

Virgil: Mixed is not like being a mix, like a mutt, but something else—It's like struggling, or hanging on, or splitting yourself from the core of who you think you are and attempting to mine the vocabulary of the self, as in a café where I am marked as Brazilian, or when I say I am Filipino, marked, actually, as Black, which is, what I am, too. All of this is surface. Loss links, and so too, does violation, and of course, so does escape, and its cousin, exile.

Editor: I do understand some of these relationships to your vexed past, but what excites me is that there is, through it all, something that cannot be captured, yet still must be shown. I, too, am tired of the black and white dyad, and because I am tired of it, I move around wanting to know more about it! But my excitement, perhaps, I must submerge. But I might ask you to ponder the exilic.

Virgil: Yes, maybe, you're right. The real engagement, after all, is a break from knowing. When I was watching myself online, I looked very fat until I saw myself move back from the lectern, looking into the sky, into the light, into the knowing of who I wanted to be. There my face was thin, so isn't this the point, too? When I don't eat, shadows.

Editor: I see what you mean, for sure, and I will consider this, but do remember I am taken, mostly by your ability to listen, and who you are on the other side of the phone, what you may be, and how you might help us to see you.

Virgil understands the source of his body as fact, as a point of realization, the connections less between each story than their being wed to a path that marks the past, circling around the desire to know, and to understand what can't be connected. Virgil's interpretation punctuates his desire for feeling, for an understanding of his own body, less grounded, but turning, into an inside, nonetheless, he makes.

A pink-white child is taking a piss in a field. This girl, who is lost, is really a boy, an innocent little sibling of one of the children in the car, driven by KQGlam, who is driving all of them to safety in her red MINI. How does Virgil know it's a MINI? Because of the power move that KQGlam makes in realizing that she won't be able to take them home to keep them away from their demise. There's a wrap-around porch that will slow them from getting inside, so KQGlam turning around, looks at the house, assesses the porch, and adjusts her turn radius.

But why do the children want to go home in the first place? What porch, like this, leads back to their very safe lives?—A life both there, and unattached to impediment or banal fact. KQGlam's makeup in the car is clear, red lips and blue eyes, and her beauty matches her insides. She's one black driver, and the children she drives to safety are fleshy pink bodies bearing blackness as a resource.

The point of the retreat from the Paris Accords is to erase the fact of a black president. It should have never happened. But because it did, it remains for a particularly dumb sum, a nightmare. Even the world will burn and melt at the thought of the blacks still swimming in the pools, and the stabbings grow, so how else would KQGlam drive but effective and simultaneously cray?

SingedheadBear in the Port Jefferson Station LA Fitness spa wants Virgil to buy CBLI Stocks—the company sells an injectable fluid that upon nuclear fallout, will prevent anybody from being radiation poisoned, but Virgil, along with them all, is being poisoned, right then, in the spa, and Virgil, who calls the OrangeBLOWHOLE a Drag Queen Clown to SingedheadBear's dumb fucking face, as well as the others's in the churning chlorine, knows that OrangeBLOWHOLE a Drag Queen Clown's hair is a crude comb over, but SingedheadBear, so Jim Jones, is insistent that that flat, dyed head halo is all the clown's own, and he's strong, 6'2" and in good shape, and the world's melting is fake.

"Look, I'm not going to change your mind, and you're not going to change mine."

Please, we could talk forever until I saw the shelf of your brow, golden.

"Listen, you're not listening."

Virgil does hush a little, sinks down, but glances at their underwater crotches, but he does not leer, no matter how much the cocks tease.

The divide is simple, the worn faces of those on T.V. supporting OrangeBLOWHOLE a Drag Queen Clown reflect a need to partition such blackness away from the possibility of their getting over. "College isn't for every-one—" *you are so stupid,* knows Virgil, and he tries: "What adult male in your life has hair like that?"

Even the spa-water laughs—

Buffoon and Clown. Pig and Rapist.

"But we want change," and the two men agree—this is a good thing.

The US will find them, and take out their leader, *bunker bust that shit.*

"I'm tired of the same old same old, politics as usual."

Burn them alive. Virgil wants to make a very difficult connection, still in words, despite his anger in the water, and because he is feeling Gaslit, he does. He understands Race as a refraction through local desires, those transmitted through the T.V., T.V. undone into naps and sweat on his fattening head post yoga synovial fluid drain—

Tonight, it is reported that a white on a train yells through a steel door, slits throats, or acid burns faces. It's so loud here: even Lebron's LA home, is vandalized, noosed. And Nigger Tagged.

Behind the steel door is a black conductor, and this conductor who's being yelled at by KeysandCard understands that he will be going no-where, no-where because KeysandCard traps the black subway conductor behind the small door of his driving compartment, screaming, *Nigger!*

KQGlam, the black driver, is going around the house not to get away from the danger, but to drive right through it, to skirt around the porch and the house, popped up, the tires turning up on the sides of the structure, and driving onto the brick walls, and over the windows. Gravity doesn't matter. What does?— the wheels sticking tight to the side of the house as she curves around, wide as possible, a bounding and barreling escape.

The little glowmer is still pissing. Watching his dream, as though it's on T.V., he, along with the rest of the audience, realizes that the little glowmer, luminous white child, is a girl because she opens her tiny legs to reveal a little vagina that oscillates between transparent blue and white, orange-yellow urine spilling to the earth. KQGlam, fully televised, is suddenly white, too, and running on foot, holds her panic in, then releases it four-on-the-floor like a blown capillary, floating in the air, walls pop open into the night as the still cold glaciers crash into a still scene, for now, an icy sea.

Virgil beats back his psoas pain by twisting his body into the pops that come out when he achieves triangle pose, and even though he knows from this, that he will nap very long, the release of oxygen from his joints gives only some relief from his hate.

He doesn't blame anyone for it, for his hate is bound to the pain that builds in his back, the very thought of it reminds him of the Hamachi Kama he saw the prodigy kid-cooks preparing on T.V.

He is so far away from home, but feels suddenly that he will work, and gain, in the arc of what leaves his body with minor gasps—Virgil's body bends into the shape of his stretching, an alarm to an awakened spine.

These are the facts, but the facts are not any better because of three white people that deliver it on the news show, *All In*. It feels so violating: one is pretty, and brunette, and her face is sculpted, her lips a fallen pink begonia.

The second, also female, is doe-eyed, and nods, and they know-it-all, and the third, the host, a male, fat head, but skinny-suited, his eyes framed, too, in Oliver Peoples. What does Virgil do to convince himself that he isn't still owned?

The skeleton in the dream is not a sign in the dream at all; in fact, the dream holds a reality: It's the roaches that will survive says SingedheadBear. *They want the war* is what all the dumb whites in the spa want, *gimme some more!*

For whom is the bully, boy yellow or orange? Virgil settles at the table to be apart from Clean, so far away, now in his mind, so far that he can properly ponder in the distance, in the series of Republican texts: "the country is divided..."—Virgil will not text Vermont, Clean.

The table is empty, or all white, round and full with no one purple in attendance, but before he sees the table he will not sit or eat at, Virgil sees what he loves in Butch, an eye around every corner to make sure of Virgil's most perfect life.

Nice people, men, white ones, with layered grey hair that look as smooth as ice cream, how Virgil is so seduced! He has even taken to eating this hair, devouring it, like a rich clean stream—*the hair fills and nourishes!*

And there it was, after the vodka and soda, or after the soda water, in the heat of the city, or after the expensive but terrible white wine in the Hotwire hotel, somewhere on the East Side, the meal he would order every time—

A triple-decker turkey club on toasted wheat, with onion rings, the bacon and the threat of toothpicks, sharp and angled into the roof of his mouth. Sharp as the bits of orange-yellow plastic wraps at the tips, they cut into him. More whites, slitting throats.

All the friends on Facebook are saying the whites are terrorists, or maybe one is, so it might mean all of them think that—Virgil would, during the stabbings, eating his swordfish over Greek salad learn: so many mowed down in London, and stabbed—

Virgil has clearly made it, rolling into the hotel lobby wearing cut-off shorts. His slim yellow shirt fit, tailored in a black jacket with a red inside collar. Some of the details he feels are in the yoga shorts he's fit in, and would later, tenured!

He moves into finally seeing and being adjacent to a family of which he will never be a part. This is fine. It's a sensation that he keeps in his mind, a sensation that reminds him that he's free with or without them, killers, ironics, decks of whites.

Virgil is free to walk down the stairs to the place where he knows that he belongs, a place that he fights for as he tries not to resist the found objects, which are at times insect, winged and black, carrying the pupa in its jaws, ready to return to feed the others.

Spit in the sink. Spit not on the walls. Spit surrounding the sofa. Spit in the seat, too. Spit as the predictive force. Virgil spits. Nose blown in the sink. Spit down the drain. Thank god for spit, says the baby man, losing his Gag reflex.

Spit so that he swallows. Spit that can't be controlled. Spit in the labor of the wire. Spit in the fantasy of desire. Spit in the belly of what's left. Spit as the fan. Spit in the face of the fan. Spit in the deliberate.

Spit in the fire. Spit in the box. Spit at the gym. Spit is the equivalency. Spit is going back in. Into the next day to see the little L.I. Aryan boys sitting there in the spa, and you can write about them docile logic, next day, they nod.

And still Virgil works in Literature. Still, he settles into the feeling of Lit, a substantial body of work he makes, avoiding the email go-ins, for fear of the signatory's claims to claim us all, *we, the white brigade defend the brown party!*

All Virgil wants is to wrestle with desire, the shade that understands that what one wants and needs must be tied to seeing the dumb cheap beats, *Nigger Clean*, Virgil thinks as he scrubs the garage floor.

Virgil's father says that writing is like being in a prison, and he's right, the back hurting, Virgil feeling that he must remain so tied to it, in case, the endurance project's angle—that he is going back to get in a run, and laundry, then to do more writing.

Virgil is going to check on the mail, then he is going to check on forms, to drop forms off, or maybe today, to see the water! Virgil wants to escape, wants to move so far from the hose he wraps around its catch.

Fuck that reviewer, Virgil thinks, and "Who cares?" he announces out loud. He's right. Virgil does have "Serious Daddy Issues." Virgil's dad was ashamed on the couch. Virgil's dad was a gambler. Virgil's dad was a mythology. Virgil's dad dealt with it.

Virgil understands there are no shortcuts. But Virgil does not understand the point of going where he does not belong. When Virgil sees a young Ed Begley Jr. and recognizes the quality of his fabrics, he realizes that Begley is a hot boy, then, and blond brow hot daddy, now!

Virgil trundles down the stairs. He decides that he will be the help, adjust the heating vent in the room, and the blowers. "Your Senator's about to cum..." is what Daddy Dave whispers in, "The Senator." And in another clip, uttered by a Cuck, "Should I clean him first?"

Seizing this allows him to take in the flat bay, and to imagine looking into a distance, where Virgil will travel and go, despite being turned down for the grant. It spares him from the arms of whiteness that prevents him from seeing or being.

Virgil is still haunted by LittleDandelion, playing on the Sit 'n' Spin. He realized, in that moment when he wanted to take the ride away from the little white boy and Little Dandelion stood up for himself, that power is indirect. It moves in many directions (Bully/Assailant/ Lover/Dream) and in different amplifications (Fear/ Tightness/Realization/Fact).

And though separated by weight and size, color and age, Virgil and LittleDandelion are twinned at mutual points of deployment.

Two boys. One Toy. But the long history of the boys in location with one another renders them forever oppositional.

As in The-One-Who-Renders-Canvas-as-Page teaches Virgil, opposition is also quiet, as in not taking a side, at all, so that not even forces, oppositional or otherwise, lay the foundation for Virgil's many actualized-routes-to-freedom.

Object A: This is the realization.
Object B: These are the facts.
Object C: This is the projection.

A: is a circle, spinning without or outside of Virgil's control. The spinning makes a pattern, a pattern, where the colors blend together into a whir of visual acuity, a mix, but still, for Virgil who grows up knowing how to fight, the victim might not have been killed because of this. B: is for blur, the blur in the feeling Virgil felt, the fear that he would both embody and absorb. It was hot and he was surrounded, this, at least, taught Virgil a lesson. C: Little Dandelion was living, Virgil, the assailant.

Virgil will give a talk. Maybe he's giving one right now. Virgil is not a slave, but often thinks of indentured servitude, or sharecropping, or gets the house in the deal, and it's folded into a salary, and as one ascends, so do the others around him. One can be the ornamentation of desire, but Virgil couldn't care less about that. Fair is never fair.

The fear he felt in that field was a buzz of emotion he still carries, a crutch, an absorptive feeling that LittleDandelion held, surrounded by his posse. They seemed so big, even though they were all children. C: is also that Virgil could have hurt him in the way he was hurt in the end, but the threat of the whites surrounding him revealed his own fragility—the Dandelion seeds blown into his face against Virgil's threat: not a wish, but defeat. TommyS describes shame as a multilayered set of streams, only stilled by what's folded around the palm tree, the feeling of the body, roped, and bound, the body bound in exaggeration, looking up brown face into a wide-eyed where?

Virgil is always moving, and sees the strangers for who they might be—in Deland, FL, he is so far away from the dream, but all the while he seeks encouragement, a feeling he cannot understand, a feeling that he knows is particular to sense, his being, his body, his posture as he gathers speed, too, is fact.

The facts are, after all, an imposition on Virgil's self-formation. He is on a bus. And sitting, he's able to assess the routes of control, and how they are tied to knowing, which is radically different from fact. There is, after all, a big problem, the problem is this. The problem is related to the facts. The facts are in. Factoids. The facts manifest as mist. The mist creates the barrier between the pain in Virgil's back and the depth in which he is unable to sleep.

Is the relationship between *as* target and *at* rest the same as Virgil's bowing down in contrition? He hates black people who feel the need to fit into the boxes that bind their faces, but he too is a black person bound by the same desires, and boxes, as a Flip, but the Flip, proven to emit keeps him moving, his eyes not on the prize, but to shift and bob.

To be understood is to be broken, to be understood to be broken is the point of understanding floating and stinging.

Is this what E-R understood when she said you must stop lying down, and stand up to face it, and Virgil took that as a sign to dance. To gig.

"The Russians are here! Look at this," Butch says, and shows the back of the *NYTimes* with their flag, shrouded over the US Capitol.

So much of his imagination is up for open critique. Politics, deft. Birds puncture the air and *race* is what Virgil wants to negotiate, and to be found, not as an anomaly, but the point where the heart is born outside of the chest cavity, and still, the organ right below the skin, beats.

Did Virgil recall this accurately? That he was Goliath, and LittleDandelion was David? Anger is both fuse and figure, but it is also fissure, and in this way Virgil understands that the haptic is something that manifests in the scene that he wants to return to.

On a bus. Below the bus. Below a crate. Below bodies. Below the porn in which he wants to hear the accent of the BBC, and the W, to see why, indeed, her need is the site of desire that includes the use of the word, *Nigger*.

The word, itself, is inevitable, the trigger, the whisper, the feeling, the space of understanding that includes who she is in relation to him, or the fact that his dick is b and B and she is o and W and the viewer, runs into the usual collisions, or at least Virgil does.

Neither are, after all, very adroit in escaping race, sex, the inevitable.

Where, for instance, is the canary in the mine?

In Australia, for instance, the Blacks there were listed among the fauna. So what kind of Animal is Virgil, beyond the shellacked hermit crabs?—He tries to get into their shapes, and movements on the gym floor, as he thinks about the multiple failures of designations, but still, is his intact self.

It smells of gasoline. It sounds like thunder. His realization is a surety, a knowing thing, like an opening in the sand that leads to the clam's foot, a way in that cannot be seen for long, Virgil understands clarity as that which quickly vanishes.

Like the plovers that dot one shelf of the beach, like the entire beach that leads to no exact return in the shore's timing, like the return that points him back into a sand wall, backed into a series of advancements.

There are all kinds of equivalencies to track. This is the way that the body learns to tug, to pull the tide back into the sea, but the hole back into the shore is never an escape: this is why, and that which Virgil dances against and drifts away from.

Virgil lets go into another scene—his body makes him feel more free than he knows, and he has found in this space a net of averages with another figure: *I can't wear that because of my rolls*, sez CatEyeLa in the costume store.

Virgil looks into her eyes and sees their surfaces, that they are the color of opal, the sea, washed with milk and sun, and captures in his perception these, and her, and even her unrelated teeth—a jumble of rot— her eyes after all are clear enough, lucid points in what Virgil does, for now.

Virgil does not think MommaSpine is frail, despite being kept together with new stents in her arteries, a mitral-valve clip for her heart, and screws at the base of her now-less-compressed spine, materials working against Virgil's memory, MommaSpine holding CeSis, a baby, in the picture near Navy Lake—*Do you remember how clear it was?* "I'd shine my car, and you'd play..."

Virgil remembers how buffed MommaSpine's legs were then, solid and almost square quads, ripped like his were, her arm clutching his sister. She is not frail, like Stream calls her, not like his father, OldStream, who was clearly strong like Virgil's mother when Virgil met him, smiling from his chair, his teeth in tiny ridges of tar, a gauze wraps around his forearms, perfect spectator bucks below.

The morning she lived, Virgil sees MommaSpine lying there, tiny, the shock of seeing her, prone, in the morning flat on the big grey sectional, not at Zumba, nor lifted into the day, out and gone, or moving in the house to pills and bags of candy, notes in Hindi, or Chinese, her iPod singing languages or electronica in her ear.

"Ronal, can you drop me off at the hospital? I can go from there."

Virgil the lover, drifting in front of the porch of Stream's house, or stuck in the night at The Lawyer's for just one night, and during this night, blood regurgitates back into his mother's heart. MommaSpine's body is going, and Virgil is busy writing, busy thinking of the thickness of his belts, whether one's too wide for the jean, or if another's brass buckle is worn enough to trigger a reaction from his copper-looking shoes.

There were signs in the night, the peering raccoon in the yard, and women in OldStream's house, brown ones, who cared for him, aluminum packs of pastry on the shelf. The bed shifts in the hospital, easily with the up buttons, helping to guide his mother back into the quiet—*no* to the milk, and *yes* to the oval lip balm Virgil applies.

The lights take too long, and this is the first time Virgil sees his mother unable to breathe, the pain in her chest, and on her face, squinching, her compromised body pushing back into Manitoba's front seat, their seat belt roping in MommaSpine for the drive.

Glide to the emergency room, park at the tip of the yellow in the emergency room entrance, deliver MommaSpine, charge into the station, elegantly, shirk the addict who was sitting in his wheelie—"*You made the wrong choices...Uhhh, No!*"—get them to arise at the sight of the standing of a son trying to save his mother.

My mother is dying. My mother is waxing her car under a sleeping willow. My mother left her entire family to be with my father. My mother lost their first child to SIDS at 55 days. My mother is a wound. My mother cannot breathe. My mother's back is now bent into an S. She worked 16-hour shifts to keep us fat. She worked to make sure we knew how to move to the front, like this. My mother will be served first.

Virgil's face is not only gorgeous—he knows because he took some of the pictures those days in the hospital and still it radiated, however dark—it alone understands how to make an argument, to move the audience, in this case, the black security, or a brown receptionist, whatever voice, dropped, to get her into the room with the physician.

Dazed and however soon, nitroglycerin pierces into MommaSpine's heart, and there is no stroke, nor does her heart or brain lose oxygen, nor do the veins cross without MommaSpine aware, her understanding how to get the medicine into her own veins—relaxed, her arm's offer, to be injected, blood drained, blood given, whatever it takes.

Virgil's invested in the fantasy that exists between them, a life that does not carry the direct story of her children never meeting her family in the Philippines, a sister never seen again, now dead, a brother rapist, her mother and a father killed, how, who, when?—How dare OrangeBLOWHOLE help to signify the ugly song, facts of the U.S.A. flags on the elevated trucks and their stickers. How dare the memory of their inclusion, hot dogs and mayo, trucks and stars, leakers and losers, and the fat wide, loud.

Public servant, he is, and Virgil rubs MommaSpine's head when her body is too hot for her hard-working heart, a heart leaking blood back in, so the doctors find out why the murmurs—MommaSpine was a runner who sometimes returned home with KFC, or they would all go to Straw Hat and she would order Thick and Chewy crust, and Virgil, then, sang,...*Time keeps on ticking/ ticking...into the future...*in the Straw Hat dining room. To feed them, and their lives, for her own, which she is willing to give up, even for dumb, busy Virgil.

"Have you fed your dad?"—At home, when Virgil enters the kitchen, MommaSpine tries to get Forgetting, To Live to go into the kitchen too. In the kitchen, Virgil's father takes many shapes; sometimes an animal caught in a cage, still able to find the tools to escape, whether rolls of mud built into a bridge topped by a rake, or stacked tires, or a lover he gets to open up a lock. Beautiful Animal—his point—escape.

Virgil dances in CeSis's old room, the room that would later be Avon's. A giant Hello Kitty mural covers multiple walls of the sky-blue bedroom. Ordinary windows open up onto the shingled roof next door, a hot-orange sky flattens onto the street, but just in front of Virgil's eyes, gnats float in the morning air. It is here where Virgil learns escape.

The story, for Virgil, is not the same as dreaming, but it is close. Once, the Activist-Belt said to Virgil, "Of course, he does research—he's a Novelist," which was meant to spark shame into Virgil, but it only bothered Virgil some, because, *the storehouse of the human*, like Myung Mi Kim says, is always in him, and wide, not from looking into himself, but from finding, what keeps his family in life.

Virgil explains to Stream that he feels he's 75% in his own imagination, but doesn't know how he arrived at that figure. It's not that he's always floating in his own circumstance, or unaware, detached from the Blacks being stabbed on sight, or the need for some writers to monger towards a prized life, or Virgil's walking in the thick wet grass under his feet.

But the 25% of the other time he's doing dishes, or reading the news, or sometimes essays, or poetry, scanning for what to place in his wheelhouse, could be a figurine in the island for the misfit toys, or whatever strikes his whims as he sorts his teas for when he'll settle into what he calls "the prosaics," which isn't a novel-in-verse, but a form that is connected to the act of making in myriad angles, in masks and dance, some forms of his escape.

Originally, Virgil wanted to layer this feeling into something more dense, an actual novel that he broke apart into prose poems, the pieces unmoored into a form more succinct than he could now imagine, but as D-Second still sits a bit on his shoulder: "just be guided by your music."

So too, the compunction of the dance, which is another form or the self gets enacted—*no, I am not a site of labor*—but still, Virgil helped lift a table to position a projector to screen images in a school where he didn't get the position. No worries—they hired a letch, someone who really needed to soil their institution. Bitter, still, is Virgil, but now he smells chlorine *whenever he wants!*

Clearly, the institution is not Virgil's world. It is his playground. Virgil learned everything that he needed to learn playing kickball, or wall ball, games that gave him *a sense* of how he would come to know—in daycare—played so much that his head hurt, took naps at the job, after plugging the kids into the VCR, awoke to make macaroni necklaces, and looked across the asphalt into his future.

At the start of the swim, Virgil feels not in sync with the lane lines or the black thick line at the bottom of the pool. That is, if he has his own lane. Without sharing, parts of his body cut into the water, parts do not, but the water does not give way to his bod until about 40 minutes in, when Virgil's body eases, stretches along the surface of the pool, just above, aiming across the water, his fingers uncurling underneath.

Move into the inner music, the wait-on-hold music that echoes in the bathroom, cell on speaker, the re-steeped tea, the form and surface of work that is not on hold, but work that has to be let open and moved, independent gutting of the self into the self: A night crawler that opens its rake-claw mouth over the hook, gorging the tip down its gut, every pull in, every inch closer to death—*does it feel a thing?*

In the pool he thought about scale, and source, how he won't be trapped by anyone that attempts to stop his momentum. He thinks of one argument he could present:

Look, I teach. And I ask students to come up with informed assertions about what they think after any given reading. If the person has only one source to support that reading, then what is "credible" is simply that single argument.

Virgil is thinking of SingedheadBear when he thinks this, and Virgil is also thinking of the L.I. Aryan boys that he recalls from his first encounter with them at the gym, and how he sees them a second time—the one who said, "I like Trump," as if this were what Virgil was asking when he posed Nuclear Fallout as one's pugilistic party gone wild.

Put up your dukes!—The problem is broader, he thinks, and because of this, Virgil escapes into his own stroke. The push of his arms through the water, extending and stretching into the future, if only the future of a single night in the late-night pool could be the equivalent of the last five minutes of his swim, where he is not pushing but elongating, and twisting his body into a shape that could propel him, svelte.

Against Virgil's elongation into what he sees as a mode between freestyle and collage, against the deep quiet that he searches for is "the prosaics"—these, he realizes, are various forms he holds in his art, a prescription towards forms of entertainment.

Does Virgil really think this? Yes. Does the art need to be broken down? No. Will Virgil be stabbed? Maybe. But to be the greatest, it may mean, swimming as gliding, and gliding, as flying. Virgil thinks of APOG Conceptual, a diviner between prose and poetry, between art and philosophy, who reminds him that the space of dreams and analysis are tied in these acts.

Is escape a place of freedom? What does it mean to embody escape as a formal mode, to get away, to move from under the weight of captivity? These are the central questions that have guided his work, which was not simply built upon expectations of brilliance.

Virgil has a real PhD, not something that he takes into his quiet, something that sits outside of his work. Again, Queen M was right to call his dissertation an "invisible scaffold," but what will you do with it? Titular, performance, as in: *It is doing me*, Virgil thinks *The Invisible Scaffold...*

Virgil, who moves through many forms, is not content with the conviction that comes with expectations of form as trap, or test. This is the aptitude that serves Virgil, the form of that project into a yet unknown, the future, a way of thinking, and perhaps this is what he wants, the dissertation as mode, not project, but meditation. Like dancers that latch onto a form—perhaps the dissertation is a fire, or a dress, or a mode through which to move into the silence of the restraint, a form, is all it is.

He sends Butch an email that reads: *Watch this, instead of reading* the *New York Times*. The link opens to a man born with a condition that has warped his entire body so that he looks like an inverted seahorse, one seemingly bred in a box, turned inside out, reminding Virgil of the black pills, "snakes" set alive at the tips of spitting metal sparklers on the 4th of July, how the heat ignites the black surface, yellow flames hiss around its circumference, circle left on the sidewalk where the "animal" unfurled from the fire, curving up into ash.

Instead of the 24 hours of life the doctors promised him, Invert-Seahorse Backwards-To-Burnt-Black-Sidewalk-Head has lived for 37 years, and in it, from Virgil's perspective, he lives it as a fold, his head bent into a permanent arc. His wide eyes look backwards and he walks forward on nubs for legs with hair.

Invert-Seahorse Backwards-To-Burnt-Black-Sidewalk-Head is unlike the 27-year-old man, who has not yet hit puberty. Red-Lex-Boy-Face-Tall-and-White confesses to the documenter that he has an underdeveloped penis, and underdeveloped balls. The doctor agrees, and tells him that he must, in fact, get on hormones sometime soon, just before the 1:35 mark.

Virgil, who has an aversion to the term "project," decides to imagine one that asks all of his senses to retreat to the back of his untrained eyes, to coalesce around a single stance, *the activity of research*. This is the song of the under-theorized. This will be Virgil's claim. It starts with the edge of something, a piece of plastic that settles into a wall, a wall that's been enacted between two places where Virgil will always remain, *Art* and *Theory*.

Virgil in his bed, alive, is watching a sequence: One, a big black boy on a skateboard is demonstrating an ollie. He sounds like a bird in his description of the trick, how to slide one foot forward while planting the other. The houses are large behind him. All Virgil wants is for Little Big Ollie to fall, or he knows that he will be satisfied at the fall, and, of course, he does. The board escapes down the street, and the fatty rolls in the driveway. The houses disappear, and all the recorder sees is his body writhing on the ground, and add to this: Little Big Ollie's moaning, and his screams.

Somewhere in China, there is a boy who has grown up into a man in a poor village. At first, there were bumps behind his ears. The bumps spread and grew, so his face now looks like he has two triple-E breasts attached, one being his nose, and somewhere there is an eye, which he uses to read.

Are these searches what Virgil has trained so much of his life for?—Examples that point to a method? Is this Virgil's own flying? Virgil remembers a story of a crazed man who broke into the house of his elderly neighbors, charging up the stairs to the couple's bedroom with a hammer. Inside, they awoke to him in their bed, above them, raining down blows.

You see, Virgil thinks, the surprise is in how the facts of the memory are embedded in the body, waiting to unleash themselves, as if to be drawn towards violence helps to locate the logic of violence, to live, alert, in its constant refrain. This is, after all, a way out of the form and into a future, and a present.

King K has been there before Virgil suspects, to Martin-Gropius-Bau, the museum where he orders the salade Niçoise, just outside of the William Kentridge retrospective, *No It Is!* To the fellowship screener's dismay, Virgil presents a plan, a plan to move around, to not be so sure in his approach towards what stands at the center of his newest project, *wandering*. Or *pacing*—after Kentridge, a restlessness that also typifies Virgil's work.

"How do I look at myself in front of a mirror?" is what Virgil asks Butch, who sucks in his cheeks, and preens like Virgil does, his head tilting up. Virgil thinks of all that he has done in a matter of weeks, having sent collages out to the other side of the country, the way he walked in the yard in his yellow shirt that finally fit, to dance.

It fits because it is J.Crew slim cotton, and looks loose. The labor of the project is the work on the front end, the making of the body into an inert surface comes from an aggressive active agent. This is the body that Virgil wants, long and thin, a body restless from movement in the morning, through the stretches that make Virgil feel like he is connected to the idea against which he can escape and return.

It is this familiarity in moving first towards, then away from the subject that begs Virgil to want the garbage truck to stop moving. Virgil finds himself in the back, ready to go, but he cannot recognize where he is as the car goes by spot after spot. He is a passenger both in the Uber car in his dream, and the one that he looks at on YouTube.   Two girls, one as grey-green as the other in the car cam both assume the driver's going to take them where they need to go after they were not where they were supposed to be.

"I have time," says the most rachet one, the one who thinks it's okay to demand things on G.P. The argument is not about race, but still Virgil is interested in the politics of race (here, expressed as masculinity and insistent expectation of worth, and blackness in grey-green) that prove toxic for the driver who yells, "Because you're pissin' me off!" Anger, white, in the body, cause and effect, and the stabbings of the blacks on sight, released in this relation.

Virgil is open to the fraternal music of whiteness that surrounds him, a sound that permeates everything he wants to be, particularly in the ways that he accepts this, takes it in, lives with it, then negotiates. Virgil is a specialist of whiteness, so that the contested space between the raced body, and his interrogated one is all the same.

At one point, he was a few feet from his home, but then the car kept moving past where he thought he lived. In Virgil's mind, he drives past the greenhouse on the campus where he no longer teaches, finds himself walking down a hill, between walls, finds himself walking through the sleet that crumbles with salt below his feet. Virgil is compelled to travel, far along the outskirts of fiction to get to the fictive as the mode that it might only grasp.

How is it that he recognizes places where he has never been, or only passed by bus so many years before, elevated in his sense of direction? This could be one of the central concerns of the project, which is one bound by passion, the passion of wanting to figure out what needs to be articulated in the search. Virgil, in other words, is looking for an unknown, looking to explore the question of surprise, the body as the mark, the spirit as the impulse, so says another of its modes, chance.

Virgil is located in the dream, in his own time, in a time that he understands he's looking around time. This means that Virgil, when he needs to, recites the exact time at the exact time it is, which means he's living in the world.

Once Virgil made it into the GForever archive by way of the curator, who had black teeth, and wanted to fuck him, and when he got in, he found boxes that had not been opened, some containing receipts, taxes, and news clippings.

"I fucks with him," is what the two blacks say to one another in the L.I. Locker Room at the Smith Haven LA Fitness. As if to prove a point of knowing, they each find a way to engage with both themselves and the world around them. Tarzan emerges out of the corner, and though Virgil is alive, he carries with him a form of fear, a fear that he will never be accepted, and a fear that his politeness along with, "I fucks with him," is a story of true camaraderie, friendship that bounces off the walls between them all, even in that instant.

The instant is as important as the forms of race, and class, and the manscaped chest of Tarzan is what sets the field into motion. Soon, Tarzan takes over the entire gym bench, his towel like the Shroud of Turin, the clothes flying out like Road Runner kicks up the dust, he throws his sweats, one piece at a time in the locker. The anxious blacks dissipate.

Does Virgil try to erase the language building around the OrangeBLOWHOLE who tweets about the "Obamacare Victims," on the day when he, Virgil hopes, will be slayed—Virgil would say to the L.I. Aryan Boys and to SingedheadBear this: "Trump is a shock jock." Which is fine, the space of celebrity being all things even, one must be flexible in one's perceived dialectics.

"This is your home." Butch reminds him, so Virgil adheres to it, and waits in the morning for the water to boil into the space between the flash of the security camera image and a text from Perfecta in Barcelona, fresh from the ice of Iceland to the heat of Spain.

The project is a lived one, the accounting for the body as it rests. How much oxygen travels in the blood? How much pressure in the heart? How much weight is leveraged into the spine, and how does one remain upright in the face of the daily stabbings, and the attacks that go to hate, unnamed. White Terrorism. White Rage. White Delay. Whiteness. White hurt. Wite-Out!—because for them it is now the time to unleash in a language other than inside, which means, *heads will roll*.

But not for Virgil, because Poetry, Virgil realizes, does something for him. Even if it is only in its music, Virgil's first form—in fact, his first language is touch, a touch which held him at some forever distance from direct connection, so that composition remains a series of *vantage points*, switching back and forth between terrains—

"Shut the door," said in private. "Don't block A. Out." or "You need to be focused," but Virgil needs to go be unhinged to write. Onwards, he looks at the white surfers suspended in the water in the wide Pacific Bay, little black dots on their boards captured in the morning of the Solar Eclipse it was all so Red. Or up close at Half Moon Bay, all of them coming into their patches and alliances, all of them gathering in the pipe or the shoal, a collective fight for their spots.

In the "Loose...See" Poems, Virgil learned that in the end, there is a surface and field that he is constantly after, a space of knowing that remains in the distance.

Maybe the reality of his self is that he is always set in a site of almost unknowing, a place in which he understands his self to be less compromised by what he might become *if he goes postal*. But perhaps Virgil *is always going postal*. This, after all, is *flow*. To remain fluid, and to keep one's eye on the ball's spinning seams. The birds on the eastern coast of the U.S. outside of the Noise Canceling Bose headphones sound like gulls.

Virgil makes so many promises to complete this or that, which in one way evens out to what manifests as his expectations. One of them is often a lecture, to give a piece of his feelings or his mind as an Academic "talk." Virgil titles his talk: "Your Micro-Aggression: My Macro-Response: Some Renderings," and he realizes that he has been there before, maybe on a subway platform, just any respite, as this could also be a crumbling sea shelf bar, or a plateau of sand crumbling beneath his heels: Red Asics on a blonde beach.

Virgil walks through the back of a kitchen of a Chinese restaurant, and on the floor are frozen fish in plastic tubs. Outside, there is a misty rain, a rain that he can only imagine is there to impede him, but still he does not find an Uber to take him anywhere. The value between the black body's worth and its livelihood is fraught with its ability to serve as cleanup, catcher, but *ain't nobody got time for dat!*

The two half glasses of wine, a Cote du Rhone, and a Pinot Noir, and before that, a California Sparkling: Blanc du Blanc (Schramsberg) roasted mussels, baby asparagus pizza, and the Tuna Tartare in Los Gatos—Virgil, Love, and Butch are pretty much rich—but it does not remove Virgil from the feeling he has when he sees what must be the human waste between cars.

Virgil—fresh from sleep—his body slow in the morning sea-air.

Was it MeanBellyLaundered that did it, dropped a load between the vehicles? For it was he, whom Virgil believes to be the culprit of Manitoba's scratched side.

On that day Virgil thinks it happened, MeanBelly-Laundered barreled through the parking lot when Virgil was returning from work, or from doing the laundry, after which Virgil decided that he would stare directly at him and go "Ughh, Freak."

Of course, Virgil would pay the price for the act, because, when he went out later, he discovered the scratch. Maybe it was the lawn service guys, keys on chains jutting out from the pockets tops, or the palm fronds?

Virgil has a $100 comprehensive, so he fixes it.

And if another appears, he will, of course, do the same. Why is he obsessed with Manitoba's surfaces?

Why does he care so much about the smallest things that happen to his vehicle, or how can he be so quickly derailed at the rejection of a fellowship, another, again and again, when he's working on what he perceives to be on such a high level?

Pacing, holding hands in the night, his face burrowed in Stream, or with Butch at the table in the morning, love is difficult in the space of what Virgil wants to call, *worth.*

Virgil is an institutional body, and simultaneously has been in a world of dreams for so long that his subjectivity is dependent upon the world's stability at every moment, so that if it is not, he will freak out at the most minor things.

A box without an address. Lost Glasses. A too tight shirt. Modern animal, Virgil is hungry for the escape he needs, but easily disrupted by the smallest things:

The rock is not a cat. The blue bird does not stay still enough to photograph. The pictures will not go undeveloped. The books remain lost. Anything might unleash the problem, whether reflective or instructive, so when shit is the surprise between cars, there is no surprise, and certainly no irony in the discovery.

That word is Nigger. It isn't said at the end of the dinner party, but it is pivotal in the desire for Virgil to understand its saliency, or use value in the morning after the game. Virgil has disdain for the YellowPlasticBlack on the T.V., the B-baller with the acrylic guard, horseshoed from his mouth, the open bite—

In the game: On the show, *Problematic*, the racists are in full view, *Get Out* and *Pepe the Frog*, are engaged in a match of racist chic, or racism chic, an old problem battling into a new one.

Blacks Advance, like Serena does, in fact, in the ease of the short angle crosscourt shot, not all power, Virgil thinks of Wilson's Suede and Leather, Venus's earliest endorsement, the resurgence is apparent in the pilot's cap in Napa, the soft leather. Tiger is fat in the picture, Cablasian buffed in real life, but in the mug shot, he is fried, and never an angel.

The boys in the locker room code themselves into a black bubble at the lockers. This is what Virgil wants to say at the dinner party with AngelFace, and HappyLa, and Virgil pretends to forget a name, or he actually forgets it, and has decided to be less politic. The sun greets Virgil's face. His goal, to simply not hurt anyone, but to satisfy his desires—

Escape into what, Virgil wants to understand the battle between bodies. Kathy Griffin holds the bloody cut head of OrangeBLOWHOLE and Sharin Needles engages in the plastic act, and then Key & Peele, or then the rubber face—

Virgil looks up at MeanBellyLaundered up on his balcony, adjacent to Virgil's—"Paranoid, huh?"

Excuse me? What did you say?

"I was talking to the moon?"

Freak, I was not looking at you, I was looking at my door, which was open,

which I can see from inside Manitoba.

Manitoba remembers when Virgil was a kid and drank a whole bottle of Ron Bacardi 151 and then vomited on SweetJane's bed while she rubbed his back, until he felt better, and then he could not wash the vomit out of his fake girlfriend's sheets, or when he damaged her keyboard and then went to get it fixed.

Virgil, unlike any of her white friends, went to the music store and had the fallen key fixed. Just like he makes sure that money makes it into Stream's account while they are both in the downtown lair.

The worlds Virgil lives in are not succinct, nor are they safe—multiple lives, and double places, and Virgil's respite will be in language. Butch braying in the morning, and the tea at some $25 for however many ounces, Virgil cuts with something mint and cheaper, and the FBI agent feels like he wants to rinse off after reading the report.

Virgil feels so much cleaner in the sauna. He realizes that he is halfway in the middle of his project, which defines his passion, the looseness that is Virgil's life in letters.

Once, Virgil and SweetJane stopped in Vallejo, at his brown cousin's house, and her henna curly hair prompted one of the brown cousins to say, "Ronal, can you get me a white girl?" The other brown cousin said, "I can make you coffee," and she did, pouring the freeze-dried Folgers into two coffee cups.

It was embarrassing to Virgil, even then, before Virgil wrote in Cafés, or before he'd been to Las Ramblas, or before Mallorca, or the Venice Biennale, a visit to Cognac where he could turn around a gawk at TheInvestors massive package, and his Latina wife would ask about his cough: "Do you have a cold?"

In the memory of the French countryside tour bus ride, no matter how rich, Virgil is restless, and again, this restlessness is tied to freedom, but in retrospect, is the life that Virgil wants to reconstruct in his prosaics a model?

It isn't precisely shame, because if it were, then it could be dissipated. Here is an example: A shark is hooked, dragged onto the shore, leaving a fossil-looking imprint in the sand below it, this ancient deep-sea species, imposing the same outline for millions of years. The shark is 93 years old, or was, before it was caught, beached, then loaded onto the truck.

The firemen, who were called to the scene, say the shark looked like a Megalodon, extinct animal, the beast must have been swimming not long before it was caught. The Earth is warming, and the animals are now where they don't belong.

Maybe it's a rabbit's? They are not rocks—
Three black, shiny pieces of shit.

Retribution for his most recent interaction—

BlondBeardHomeless is at a corner, and he turns Virgil on, the burst of orange in that beard, his face, angling for what he needs. His fat hand, pink and crusted black, the sweet smell of something that Virgil wanted, his hair wheat, a golden field, a promise, is indeed hot, for him and for the United States.

Where are his teeth?—Was the question raised between rich Virgil and the even more wealthy Butch. This is old news for Virgil, for certain, but in this news, he attains, a feeling, but goes immediately to his Purell in Manitoba, then rubs away anything he may catch, but wants to pay BlondeBeardHomeless $50 to flash him his dick, which is why.

Rarely has opportunity for public visibility limited Virgil's sensibility, particularly in how he delivers his work to an audience in what appears to be his being in a state of seamlessness—if, or as long as he can succumb to his vision, one that finds itself most precise, underwater.

Virgil's vision remains as clear in the pool as possible, but in order to engage in critique, he must return to some basics. Does he pound on a table to make a point? Does he present a song of addiction and recovery to mark his emergence as a worthy body, or is Virgil a taker, and a big mouth, a leaker, or even, a Diva?

In one video he watches, Virgil learns (or in this case relearns) what his father taught him: how to both self-protect and to violate. This, Virgil thinks, is what makes him fight-ready, most anytime.

To shield his face with his arms, and to strike with the hardest part of these, the bones in the outer forearms, the elbows.

These are the weapons he uses to open up an internal monologue.

Here's the thing. Virgil is full of a need to be alone, to enter the quiet of his imagination. But also, he likes to be stretched, and to have fun. In this sense, Virgil is always equipped to do battle with whomever, and is by nature, confrontational, perhaps, because of this.

The luxury?—The anger he holds at the periphery of his awareness.

Virgil has often had to use the skills that his father, Not Forgetting, to Remind has passed onto him. He uses them to do damage as he can, in defense, of course, leaping in the air to land on someone else's collarbone on the dance floor. Dumb, but still, rather than return to the club to be stabbed, he was 86'ed for like two weeks, and in between Virgil ran for miles pretending to encounter the assailant, guards held up in the air—he was warned by BottomFeeder: "He was up here looking for you, and he had a knife!"

Tough, maybe, but only enough to protect the stomach and the eyes.

Skills Virgil holds close to his heart, skills he hones—
In other words, Virgil practices to be ready.

In one sense, his readiness keeps him directed towards a future that includes moving as easily as possible from defense to offense: *to slay* is to move forward, to offend in the face of casual and daily assault, right?

Do you find yourself pouring out the extra coffee from the cup, or are you concerned that there might be syringes in the trash at Starbucks, if you are so employed?

Did you think the world that you wanted to enter was there? Did you understand the fantasy of your neighbor's as your own, or did you snatch groceries from a porch as a paperboy?

Did you want to sweep out the store for pay?

Do you still imagine opening and serving wine with aplomb? Do you pound and pound?

After the meeting in the basement in the City with the Metal Sky, Virgil received an email from Wite-Out that he mostly expected, because in the end being a germ is a way of life for her. Tone: Lunatic. As the Race Drops began to build, there was a warning that Butch sent, a warning of severe thunderstorms, the urgency that delays any haste, and the rush of the rain pushes Virgil into a useable past.

President Curious has died.

It's not the fault of anyone, but the black president, former—is to be erased—Virgil's anger in what is gone, and who is lost, his body gone, too—the feeling is not the mourning, but the complexity of its attempted erasure, in his, and the joke in who replaces whom:

We've forgotten about the "we."

In the video he shot, Virgil wears his silicone swim cap in the basement, trying to look out at the fists that are not coming, but still he dodges those, and weaves, still he feels the pull of the transmission as it jolts between gears, seemingly involuntary movements, and then propulsion.

Apparently the Metal Sky had other plans for Virgil. Plans more urgent. The drops came out of nowhere. He sensed the sky was tightening, but Virgil had no idea how to react, other than with fear.

Are they coming for me?
Will they vestibule my black azz?
Will I, in the heat of the paint,
chew on my horse-shoe-out-open-mouthguard?
Will my team, refuse to go
to the OrangeBLOWHOLE's new home,
after winning it all? Will we?
Will I be shot, pregnant while holding a knife,
or will I die from a hip wound,
rifled in a baseball field?

It's not as if these events are even in the same universe as Virgil's encounter outside of the basement post-performance, panel, whatever it was—but still, his encounter felt real, a track, a pattern, a record of publication that is already filed in "DivData," Virgil's University Work Aggregating tool: for later reference, and ultimately *mo' money, mo' money mo' money*.

Virgil walks far ahead from the writing, or moves far enough to take a call, to find an insect's white egg sack—*is that a sweet pupa?*—to reveal a date, to promise something out of the urgency of the line drive which is actually Psycho Democratic Gunfire!

To extract himself from the scene and subject—Here is the scenario:

Wite-Out wants to command everything, and so sometimes does Stream, and so does Butch, and so once in awhile, does Love—

In another sense, all of these characters attempt to corral another body that, arguably, can't be.

So any agent against, is an offense, and in the end, out of the periphery, cartwheels enact, and given the pattern of their surprise in most formal occasions, these are understood to be asymmetrical pieces put together as the rationale, the project, the grant seeker must be aggressive for whom, exactly?

If you fall/ I will catch you/ I will be waiting... is it for the promise of what might be assembled, won, the pieces of the self in constant defense, so clearly, no fun—

This is the thing about an ambush—while Virgil never expects this, but always does—*at the same damn time!*—his ability to record and to present allows him, even amidst many competing circumstances—found or self-induced—some form of lasting documentation.

Virgil thinks maybe the draw for him and the others is pure stardom, or something, pure drama—whatever the case may be, the effect in his discovery, after sliding the timeline bar back, was that Virgil returned to an unusual place of intimidation by the impending Race Rain.

But there would be no storm, because Virgil refused, partly, and was afraid, partly.

Would this attack somehow hinge against his standing?

Would he absorb the encounter? Would his career?

Virgil does not want to relate to The Others, Flop Tops and Fillers, with a sense of anything other than rage, because for him—in Virgil's crazy imagination—there's no record but being a series of advancements.

Outside of the long closed gay bar, Bojangles, there was a dead white boy found in the parking lot, whose black friend, left living, had platinum blonde style. Another black, BottomFeeder, is pussy up in a room in a bathhouse. And Virgil thinks this is the illuminated space from within which the fictive must continue its assaults.

In the Manhole in an early morning, Virgil moves in for a kiss and his eye is not burnt, because the tip of the cigar, oddly, is cold ash. SLUT or PIG is written in black marker on a white belly, and a cold white man is bolted to a wall. He snorted coke off of Virgil's cock down there. Virgil escaped to another room, hearing his name yelled in the dungeon—

"Virgil! Virgil! Virgil!"

It's too dark to see down where he was, but not dark enough for Virgil to recall the smell of DaddyJoliet's pipe filling the hallway in Millington.

DaddyJoliet spoke Latin.

In the house, there is no direct access to this story that is fixed across the Meatpacking District, NYC, when only a glance informs Virgil's need, his need to be right, to be stroked, and to be held, for if not, who knows for what?

This is Virgil's stance, at least in his first look, a swimming stroke, to move under the water until his body becomes loose and open, stretching forward, in his own lane, preferably.

Pool aside, or chlorine left in the nasal cavity: Here's the thing—Virgil does not need Wite-Out to move through his imagination, but in reviewing the scene in the privacy of the Red House's yard's deck, it seemed like a good idea. Still does.

The recycling can rumbles, and so too, the cup stirs, and the neighbors "Avatared" the forest that was previously their tree filled yard, and the buzzing drones of lawn gear hum, like the rinsed teacup is rinsed during the session, and the rumble of the dump truck that leaves a pile of dirt in their yard.

In retrospect, Virgil understands what builds as something that he has to follow through the memory of the City with the Metal Sky, sure, but even as he is so far from it in the midst of the containment, it's still a trap and set-up.

Or maybe they were just kids, then. Virgil will forever be tied to that existence, but despite wishes from Stream, Virgil will seek composition and meditation as formal strategy. This is one way to revisit the scene of embarrassment. The space of recovery is not about addiction for Virgil, it's about recovering a longer past that has nothing to do with CinchGutBelt"J"-in-da"T"hotBeard, nor anything ever to do with the white brigade! Fuck the white brigade!

It's too bad that there was not any real follow-up after the capture. Because Virgil would have played along, but because he has his own thing going on, Virgil leaves for the suburbs, and decides to make what he wants, when he wants. So see-ya! *Ballistics!—I gits this*, Virgil freestyles.

The animal that wasn't hit by a car on the road; instead, was shot in the face with a BB gun. Some of her teeth were shot out. Some of the BB's ended up blowing away parts of the roof of her mouth. And since there were no exit wounds to prove otherwise, it would appear that she swallowed some of the ammo.

"What happened? Maybe, would you feel better if we watched it together?"

Wite-Out was not ready for the battle, or for Virgil all hyphy at that underground reading as official panel! In the footage, Wite-Out makes hand gestures like *I am manifest, oracle and start*, akin to the PodBod in the Porsche, who parks in the yellow zone at the Starbucks in Miller Place, and whisks in with his bad self to uproot whatever he needs to jumpstart his evening. And so does another van, and even in the lot, a mini-CAT tractor winds by!

Look Bitch, the dismissal has to do with the understanding of those in the perceived bottom of the frame as "property" and within the bounds of "development," the moment where the truth is caught on tape, FineJoke told a tale:

> *Terror is funny, to some, and it can be realized through a number of formations that are familiar, and one can say something about the state of the art, and art making, but there is a history of terror that affects some of us more than others.*

Which means not you! Which means there is a problem, but it's not yours to interpret, Virgil was not taking notes, so he did not write or say this then, but he does later, notes around the collection of pictured

fists semi-closed in numerous shots and cut-outs—
Some come up in Virgil's quick blue pen sketches, to
help him see what he wants to say. Some fetal closed.
Some bodies are shot because of consequences. A
Reach. Some are shot in the summer. Some amplify.
Or silence.

There are various formations that could work to
illuminate these:

A Little Glowmer decides to play. A Little Glowmer
attempts to make a screw act like a top, little girl
hands flicking it into its activity. HappyPetSitting
Dad ignores her, but also, you see, he pays attention, enough attention to keep the excitement of the
Glowmer alive. Is the Glowmer impervious to Race
Drops? This is a casual and constant pounding that
Virgil wants to block out, but it is against this pounding that he figures his resistance, and his typing, which
after all is play, joy, and cartwheels!

Virgil was working on something in that basement.
Perhaps working towards the space of what it means to
mask. Forever. In goggles and a swim cap. To signify the
difference between the swimmer and the germ, this is
the story, a story of power and time, and moving around
the document, a motion, really, that has found an epicenter, an epicenter in what he felt to be risk, breaking
and breaking and breaking.

The possibility in there, Virgil sings:

...*I've got to run away*... Virgil would like to sing
along, but what are the ethics in returning to the notes
that are in a video hidden away, perhaps, now, even per-
manently lost, a video in which one says *I am the germ.*
And my role in this activity is that I am tainted love, and
what are the alliances? Language?

Are there security cameras in the Red House that will protect the machines left behind in the morning's grey light? Is there a burden against which Virgil will feel less, now that he's free, and holds a card that says his employment is indefinite?

In Ta On Mwah Video, there, too are germs.

These germs are cast in a sketch where power triangulates. The world is often perceived and presented as a stable one, a world of understood pressures, a world of steady beats, a world of synthesizers, a world of regular sounds after all, forever big brother to the Beave, Wally—Virgil looks into the Race Drop's pressure and moves inside where it's cool, and marks.

Virgil realizes that it is most polite to sit as witness. The witness in the dunk tank, the one who runs ahead and pushes the button—no ball will be thrown, and in fact, during practice, there will be a shooting, and the shooting will presuppose any decorum across partisan lines.

A jet will be shot out of the sky, and the sky will darken until there is no leastwise survivor. The safety dance is only for some. War is coming, and so too, is the ejection of the pilot from the cockpit. Safe?

Wite-Out! Listen.

But only Dakota appears white in the seven Sailors killed in the collision.

Noe, Xavier, Shingo, Carlos, Ngoc, and there's Gary, who was 37. Maybe. "Adventure on the Destroyer," "...an immigrant from the Philippines....poor teenager from Guatemala...native of Vietnam...a fire fighter's son from a rural crossroads..."

Wite-Out has a friend who is a drunk, who even at a party, later, wanted to engage in a fight, on the street! Between Tenured Faculty! Imagine!

The arrangements of power are often clear, but even GradStudGlowmers feel the impending need to rule.

Thing is, this is not your world Hoe, and I am here, Virgil says, *to tell you what*

Ah think!

Virgil is often seen as a machine, prolific, a high producer of product—so much so that he can even joke, when the birds cut the morning against some form of white buzzing or drilling, a snag on a corner, a nub—

Butch might think it's funny, when Virgil plays a "drug pusher" in the nap and sleep room of the Red House. Virgil has so little patience for many things, but he does see connections between what BlueLivesMatter might be thinking and the ProudBoys, and White Power, too—

Mayo-Consiousness is real, and it's enacted
in Virgil's own racist imaginary, one where
he looks at the two (FetalFatArmeth and
KaptainPointeePoo) discussing the future:

...a hold onto the suburban Atlanta district...
C'mon man, you want to get high?
You won't feel a thing. Virgil needs stability,
so it's stability that he will create.

FineJoke once invited Virgil to a performance before the one in the basement in The City with the Metal Sky, and even neutrally, Virgil realizes that it was better than the one he got caught up in. That performance was at the New Museum in NYC. In it, Virgil revealed the world of his neighbor's dead cat that TheStoryTells turned into a movie!

It exists!

There is no story to be unveiled in Virgil's recounting of the events in the museum—not here—other than to say, he learned about voice.

It's not a persona, it's the fear that he will be seen for what he is, a floater.

He doesn't care what others think, which makes Virgil a very active reader of circumstance and perspective, but the threat of his being perceived as a floater is maybe like being called lazy, so this is why he works constantly.

But did Virgil think with Tenure would also come release?

Did Virgil find a way back into the heart of his most never to be fired self?

Virgil looks into the grass where he tried to dance, but felt that his body was so fat. For The Treatise, Virgil's mask is yet to be bought. Collage-Knowledge, is this a thing? So. Why fiction? This is a question that Virgil wants to answer, but being a floater means that he is taken in multiple directions, but he's not distracted.

Look, Reading is Fundamental, we all know this, thinks Virgil. But Reading is a matter of choice, abortion counts, and so does porno, and breeding, and the collapse of sense into form, say of the confession to reveal the measured girth of the first object in how a Brut deodorant bottle opens the ass, then a fist, then the real raw contact, Virgil hedges—

Virgil attempts to describe this to Stream, an example in the case of only his being semi-warmed to *Moonlight*.

It seems that, for Virgil, the movie moves in multiple ways, but he realizes that it is not what is being presented as its public account, given the color composition of the film, the blues, the blacks—this isn't new, but this isn't the point.

Black culture travels, TheBlackUmbrella reminds.

"Under the sign of fiction" is a phrase that one of TheOracles[TB] taught Virgil, so in this formation, he feels, more or less enabled.

Boxes, and lockers—

In one still of the unpublished reading video, Virgil and FineJoke and TheNewLing are on one side of the group.

Virgil, the coolest of them all, is going *mmmmmm*. A lot.

AYYYYYYYYYYYYYYYYYYYYYY, sez Fonzie, thumb up, and sways.

Virgil is afraid to see his own anger and to consider what he says on tape, but will over time, alone."

Right now, he simply has to understand a way back in. It's like how he gets into the swim. Virgil is after a line of feeling he only achieves near the last fourth of his session, at the forty-five minute mark, out of his body.

FineJoke looks serene in the corner, staring into an inner, and TheNewLing is painting a black cup white, or spitting out white milk on the floor. Virgil is hungry too, not for stardom, but an answer, and he fears, for some reason, to sweat Wite-Out.

Wite-Out is elevated, moving above the audience, hovering as if a drone
on the art scene.
In every case, the body is marked and, too, it is resilient against, or:
Down
Down
Boogie on Down
On Down
Of course, it makes sense, to be compelling is to be an obstacle. And of course, there is a radical difference

between the synthesized existence, and the bass line, but Virgil, who is not a musician, is unaware of the differences between the two when he's pressured.

But in his "freestyle and collage" analysis, he realizes that there are clear similarities between The OrangeBLOWHOLE and Wite-Out.

Their brilliance circulates in their ability to vanish into a collective, of memory, and over time, fade into positions of what we all know, type.

But Virgil is a Master. Virgil understands the role of performance, and the heat in the humid mist also knows, and understands.

Birds warble into the late morning, an indefatigable heart: What matters?

"The kitschy thing," Wite-Out says in the anger, or at the gang jump-in, in the battle, something that time has, in fact, healed.

"It's Kitsch by perspective."—this is what TheNewLing says, and when one is hurt, one turns away.

In one still in the hidden or lost video, there is an arm, and the arm is folded up at the end into a hand. Virgil moves back into the document. Sees it. Virgil decides he can draw from parts of it, if even fragments, becoming both point and aggressor, figure: *Suck on my machine gun*.

The Joke is always a rupture. The joke is a wound. I want to get into language, Virgil thought about all the times he was yelled at—

Rolled eyes. Smell. His mother's language—
We have that here.

AO smiles at Virgil across the Green Summer House for EXBPs, from one room to another. The EXBPs don't know each other well, yet, and it's late, and the light at that moment is not natural, but still. The smile between them reveals curiosity, even some concern. On Virgil's part, he realizes that his poetry has taken him to that location, in the room across from AO, because he is, indeed, a floater, wandering after the ruptures into the knot of what connects them, their bodies of work, and their bodies.

In the SBucks on Nesconset Highway the prints on the walls differ from those on Broadway or Florin Road. In the earlier, white people are making and buying, and in the latter, black hands are laboring and still—but this Virgil documented in a different time. For now, in the Radical Sabbatical, Virgil enacts in a constitutive mode through which he is able to reconstruct his life in a world, primarily, of Letters.

In the large lecture hall of a Lit Course—when Virgil was nineteen or twenty—he thought he would appear on a book jacket, his picture small but handsome, tucked away in the inside front cover's sleeve. Virgil figured that what would haunt him were the questions the Professor posed around reading Sethe's back, tree limb scar, a shape self-serving for Virgil, who also thought in another class that the PhilosophyNubile teaching cross-legged on the table is how Virgil would sit, one day, if he were the instructor.

Someday is an illusion, for some, but Virgil never had a doubt, and did not even think about the few dots of brown in the sea of white that forces the University's life into a coma. Yes, the captors say: We will release your Auto. But we will send him back, his stiff, vibrating eyes will be a reminder that a white dinner jacket can cloak even the tallest of whites, tortured citizen switched from son to father, the dead to the living.

Virgil, now, has time he's never had. He fills it with an anxiousness that radiates through him, the acupuncturist's needles directing the flow. One needle hurts. Others don't, and open the path from his neck to the backsides of his knees. Obamacare, the OrangeBLOWHOLE tweets "...IS DEAD." Angel Face asks how we feel about Auto, and Virgil spews disdain, like Auto deserved it.

Fair is not fair, ever, and the white brigade uses their sense of impending death so often, like a prop—the threat in understanding that Blue Lives do matter on the sticker on the back of a pickup. Virgil's blue X's cover the eyes of the WINNER in the photograph in the *NY Times*, The Victorious in a red dress pointing, her hands, not a thumbs up, but her index—*I have lived here all of my life.*

When Virgil wanted change, he grabbed a box-cutter and slashed the paper through the eyes, rage and packing tape, then tape over her face, the winner, bold blue X's sharpie'ed over her eyes. This is the only way he can read the news, by defacing it: 5-0 as it were, says President BLOWHOLE, Orangina, a Mouth.

In the movie, *The Town*, the two old boss mobsters in the flower shop front must be lovers, one cutting thorns off a rose, threatening to chop the nuts off Ben Affleck. Before this, to protect his WGF from the projects, he says— "Come with me, we're going to hurt some people...You can't ask any questions."

Bust the door down to wire-rod-break the bones after slamming the fatso onto the floor of his own apartment, and before this, shoot him in the knees. Say *oh yeah* to this, but how calm the sistah recounting the ID asked for, then another, four bullets in another BlackCastle, this one finding the heart.

Bully-to-death is the mode of the white brigade, despite the brown body's impermanence, and Bully is the shrinking belly that's ever-cinched to remind the viewer of the importance of his weight loss, to request us to look at his disappearing body with compassion, and for him to say, "Your work should not be so much about you," is really saying, "It should be about me!"

Virgil hears, *Me so horny* at the sight of white laziness, a belly, a plaid shirt, the ease of the self in public space, split bulges barely notice. Clean, the former President and CEO of a luxury paper line—"My wife is on a cruise."

"Oh yeah? Where?"

"Ah, Bermuda."

In the Green Summer House for EXBPs, the artists are aware of time and circumstance in producing work while in the presence of one another's constructed leisure. E-R once kept talking about art, or space, or maybe befuddlement, while asleep. The black mind cannot stop. This, is a theory. Sometimes, meditations on freedom must include the time it takes to retreat, as well as to ponder.

"Why do you feel you have to create so much?" asks the Tracker Jacker.

Have you seen Lost in Space *or not?* The body and mind that's unknown and brown, precise and mean, for a while just doesn't exist, and the sites of evaluation will shift to debase it as it becomes, before recognition in increments pub by pub, gouge by gut, by gall, "I'd like to praise my God Jehova," Serena always shouted out, at the French, US, Wimby, Indian Wells, Anywhere! And Newsflash, unmoved by the permanent site of Whiteness, one taps a straw sticking out of a Dooney & Bourke—

One Black is pulled over, and another has to drive. One figures out a way to buy a bottle of wine at a restaurant in the hours when liquour's not for sale in the Berkshires, another figures out how to fly, running up a hill near the Green Summer House for EXBPs. Several sleep in the former ski lodge's lowest floor, and another does not recall where or how the other slept, or when they did fall asleep to get up and to write again.

Virgil is shy at times, but he looks into the Berkshires sky in anticipation of what he'll make to add to his file. Could even be text outlined in a leather watchband, refuse, deteriorated ostrich could spark the collage, whatever possible angle to note, to aggregate, to fill one pool, because the others will be drained.

When he was young, and even more disoriented, Virgil's host at Squaw Valley thought Virgil could be embarrassed for not cutting his own tomatoes, that he was dependent on the other scholarship poet, GermanTopless, who cut the tomatoes for him and even sketched Virgil. But he'd not eaten a Caprese salad before, and eaten with such whites before that moment, his knife, maybe dull all the same, as was his maybe forgetting how Daddy Joliet did teach him, many times, to eat in *The Continental Style*.

The competition might be scored in multiple ways. One way is in Virgil's need to draw comparisons between then and now. More images—the SBucks print shots he keeps in his iPhoto caché show the usual plans and blacks, shadows and labor. One black body rakes the beans in a Zen garden, the other is a silhouette, and may as well be the leaf, or a lip's pout, or the color of azure and black skin that belies the broken tooth of the rake in the picture, and this must be how coffee beans dry.

Virgil don' know nuffin' 'bout no labor, but he did. His feet stunk from Rice Bowl, where he would mop the floor, and once cleaned the parking lot overflowed with sewage, and other shit, and the floor inside was greyed in the tile, the color of dried clay, and the sea cucumbers sat in vats in buckets. "Do it now, or you'll be doing it later..." beamed MommaSpine.

Black Lives Matter more than ever because the resiliency of these bodies in the Green Summer House for EXBPs leads to light, butter lettuce and saffron, to fuel the art. Bodies to be logged. Black and brown bodies toil away and are suspended in Virgil's SBucks photo stream, whether a field or on a farm; but there, in the city, white hands hold instruments, filters, sheening beans—Whites roast, wait in lines, and belong.

Before AO died, Virgil gave her a casual warning from the couch beneath soft, artificial light. "I read that you should not check your work email before bed, because it can shorten your life." AO, like several others before and after her, was discovered dead in her apartment, yet she has also visited him in this dream and is laughing.

Even though Virgil did not know AO well in life, she, like many of his mentors, is dead, and he carries her in his psyche. In the dream where they most recently met, he has a feeling that he wants to wear his glasses because they keep his eyes "cool and relaxed."

All Virgil wants to do is make sense of the pictures he carries in his phone, some downloaded into his other machines in various timelines, but mostly they are left in one that he only now has time to sort. Two of the photos he sees are with Virgil and Butch on a boat that took them from Venice to the island of Murano. The sun coats Virgil's body, and his grey suit coat looks great and his stomach is relatively flat in the jacket, one he does not wear seriously, even if it says micro-fit, the slim cut of the suit not thin enough for the pant that reads as too broad, down to the wide cuff.

The boat leads to the vase that Butch will buy. However many Euro, the glass looks dusted matte, almost, but still lets in the light, tangerine, and orange swirls against a Mallorcan blue sea. The piece is a small, thick heart, now the center of the Red House, backlit through the night, sometimes its eye. When Virgil receives the text with the cartoon of a red monster in the basement, it's getting a haircut, but clearly this is a scene of torture. No scissors, also a narcissist: dynamite is planted into the top of its head, like six sticks, and the fuses are lit, the blast obliterates the hair, leaving behind, a smoking scalp.

Of this, he is certain: Virgil, too, will lose more hair. It is his hope that he eats enough fruit and drinks enough water to keep the bones visible beneath his face, and in doing so, his content, subjectivity, will be noted as a form of erasure—not to vanish from not eating, but to render Virgil's particular expectations as a person, a human, a being.

But like his beautiful hair, he realizes his sight is going, too. For sure, Virgil will have to feel his way to the shore, live in natural causes as he hopes to die of them. DSecond, one of the living, white but not part of the white brigade, gives him advice, "I am never everyone's first choice, but I am always everyone's second."

When Teacher M wrote to Virgil in H.S. in his yearbook, that he "would excel not in terms of money or status, but in terms of compassion," it drove him into a place that, by default, continued to elevate him toward first class. Virgil was, in fact, quite jelly, looking up at the seats beyond his. The Most Musician, up there, was in first, while Virgil remained several seats behind, making Virgil think: "It is about Fame."

Against a cold wall in Asia/Pacific/Coffees, Virgil, in leisure, ponders temperature. At a performance in California in a black box, The Vision told Virgil and the rest of his MUTUALGANG that they needed, first, to understand their lineage, particularly other performance artists, and secondly, she asked a question Virgil always holds: "How did your bodies feel during the show? Were you hot? Were you cold?"

Of course, The Vision was not asking whether or not MUTUALGANG was hot or cold, but something else. It had to do with how she felt she could direct their bodies toward whomever they needed to become, one day, and of course, who they were at that very moment. The force of the question returned them to their bodies, and some might say, to earth.

This is why the performance in the basement in the City with the Metal Sky was much easier than the one under the California sun in the black box. Virgil was aware, then, of his body, and though his crew was away, doing them, he had some homies in that room that had Virgil's back, a communal force that shaped the turn of his ear into a flattening sound whenever Wite-Out tried to reason out of what seemed all to him a come up.

Did The Vision ever meet AO? This question undergirds the longer history implicit in the retreat in the

Green Summer House for EXPBs—how to mark the lineages of who is celebrated and who needs to be, all the same. History is not archival. The Vision was also very clear in her accounting of the fact that, in addition to lineage and temperature, she felt that MUTUALGANG's work took "Risks." This compliment still fuels Virgil. He sits with it forever, because he admires it, in her poetry and prose, The Vision's ability to hold anger so deftly in the space of critique, and then, on a whim, to unwind it through the failures of institutions and triumphs of questionable literary stars.

Virgil knows this crucially as being on offense, informing his attack on the transparent lyric: *why-not-kill-me-now—just playin'.* Clearly, Virgil understands "Risks," and maybe their swirling affinities with interruption, too: weight gain, fat-phobia, pigging out at the pastry grabbed from a bag, and all the while, Virgil does think: *Should you be eating that?*

Virgil is hungry. He wants to eat, but he eats only almonds after kale and blackberries, yogurt, cheese and chips, drinks tea and San Pellegrino. In other words, competition is not completion, because once captured, the victim needs to adjust to the circumstances, to stay tight.

Virgil also likes to remember J20+andFLYTHEN&NOW in a crop top, or once at the front of the small seminar room, the same time he was nineteen or twenty, her students sitting in a circle to face her on the first day of *The Reading and Writing of African American Poetry.*

Airdale, Armani, and Full: the end of the Academy all. J20+andFLYTHEN&NOW CAME IN FULL PROFESSOR!, and teaching the centrality of black dialect in the American Poetic tradition, its capacities, histories contained and dispersed.

J20+andFLYTHEN&NOW smoked Nat Shermans in front of a Grand Piano with all of her poetry students around her in the restaurant that looked like a mound of white clay inset from the road that led to the university where Virgil would one day lecture about temporality, abstraction, and violation.

At the buffet spread in one of the parties after a student reading, J20+andFLYTHEN&NOW, making her plate, confesses to Virgil—"I haven't slept for like three days...A PhD?...Watch out, they'll try to book-you-to-death."

In competition, there is no running, and there is always a trap. The potential for the self's unwinding, into say *The Wall Street Journal*, *USA Today*, or *NEWSDAY*, is that you *are a mystery in the zone of belonging*. It was a very good year when Virgil achieved tenure! But this was, Virgil felt, not much of an ending, but an invitation to not go insane, and to not die.

But Virgil will produce, and the production that he attempts to mark for himself, and in his "Biobib" has everything to do with the ropes and hooks he saw in *G.I. Joe: Retaliation*, over the roasted vegetable pasta he made, the hooks that latched into the sides of the rock face, hooks shot into a marbled black and white cliff face as the fighters soared, holding onto the ropes, feet racing across the impossible surface, kicking and sword slicing one another until the non-stars plummeted and the stars remained.

Of course, it's clear, Virgil thinks—*We write out of fear, or fear is the tramline that hovers above us, tugging us from one range to the next, but fear, at least to me, is not the same as sorrow.* Sorrow is a Long-Duck-Dong song that plays through Virgil, who jumps at the smallest things: the garage door opener falling in his lap in the black truck, or four-eyed-curl-frames-in-royal-blue-polo who slips his arm around him to grab a ring charger from the community table.

He got this. She got that. She is suffering, poor. She is dead. He is on sabbatical, almost, but for now (because he's doing homecare) is on F.M.L.A. *Ganstah*. Virgil improvises. He is not in competition with the normal, or even the normalizing desire to be embraced, because Virgil does not have any particular home-town, so he often looks across the S.F. Bay from where the Mudflat sculptures once appeared, lost like the piers, ruins pointing to where?

Stardom? Virgil has it, maybe wants more, but in the end, all he is after is the quiet that provides him with this view:

I just wish they would stop acting
like things are so stable, and, arguably,
that some domesticated "we" connects "us"
to the speaker's designated events by proxy,
because in the end, all they want is to be heard.

Some artists and writers, and fewer critics, might argue that this is "making some way out of no way," but Virgil understands the material consequences of being presented with things bent, torn, and already spent before it might be reconfigured into experiment.

One example was in the cardboard boxing of a "Baby Wet & Care" doll and wire hangers that Naldo and TheThenBuildingBlackDad fashioned into a catcher's facemask, other toy-train-track boxes triple rein-forced and stuffed with foam from somewhere, forming the body-armor, and the headgear padding to absorb missed catches.

"Naldo," what Virgil first called his big brother, had some pitching arm, just like the sweet serve that whistled by Virgil's ear, in doubles. Naldo calls tennis, *a game of motion*. Naldo pissed on Virgil in a bathtub. Naldo looks like Virgil, and for this, there are consequences.

Virgil burned Naldo's arm on purpose with the soldering iron as payback. Virgil broke the window. Virgil did not tighten the front wheel of the ten-speed. By this, Virgil means that he is engaged in the *activity of performance*, something Ralph Ellison calls "tinkering," in the tradition of Edison. Virgil thinks he mentions it, but it's something more, something that won't bind Virgil into being absorbed into simply wanting to tell his story.

Living, To Play (Virgil's Dad's always morphs in Virgil) and MommaSpine taught Virgil and CeSis everything they could for them to constitute their most original lives. The roaches scattered at the roadside hotel, or sleeping under the sky of a rest stop between Millington and Alameda—and to add, for six or seven months, LivingToGive, another name for Virgil's dad, was away at sea, but MommaSpine was there: "She raised you guys alone. "

In Alameda, Virgil remembers the windows were open early in the morning, voices, and the house was cold. Maybe one of Virgil's uncles, The Twin or BAMA40 was in the house.

Maybe BAMA40 came to protect his brother's wife after he found out about the break-in. But it was no matter, Virgil, nine or ten, was unafraid of who it was that robbed their home. Dust the windows for prints, black dust left on the white sills. The fingerprints were only marks to Virgil. Not peril.

Naldo's arm, which is like his father's, is akin to Virgil's—all of their arms, like their skin, is loose, especially at the joints. "They all play tennis the same," the PI Tennis Prodigy says, their strokes swinging to make forcing shots, bodies taught to propel opponents into compromised positions.

The weight of the ball comes, too, from the hard quads. The speed of the pitch comes from the elbow's rotation, forearm's aim and finger tips flick. As in tennis, "Go up after it!" BlackDad coaches, Virgil's serve crisp off the strings, his racket head slicing the air. Through impact, his body flowing out, and into the court for power and position.

This is not a White life.

This is: TheCurveButtDad is advising LanternShortsYellow to NOT GO TO STANFORD, as if the same rules apply for her AZN AZZ, especially the specific reality where TheCurveButtDad's white son just graduated from a school in the city, so TheCurveButtDad could save enough to buy an apartment in Queens. "If he decides to go to graduate school, we'll think about how to pay for it then."

In the park, where Virgil runs, chatting with stream against the wind, One WMD throws the ball in an arc, and mimes the full pitching swing, as he releases to his softball daughter, who throws the ball back in the same pattern as her catch, reversed.

This, too, is social capital inheritance.

Virgil does not explore this directly, but he puts together route, meditation, and order. In doing so, he relishes beating them all.

Running the longest and outlasting each, he will not be attacked in the park, but the fear that he feels as he runs around it is bound by the white children holding hands, two girls rolling their whole bodies down the side of a lush, grassy hill.

Randomly checked his wallet as Virgil glances, up. Predator?

A PudgyL.I.DAD coaches his son to "juggle" through a small maze of pylons in the soccer field, the centerpiece of the park, and the canvas portable chairs dig in as the sitters watch their kids play. *This is livin' really livin'.*

A large flappy catcher's mitt opens in a garage.

And SinewyanabrownedlegsandarmsANA thieves the Sweet N' Low in the SBucks on Nesconset Highway, and the Splenda, she saves for later, or to never use at all.

Vestibule

Malcolm has gone to another level, but Virgil is still communicating with him in dreams by phone, but maybe more than this, their communication is a way of seeing into what needs to be reckoned with, because often what remains of their conversations are the shapes the silhouettes of the trees leave on one of the bowed walls in the Red House where Virgil and Butch have forever lived.

Virgil wants to return to their patterns when he awakes—and since he is a figure of several skills—he fashions himself after William Blake—Virgil thinks of making an etching of muffled snores edging into the quiet fountain flow at the Harvest Inn. Even though he's never made an etching, Virgil understands that—working even in sound—his vision is only compromised by stretch and material, while his "hand," so often seeks the potential of both.

What strikes him about constructing just what he sees are how shadows function within this potential. The gesture in remembering this is enough, but too, it's fleeting—the shadows vanish with the bird's pitch as the day emerges in the Red House, so how will Virgil cease his behavior enough to capture both the forms on the walls as he considers the sonic?

Start with the bricks in the sunroom in the Red House, the way they start to crumble. What expensive home will they finally move to when they leave the Red House to go together to California? Will Stream ever add to the life that Virgil and Butch share? Will Virgil learn to kiss the walls in The Condo where Virgil now lives, as he does stranger after stranger, and will he carry these "butterfly kisses," from beneath Stream into the density of voices building at the Mount Sinai SBucks tables as much as the strain of the Cicadas and Crickets in the East?

"They shoulda sed that…." "………." Virgil has many plans to destroy sentiment. In fact, he has written from found voices before, but to collage with the light and insect wings, or a bottle opener/refrigerator magnet taped into a notebook; or on another one of its pages pine needles, twigs, little leaves, sap—

Touched belly, he will never leave Butch, though the possibility calls as Virgil splits on the studio floor, or dashes out to grab the Saturday *Times*, just before he reads that a story's plot could be entirely internal—AntColonyArtColony—

"You're with these people for a month!"

And when he even imagines divorce, it's as if he and Butch are Siamese twins fused at the top of one skull or sharing one heart, a fine sheen of fur grows over the thought.

Maybe Stream is the blood?
A Stent? A lifeline, but to where?
To the objective, and as much, to the fiction—

"I cum like a horse." This is what The Golf Attendant tells Virgil, his khakis somewhere between silk and nylon, his Polo, wide panel horizon yellow and plum stripes frame, as thick buttons dot down the collar. Grey hair dyed red-brown, some waves, but not Corn Silk. Shiny skin. Conditioned. His pubes shaved, a desert, or like The Smile, another in a long line of men to lighten the missing, to heavy the loss. The Golf Attendant's stubble cuts into Virgil's face, a black sharp lawn. The soil is black below the stacks of sod that Virgil remembers staring at before the neighbors across the street laid it down, and ran a train on their trees, trees that used to shade the Red House, even from afar, they cooled.

Virgil's desire is bound by touch, to love, if Virgil thinks of it more delicately—is love like the creeping breeze, the dangling of limbs, finely swaying as signifier, or at least a reminder—as in squirrel plot or crow's salute? One's black talons latch to the hammock for a sec.

This helps to unveil what Virgil wants, and has, the tender, usual Butch refrain:

Let me know what's goin' on.

"I'm livin' my best life."

Freedom in desire, or in a joke—perhaps this is the station between what Virgil wants to say when he writes of Butch/Virgil life in the form of an extended ellipses—for Stream, too, is the plot—and what he wants to say now is ever conscious of a form beyond shape—say the paragraph, the collage, the line, and its extensions into expected forms as much as predicted desires.

White Space is constitutive of White Bodies, what you/we know about dat?

Cash me outside.

Virgil's glances into the square belly, of what he wants to touch, even there, out in the open at Cat & Cloud—

"They do have a good sand trap."

Virgil tries, in a way, to convince Stream still then, a new lover, not to doubt his focus on him, however fiction, however, love, too, it is a form—*We work in one vector for our entire lives.*

But Virgil also thinks about being bound by the inanimate, a form triggered by trains, or sex, or T.V., or pasta, or the wind that plays at the fingertips of Virgil's deductions, his hand undulating out of the car, fingers press together, snaking to give the illusion of a wave centered by its axis.

To be bound, Virgil realizes, is not to be trapped. To be bound, Virgil learns, is to be connected to the force of what one is intentionally pulled by. The issue Virgil has is that *craft,* too, is an end, one that often traps the maker by race, gender, and class. When one expects the form of the executing body, as in knowing its "periodicity," or maybe even, "Where's the argument?"—one understands the deal, is settled, satisfied, and not "shocked."

I come from a shocked past, Virgil thinks this as he recalls the dinner party where PredictableBoots accused Virgil of "being shocking," just to be such, and from that moment, Virgil realized that he would forever be annoyed by PredictableBoots, and realizes that, in the end, he tries as hard as his wife, TheBlondeArt, to make everything clear, and realized, too, then: *Whatever. Everyone gotta eat.*

Sometimes Virgil sees PredictableBoots and The BlondeArt at parties. Their boy, A Son Somewhere Raps, though, is a teen dream, so not so bad. Their anger and curiosity suspends them as satellites for Virgil, though they offer some kindness, and Avon, too, thought PredictableBoots's shoes were so wrong, so Virgil does not hate PredictableBoots, The BlondeArt, or A Son Somewhere Raps, but Virgil thinks for a time that both PredictableBoots and TheBlondeArt are generally and over time, loosely WHACK, but that A Son Somewhere Raps is an eventual star.

The Word in a blurb called Virgil's second book, one of hybrid forms, "a pillow book," something which anchored Virgil's mind to a story he had to forever tell, and for the first time in a while, Virgil takes notice of how indifferent and ugly he sometimes feels in the morning. This is a perk of the Radical Sabbatical, for sure, the time to stare into the mirror, which is both looking into the present and expecting a future with no immediate deadline, nor leading to any real place to go, besides *Movin On Up...*

To
The
Sky.

The Flower Prisoner Virgil meets at the Sugar Hole works on CSI sets in NYC. The Flower Prisoner's face, another bearded smile—or an alternative lay—is to be sealed behind a thin, plastic shower curtain at the Smith Haven LA Fitness out of view. But still, Virgil is jealous of a make-out session Stream gives to a woman at a party; however rendered and in whatever detail, it pulls at Virgil's jelly heart, even when he is far away in Peterborough, NH, far from that make-out session, which Virgil tucks away in the surrounding green, turning orange forest.

Combat cock blocks The Flower Prisoner by hurling his club-dick in Virgil's face. Virgil tastes it, but is turned off, just as quickly, by The Flower Prisoner's inability to socialize during the hot play. TheDadWhoVirgilOnceDrew does not change his face, but Virgil gets him to find his way into the exchange of white bodies on brown boy action, where Virgil, finally, is totally naked in the Sugar Hole.

It was, Virgil felt, a time he saved up for, but it also became too much to temper, as Virgil took on, maybe too many men, more and more distractions, but lays, as the long reader of Virgil's growing corpus could surmise, takes Virgil to where he arrives, in the same damn recurring mirror.

Sir!

Pink Skin.
Sacks,
plugged
between
Virgil's
top
teeth.

Virgil's face was puffy that morning, the sugared blood fattening it, his dreams tugged between several occasions, a car with no breaks and L.E.D. or otherwise signs on the dash to indicate the crash about to happen, a car, they are tailgating, without much choice—in this Virgil collides smack dab into what he does not want to remember—

I must remain in the fiction.

For Virgil, remaining in the fiction is a dance between lived experience and the truth, the walls of performance bound by his characters, ones he maps against, and how he improvises, ducking into form, coming out, rendering.

Is fiction a line of events? Or is it the life Virgil simply lives? Memoir? Logorrhea? Whatever the case, he learns to construct this writing life by acting out, however he feels, *as his primary mode of research.*

This is one intervention.

Virgil, as a boy, carried MommaSpine's wallet when they went to the base commissary. The wallet was suede, olive green. It was soft. It was as soft as the time she and Daddy, Who Loves made him and Naldo and CeSis fried cow tongue for breakfast, and before serving it, made sure to show the thawed meat to his children, peeled from the cold butcher paper before MommaSpine cooked it.

Virgil calls the kisses Stream likes, "Jackie O Kisses," the pecks they imagine like those from that first lady, but Virgil's are more like the cow's, Virgil's thick tongue dropping into the lover's mouth slow, to drink the saliva, especially when the lover's man paw, thick and ready, hovers, then into Virgil's other black hole.

MommaSpine did not "lose it" when Virgil lost the wallet in the base commissary that day Virgil recalls searching, not aimlessly, but on his own adventure with the cart, which remained full of the food that would still be paid for, no matter what. Looking for the wallet in the low freezers, in the bins, then back in the basket, "all around" is what Virgil holds onto, searching in a way, forever.

"You think you're rich."

This is what Virgil would often hear from his family, and he wanted to be this, the spoiled rich white teen, the son of the KTVU anchor, the only boy in the real Lacoste

Shirts. Then, Virgil had no idea about the difference between LeTigre and Lacoste—

Virgil's poetry and close attention to *the drafts* of poems, essays, of stories, however, one day, would lead him far from needing to care about such difference.

"Only the best, Got Rocks." is how his family teased him. "Whaddyou Care, You're Rich," is what Butch says.

Virgil was sorry to have lost the wallet, and he cried to his mother and father, as though *he* were the lost object. Those tears, then, Virgil feels may have been because he had no idea that all he wanted was to be under the chests of men, what he could not explain, then, was the reach of a much longer memory under the broad, inevitable cover of white bodies cupped in a field of green and sound.

In the SugarHole—The Flower Prisoner's body is fat, his tit in Virgil's hand feels like a soft missile. To be so soft, and free is a right of that kind of white body, *a baby body for life!*

To cum for such men, for Virgil, is to be enamored, held, and torqued, under a chest, or even, to gaze at a micro-penis—*who cares, the bush is enough*—to ponder, in others, the "SU-*frace*," as Rafa Nadal calls it.

Virgil, with tennis-trained reflexes, catches the baggy that's fallen out of The Flower Prisoner's shirt pocket onto Virgil's chest, and crams it back into the Flower Prisoner's pocket, "Are you 5-0?" Though Virgil is not, this is the start of what leads to the punchline of a joke that Virgil tells to The Flower Prisoner—"We'll stuff that weed up your anal cavity, should someone come into the theater to bust all the fags....It's 5-0!!!"—and though he is joking, and though he thinks it's funny, should the Po Po pop up, Virgil would never want to be caught up in any actual case.

Poet's time, it was, as though Virgil might rework any moment over and over again. No matter. The Prison-Industrial Complex—Ruthie Gilmore, and Angela Davis, their names arise in Virgil and The Flower Prisoner's soft conversations in the porn theater light, but what stands out is *Keefe*, which The Flower Prisoner says makes everything in the commissary.

Virgil searches: "private label foods," "skin-and-hair products," even "athletic footwear, electronics, and personal items." The Flower Prisoner reports: "Our tax dollars are going right to Keefe" to which Virgil offers a list:

Sharecropping
Carpentry
Unions
Rehab

And suddenly, Virgil is re-struck by how imprisoned Black and Brown bodies are always worth money, precious in their labor, precious in their ability to entertain, to satisfy violation, and speculative violator, which may explain some part of Virgil's heat on a couch, how he is liked, against the Flower Prisoner's shirt, sunset tones in the SugarHole. Virgil, in his research, goes from the Keefe site, to the Pew Research Center's "Fact Tank: News in the Numbers," to learn:

In 2017, blacks represented 12% of the U.S. adult population but 33% of the sentenced prison population. Whites accounted for 64% of adults but 30% of prisoners. And while Hispanics

*represented 16% of the adult population, they
accounted for 23% of inmates.*

It wasn't or isn't pathos. Virgil cannot stand thinking this, but now that he knows, he realizes the question—*Where my Azian's at?*—but some love shared in
the vestibule is what he wants, in a corner, a corner out
of which he peeps Combat standing there all sex-zombie
-like, and for a second they were all together as one
mass. But no anal, not then.

*I was this.
I was that.*

It was, and is, however, related to texture, understanding Virgil's will, a will he feels might conform under
what he lost, but he will never pimp it out by revealing
the act that leads to his weakening into a singular frame.

It's not as though Virgil is too thick with pride to not
allow him to reveal himself as the suffering subject, at
times, but for Virgil he likes to remain fit, and found,
and *in the drafts*. Virgil, instead, will move more explic-
itly into the interdisciplinary arts!

It's like when he was lost in the middle of a shop-
ping square in Hawaii on a stopover between his family's Navy move from Guam to the U.S.A. Lost, in that
square, when a group of brown men told him to stay in
one place until his parents came to find him.

The brown men had faith. Faith that Virgil would be
found, a faith enough that was transmitted to Virgil who
did not go, as usual, to the registers at the front of the
store to page his mother. For there were no registers,
and Virgil did not feel ditched, maybe knowing, too,

that he would be found, knowing that these brown men would and were there to help him, knowing how *to stay in one place*, was how he came to find his voice in the midst of always being lost.

It's okay, it just had sentimental value, or *It only had sentimental value*. His parents did not say, "It had sentimental value," because the suede, olive green wallet, and its forever being lost, would have signified how some bodies are made to expose their feelings around the self, while others exist between the life of the body—say in this case, the child—and the wallet, forever linked. However, for Virgil, his past child "losing" the wallet illuminates the implicit safety in not holding onto things, as the body, itself, may one day be snatched.

Things vanish, and things can mean little. Or perfect conditions are rare: the tiny white dog meets a tiny white girl under a crisp fall day in Peterborough, NH, and the tiny white girl eats a muffin, and the tiny white lady, the tiny white girl's mom, ectomorph blonde, pops out of the big red Ford Explorer, along with tiny white dad's feet, and a round child too, emits, pink ribbons vs. cancer, such being the politics of white, white, white, the leaves are so brown and orange.

On the stage, Virgil is not Lucy. Virgil has not purchased a mask for the evening of his performance, and in the morning, when he wants to leave the Red House to escape to California, he realizes it's because he's never afraid of rendering his confusion, but still, this rendering consumes and controls.

To rend, the Linguist tells him, is not to build, but to take away, and for Virgil, this means, to move away from the object, further and further, until the assumptions become less and less, until what remains is more and more real. More and more of a drive towards etching or drafting or even, *ticking*.

Clear your mind

Clear...your behind...

A body made in feeling—something which exists between words that are broken, and those which aren't. Virgil is writing as Black Bodies continue to endure. If this is fiction, it's also the usual. Hence, Virgil is assured in moving between forms, and beyond them. The black body as source text, the black body as field—the black body moving further and further away from that which—

Missed diagnoses? Can these exist for bodies that are banged around, but still heal? Virgil's father, for instance, is gaining back his memory, or maybe he could care less, and is now no way dying in what he describes as a prison, his wish, to drive, with a fought-for license, wherever he wants, in other words, for him, is to be free. *He got it!*

Fantasy—Virgil hears someone read a poem that parades as hurt, and needs confirmation. Snaps. Or "Uh-huh..." Or... "Mmmmmmmm" Or an award. To a Lunatic. A stage, a ladder left in the yard overnight, and it's still there. Virgil isn't mourning. Or complaining. He has resources. That is, he also isn't sad.

Virgil is simply curious. He leans into abstraction, because he and the suede, olive green wallet and the cow tongue are suspended, soft, crafted into a dual-form of what remains, a story, one bound by a search, for dick, for dads, for money, for love, for release into more and more security, and saying in a saying system:

spit,
 freestyle,
poetry,
  sketches,
drawings,
and
  dance

Virgil understands that for him, *station* is close to *static*. But Virgil recalls, also around the time he lost his mother's wallet, looking up into the telephone lines above the car window, while his family drove along the quiet roads in Tennessee:

To where, doesn't matter—

Virgil looking up at the crisscrossing and waving lines that dipped above him, lines gathering and bowing above as he lay on the "jungle" full-spread custom mattress his mother upholstered for their Pinto Squire, and for her children:

It is the light, itself, in the gaps that constitute
the space of the fictive,
so that Virgil makes something up,
slips in the loss, the wide wind
blasting against the carapace—
of the imagined—
This is Virgil's own
history of risk, and of flight—

In the street, Virgil and C... stop where Virgil first stopped on a walk after a day of moving from the collages to the ink and water-soluble oil pastels in the Berlin loft. During that visit, Virgil was in two lofts, the first larger than the second. The second held a window to the street, where he set his iPad Pro on the ledge to record others outside for a track, Berlin kids talking on their way to school, he caught—this he would set as the background for his slowed down and antique filtered body backstroking in the pool at the Hotel Lafayette in San Diego.

The Musician, For Real, during a recent performance thought that Virgil was a synchronized swimmer, which is funny, as he never was, though in the paused image, Virgil's arm pointed up out of the water projected for the audience before it struck back in to propel him through the pool, serving as a visual backdrop of the performance.

Virgil did not think of mimicking the move in the performance—he could, easily, as a dancer—no more than he thought about his stroke while swimming. He just felt a need to manipulate the memory both in film, and again on stage, and he wanted to show what he was after, something he understood later, that he was working in gesture to illuminate the line, for sure, but ultimately towards composing the scene with the sculptural.

Virgil and C... pause in front of a small gallery's exhibit, *Prince's Berlin*. In the portrait, Virgil sees that the bones of Prince's face are pronounced, even more than Virgil imagined, his skin powdered to white, smooth, yet still angles—shrieks as song, song as call to the whir of the AC fans, these sounds cancelling the birds that he doesn't hear in the morning of which he wants to remember, because in the Red House, the air is cool.

At night, the taxi driver does not want Virgil to put his pizza box on the seat. To Virgil, Berlin was so full of starch, rolls after rolls, croissant, the mornings of flat cheeses and separating eggs, and fruits, nuts, and toast as bland as the day, as grey as the streets, few trees, save in a large esplanade, a park where Virgil felt like Narcissus with no pond to reflect in, because the only pond he encountered on his long run was thick with algae.

Virgil was going internal in that loft, too, and even though his home institution did not forward his grant application to move to the next round—so dumb of them, that round to say that his work had no singular focus, and three years later, after Virgil practiced even more, to say, his work was now too developed —however not their type, or whatever, Virgil's vision will remain intact and expansive across however many disciplines he wishes to practice, or needs to:

> *Discipline for Virgil is compelling—*
> *it represents escape into one form*
> *or the next, not because he is unsure,*
> *but because his wandering is specific.*
> *It is not a choice to wander*
> *for those displaced,*
> *and further still,*
> *to those for whom trauma travels,*
> *the line is zigzagged.*
> *E.g. Jagged knife finds the liver,*
> *fatty, rich and free, toes point*
> *to connect, the lines,*
> *guiding—*

Virgil's move into the second loft does allow him a different point of view, views into the German homes across the street, the stacked scenes opening up to a morning in which Virgil realizes he has as his process, without reservation, a morning chock full of lives, those he does not know, those lives that may lead Virgil to a future worth making his way through and into by layering one performance onto another, as a means of seeing what might happen over time.

For Virgil, the sculptural is a mode of understanding the line, something he finds in the poetry. But for Virgil, fiction, and maybe theory isn't about connecting meaning within any one given form, it's about embedding the form in the tempo within the sensation of life, of the news, of the accounts of the experience of what it means to alter the site of what's found—

This special counsel. That special counsel.

What Virgil escapes from is found in the psychic shapes that the repeating and altering structures of language allow. The patterns of a poem can form a story, so that the sense of what Virgil learns to render is also what he hopes to find in paragraphs. Crotches sometimes come into view, or a dissipating voice in a varied field, the advancements of Virgil's longing.

LayeredJabbaWhoSmellsofWaterWash is obvi jovial, when he describes his time in the wet saunas gone in the new LA Fitnesses on Long Island. Because of black mold, because of bacteria, because of expense, the dry sauna men speculate, the wet ones had to go. But LayeredJabbaWhoSmellsofWaterWash has another theory to share, one that Virgil knows to be the right one— "In every one on them on the Island, men were having sex with each other." "Is that what they mean by hot steamy sex?" LayeredJabbaWhoSmellsofWaterWash asks, adding, "Why would they do that?"

It could be a coy invitation Virgil thinks, to press his towel more into his crotch, the sign, then or later, but he concludes the question should be, instead, for what other purpose is any men's sauna?

Callers calling into *Shade 45* announce what they would want on their last day before going off to prison. What a question, but so many of the men tell how they want three-ways, orgies, but clarify, "without men," a map to the life of being fully satisfied, but what they want are such, Virgil thinks, lame prescriptions, dumb blacks as dumb as whites.

In *Django Unchained*, Hilde (Broomhilda) is trapped in the hotbox, for running away, and when the rusted, iron lid is ripped open, she lays prone, but is just as quickly roused by the daylight as she's doused with water.

In her screams and gasps, Virgil, as a filmmaker, understands that the water thrown from the bucket into the hole onto Hilde, before she is snatched out of the hotbox reveals an impending set of heroics *before* Hilde's naked, struggling body is cleaned up to serve—slaves in medieval collars, "Shoots" corrected to "Schultz," the camera trained between the box in the distance and the tear, driving hot down Django's face.

For this reason, Virgil feels *Django Unchained* to be more compelling than *Moonlight,* because the depicted black forms in the latter are somehow, squarely familiar, not that *Moonlight* isn't gorgeous, but it's precisely this familiarity that allows Virgil to see that he is not as deeply taken by the utter beauty in blackness as he is in its mixed-up amplifications, that is, in how blackness is violently embedded across time and space, an impossible corrective.

For Virgil, cinematic tension in any movie equals the potential to move along the line of his wandering, yes, but wandering in the form of examination and retreat *at the same damn time*. Hence, for Virgil, his walks are as crucial as his feelings while on the walks. To get lost along a river, to have been traveling along rivers into a hollow that reminds Virgil his path is a series of movements around the subject, movements away from a history of what he might record, for then, for now, for them, why?

Even in the sound of a saw in the distance against steel—even at the sight of a boy in the East Setauket Starbucks, wrapped warm in a beach towel that reads in blue, *Joint Resistance* against a muted red, a back print of assorted artillery. Virgil as a construct, made of diametrical parts, a body of slavery, and a body of exile, a body of resistance, and one of resistant assimilation, and then, a body that desires, one who is longing, or one who longs until he gets sick.

PoutBrilliantModel AKA Hollow G says, on the river cruise ship, "You are sensitive." PoutBrilliantModel AKA Hollow G does not say this as though Virgil is overreacting. She says it because she notices that Virgil knows how to speak at a dinner table into white wealth. If charm is an attack, it is also a kick-turn, returning the body to the pool's present, the kick-turn as a way into the source of what needs to be maneuvered, not out of hate but out of the desire to jet, quickly and smoothly through the lap.

However, Virgil, by consequence, is not free. And this becomes obvious when frog-tan-fat sits across from

Virgil, and the OtherBlackwithBoseWireless sits down to vanish into the shield of Virgil's internal life. At that moment, frog-tan-fat, OtherBlackwithBoseWireless and Virgil form into difference, a broken triangle that marks Virgil's body as a mode of being in collective asymmetry *with all of them.*

> Giant winged sculpture
> Berlin?
> Virgil?
> Short grey statues—
> Men hide in the dark.
> Faces morph,
> Faces block sites of being held,
> and then the fear of being hit, or stabbed—

C... asks Virgil about the election, and by this point, Virgil is filled with pistachios, jalapeno pretzels, and dry Italian white wine, and sits on the top, outside deck of C...'s Berlin mansion that was once many apartments, gutted into a giant open hall, with just a few perfectly syncopated rooms, dry sauna, spa, and a yoga studio, sculpted lights, elevator and a succinct alarm system. In the now Berlin mansion, Virgil is so far away, too far, from the Red House, in a place, taking pics he is asked not to post, a place where Virgil leaves no trace and of which he makes no record, save a few drawings, from memory, of the large, opaque, oblong chandeliers.

Virgil exits into the Berlin night with a native tongue, which is sadly English, and other languages that have not been handed down, or been taken away, languages that have followed him into the edges of ascent, languages that pull him into the heights of what he's made: stanzas that came to him on the river cruise ship after he saw the gargoyles from the 13th Century on the walls which compelled him towards water-soluble oil pastels and pasting new things against the ancient.

Virgil presses into the paper, pushing business cards together from restaurants he went to in Paris, and one in Cognac, layering them into his collages, and then writing over them, blending paint with water and green tea to seep in. From making these works, Virgil's visions alter. The dogs outside even look different—But even so, Virgil is afraid to travel towards what he sees, to go to the Philippines because he has seen bodies, random drug dealers and users shot on sight, their corpses flooding the sidewalk as does their own blood.

The Loire Valley is filled with men who fish, and in a town near Amboise, Virgil runs through a small alley. How quickly Virgil would tire from being so far, so far from each day, of not knowing what one would do without the threat of being shot or locked up as punctuation to a free life before getting caught. Sway on *Shade 45* says on his last day before being locked up, that he would like to fish in a crystal-clear lake with his lover, relax in its enduring quiet, a quiet Virgil would also draw from, and he does before the pops of hunting rounds carry towards him in the amber-orange forest in Peterborough, NH, as he constructs on the screened-in porch, the leaves below him, soft carpet catching the scaled autumn light.

The white man and girl who bought Desiré expected a scam, and so did Virgil, who asked them to meet him and his 2005 Knowledge Blue Subaru in front of the Whole Foods parking lot in "Midtown" Santa Cruz. Desiré's A/C was brand new, and so too, were her tires, and so too, was the timing belt, and so too, was the car gently shipped from Port Jefferson Station to Sacramento on a truck bed to save mileage, wear and tear.

The binder he gave the white man and girl was thick with pages of Desiré's past, mostly of routine services, any repairs, or body work, minimal and minor. All along, it was Virgil's plan to sell his car in excellent condition to any buyer before he would meet Manitoba, his come up. CeSis thinks inside Manitoba it smells like fresh paint, so crystal clear his need to save the things that matter, like such a familiar smell that Virgil, too, recognizes as linked to his need to keep everything in his life new, and clear, free, open, and without stains.

"Ghastly" is what Clean called the thick fluid Virgil left on the white hotel sheets, fluid shit, of pink resin of polyp leak and lube, Virgil's insides mined from Clean's plowing. The day the OrangeBLOWHOLE won, Virgil and Avon ate calamari under the sun in a courtyard not too far from the ocean in Santa Cruz. Avon would soon travel to South Korea, and Virgil would be sitting in front of the shadows of the Port Jefferson Starbucks, a few seconds from the Sound, the Atlantic heat grounding him into submission.

Virgil's comings and goings, seemingly every day, revolved around the Google search "Trump/Russia,"— the comment by L.I.Proles in the spa left him feeling a little broken, announcing, "nothing will come of it." What's important, though, for Virgil is the black mold the L.I.Proles discuss in the "No-Homo" Saunas they say they want. The fact is, that in another world, in the Miller Place Starbucks, cargo shorts were the culprit in not allowing FatHandInLexusAWD entry into the links.

"I had to buy a new pair of shorts... I mean, I was there anyhow."

Virgil is now so far away from Clean, after his dumb vote for the OrangeBLOWHOLE, and in another increasing love, he drifts away from yet still with Stream for as much as he can, and for the day, away from his texts, FB off, to examine the densely green trees gliding by him on the train's top deck on his way to Huntington to meet TheOrb.

But away from them all, into the quiet of the prose, so far from the parking garage below the Sheraton, the little clicking ticket, the hot wind, the tornado ripped apart trees, growing into the humidity of Western Mass—Virgil is no longer in the city of low-lying factories and almost invisible houses hidden in the brown trees along the Connecticut River.

But by Clean, Virgil, at one point, was sprung. Clean likes "Brown," starring Virgil in the video wearing only a yellow polyester baby doll, running along the cliffs, and "skiing" down the Marin Headland's loose soil, his buffed calves and the club he holds to the sky, preventing his fall, running shoes digging into the coastal dirt and plants, but for whom?

Clean loved the video. And said he imagined seeing Virgil in that dress, in his car, the one he suggested he'd sell to Virgil. But the Black Jaguar XK, Clean said he might sell, maybe was a trick—Virgil could have given him the 30K, but in the end, Clean sold that vehicle and the Audi Crossover SUV to one of his employees, a manager of some heft who wanted to fake the fly life, a series of fronts in a fake world all with two used cars, one perhaps for him, his new-to-him XK, the other, for his wife or daughter, their new-to-them Q7.

In his refusal of Virgil's offer to buy the Black Jaguar, did Clean think that Virgil was no good for an easy 30K loan with his perfect credit history and access to the moon should he want any car to secure a ride in what Clean would later call Virgil's *California Life*?

"Do you think I am mellow?"

"I think you're fuckin' psycho."

This is the exchange between Virgil and Butch when Virgil thinks he has body lice or scabies, after his back and boy pussy, juicing and exposed in ShowWorld, flowering out of a split mattress, was banged out by PinkLipped Dad-Knob who fucked like a robot. Virgil could care less about PinkLipped Dad-Knob's body or his lips, but to be lost between TheGerman and KennyRogersMealWormTongue in a white room, and almost spit roasted, and then to seek lice inspection by Butch is prolly why Virgil was dazed for a day, left searching his skin for bites in the several days following his activities.

Virgil saves the casts of his teeth, two cement pieces, upper and lower sections that interlock in a box, now in a bag of material for use in what he imagines will be a new series of self-portraits. Virgil saves a fast sketch of Butch in brown crayon on a paper table cloth from breakfast in Sayville the morning they missed the ferry to Fire Island. The sketch is rolled up in a basket next to WildBoy's baby pic—In the shot is the cardboard sign CeSis made that, her son, WildBoy holds up: I WILL DROOL FOR FOOD.

Virgil throws the Oliver Peoples ad into the recycling with like 50 lbs. of PMLA journals, and returns his psyche to sudden freedom as he tosses out the possibility of spending another $1K on more frames and lenses he'll buy when he can afford them, and journals he could give two fucks about; but ultimately, he tosses everything out because he grows exhausted by the ad thick with whites, leisurely styling in the palm-treed sunsets, indicators of what he does not want to be, but still he longs for something within their radius.

Read more.

Try Audible.

Virgil's Radical Sabbatical is giving Virgil the opportunity to think about his future in more concrete terms. The teeth knock. He imagines his night guard *a pacifier*, which is what he calls it at the dentist's office as he discusses transparent pay scales, salaries, and how hard he works to be the most actively published in the division, hence Virgil's grinding. The Dentist and his Assistant are surprised that more publications mean more cash, and are rocked by how Virgil knows his colleagues' salary and rank; and they, too, know his, but *what do you care?*—Dad,OnTheMend's favorite saying.

How's California? It's a question that Virgil often answers on Long Island, not always with the weather, or what he's acquired, which would change once he buys property, but Virgil makes a pact with himself, that he will not chase what others have, will be direct, and stop showing off. Instead, he'll make his work, looking inside to create what he wants, and to build opportunities for advancements in what he needs. For instance, instead of applying for a new position, Virgil will write sentences, and dance, and build, and look into the mirror of his unknown future.

The black bird trapped in the garage should have been afraid, and it showed its fear by shitting on the no longer used racing bike, and the grey epoxy floor with the water drying in its center. The hair clippings are in the bathroom, and the house is sweating, and Virgil is in a very expensive intentionally worn out and holy AG T-shirt and fitted ripped jeans. Another AG shirt, grey linen, hangs in the window to air dry, and he leaves Butch voicemails, emergency call after emergency call, before throwing Butch's old, grass-stained white Champion kick at the black bird too scared to drop from behind the retracted garage door to fly away.

The black bird remains caught like the ant, "stunned" with a flick, and captured by cell cam. Its crime? Crawling on Virgil. Virgil thought he broke one or more of its legs, because, the ant stirred in a circle, dazed, but it was only that, no broken leg, because quickly it "fixed" itself like the crazy queen in the club did after Virgil lifted him in the air and slammed him to the slippery, steel dance floor at FACES.

Virgil is "a Mean-Sommufabitch," like Butch often tells him he is, and further qualifies this by saying Virgil couldn't have gotten this trait from his parents. This is true, but he did get from MommaSpine and VolleyDad his sense of responsibility, which is why he calls Butch so often at work, in between startling the black bird, so he can move on with his day, into the possibilities found only through his thinking without stress.

In the film *Land Ho!*, the story circles around a journey, a lost Doctor, and a sad Banker, Silver-White traveling across Iceland in a big black Hummer—The lost

Doctor (Mitch, U.S.) wants to dance with his sad Banker (Colin, Aussie), and love him, because he is alone in his heart. Though he has money, we learn the doctor, was "forced out," and still sports a stethoscope—so the viewer knows the lost Doctor's got some questionable past, but still, he can have most anything, and finances the vacation for them both.

There is no sex between them, the lost Doctor and the sad Banker, Silver-White, but the sexual tension is obvi, a need to return to the playful boys they once were, even as young married men, in-laws sharing relatives, a family dynamic Virgil does not have, or want, so perhaps he connects across a fantasy he observes in their fictive lives without this deet.

The lost Doctor and the sad Banker, Silver-White's desire, refreshingly, is triggered NOT by a white blonde ingenue (these do come and go, white grandchild/niece and her BFF away at college, meet up with the grey men, who treat the girls to dinner, and a Disco), but by A Black Woman, OMG, Her Face, Broad Teeth and Her Head of Kitchen, Some Do in a Jacked Bun, in the white, too, steaming water of the hot spring, who seduces the sad Banker, more directly, than the white grandchild/niece's BFF at da club.

"There's a warm spot near me," beckons A Black Woman, OMG, Her Face, Broad Teeth and Her Head of Kitchen, Some Do in a Jacked Bun, and maybe this is how Virgil longs and catches too, the easy seduction of this kind of man, these kinds, Silver-Whites bonded by a simple sweetness, however complicated, and loaded.

In the margins, one might be wedded, but also in the margins, one can climb. But the black bird remains trapped in the garage, first, unafraid to fly into the day to look below the levels, but now unable to see the obvious freedom when Virgil leaves the garage door open where the black bird came in.

The lost Doctor and the sad Banker, Silver-White end up, one night, in the same bed, atop the covers, or clothed, after sharing a joint, drifting together. The lost Doctor is afraid, the sad Banker is high. Geysers often shoot. One old man strips. They are not grumpy, though one remains deeply sad, the other expands as a field of regret. But the movie does offer an important intervention: OMG, Her Face, Broad Teeth and Her Head of Kitchen, Some Do in a Jacked Bun (a lawyer) takes photos of the lost Doctor and the sad Banker, Silver-White in the hot spring, using a silver vintage looking boxy camera, as the two men relax and laugh.

Even though Virgil can be a cynical byatch, he loves how OMG, Her Face, Broad Teeth and Her Head of Kitchen, Some Do in a Jacked Bun is often depicted alone, clearly independent, and ready to hike, mountain trails, hers, not a story of pathos. The lost Doctor and the sad Banker, Silver-White, however, on the other hand, move somehow, aimlessly, in many places, but pivotally; in fact, in one scene, the two are lying together against a rock, awaking to greet daybreak, a short distance from their luxury campsite they thought they were miles from, lost in wine, weed, and darkness the night before.

The lost Doctor and the sad Banker, Silver-White, who find their way by remaining in one place, are greeted by the view of a wide brown range of mountains, peaks of white, and their compound, first class bungalows pop out below, on the horizon. Virgil remembers this time while encountering *Land Ho!*, the long days of heat, the one train ride into the city that summer, maybe one more, but more, the insects, the humidity, and the quiet.

Journal as Fictive. Black Bird in the Garage. The bloodbath he could have suffered were Virgil cruel or spiteful. Virgil can't unkink the hose, at first, but when he does, he tosses it in the shallow bird bath, pewter, or steel, green algae, patina—Virgil goes in the Red House to silence the tea kettle, stainless steel Alessi, a shiny cone with a flat edged spout with no whistle.

Virgil has a theory. Post-garden. Post-pool. Post-line. Post-rush. If he takes the time to think about the desire between the lost Doctor and the sad Banker, Silver-White, and to look a lot into the sad eyes of the sad Banker, while watching the movie, it also gives him some time to think of the teaser on the Independent Film Channel that got Virgil to watch *Land Ho!* in the first place:

Across the screen, mist seeps up in the water, and the fiord was flat. Melted ice: In any case, they were in a stream together, this old white man, and that black woman, and her hair was pushed up, and like Stream says of Virgil, she may have been "of a certain caliber," but all Virgil wanted was to see them doing it. It was with anticipation that he fell for the trick of difference set by anticipation in the young black/old white/man/woman bait. No frontal nudity, but there's a kiss, and the promise of such in how they were placed, in the water, sexy with one another.

Is it normal to have your feet slapped, mid flip-turn, by a MeanWhite-as-a-Line-White-Swimmer who's on the ready, crouching on the pool deck, even though you glide with self-wrought power after the push, kicking underwater into the 7:30 PM mark? Virgil knows what time it is, when the pool closes and finally, in his writing chair, he is able to consider how to move within the reflection of his own swim.

His speed he does not think of, because he once swam in a place where the sea was walled off into a giant man-made tide pool. No need to be jelly. It was like being in the woven print shirt these white men wear, olive and muted rust flora, like The Flower Prisoner's, but Virgil knows he was in that water in Guam, so he would never recall a dull colored thing to inspire what could be worn, should he ever choose such a print.

In the man-made tide pool, coral grew along its living walls, and Virgil's legs feel long, as long as the Portuguese Man-of-War's tentacles he first sees on *Flipper*, the underwater stock footage revealing the stinging-to-come on Sandy Rick's long tanned torso and limbs, while Bud Rick, his little, lighter-skinned brother, in the dingy screams in terror. Then, of course, Flipper goes on the attack, against the tentacles, to save his white boy. Does Flipper get wrapped up? Virgil can't recall, exactly.

Virgil does, however, remember Sandy stung, wrapped up by venomous cords, the jellyfish's white, floating bulbous head at the surface, untouched, before and after the attack. For Virgil, this is quite a powerful constraint, for what Virgil is clear about is the ocean walled off by cement, in Guam, the tide coming in to fill the pool up at high, and releasing at low tide. Virgil feels this pressure, and in his attention to stillness, he asks himself: *What if I held on, to only this memory as stress? But I grew up near the deepest natural trench in the world, in the Marianas. And I will, forever, be safe, secure in this fact.*

Virgil has not yet entered the ocean, at Seabright Beach, near his place in Santa Cruz because he is afraid of what he'll find. Needles. A shelf. Rocks. Virgil understands his memory as currency, a time to think of when he walked along the beach in Guam, at the only "day camp" he ever went to, one in which he never found the poured wax and wick he left cooling in the starfish shaped hole he sculpted in the sand.

On the bus ride home from camp one day, a story was told. A boy cinched his neck to a telephone pole with his belt, when the bus was stopped, and his head was torn off as the bus left. Or maybe a boy's head was knocked off by a telephone pole when the bus sped by it, as the boy stuck his head out to feel the air's rush, or to yell.

One year later on a field trip to a museum somewhere in Tennessee, all the kids are shown the skull of a boy whose teeth were blown out of his face after holding a firework in his mouth and lighting it. Bodies of quotidian violence connect, across territories, states, and into the future that begins with Guam, T.V. Everglades, FL to Shelby County, TN fo' real.

Virgil military shuttled between Tennessee and Guam, back and forth, near river beds and the deep heart of the ocean, his life under or near the water would make him, *special*, as the PoutBrilliantModel AKA Hollow G called Virgil, despite her riches, how down to earth she was. Base kids? Maybe, but in any case, this was his playground—the site of his origins next to any ocean to be made always, wider.

Butch finds a way to free the black bird. He and a staff member from his job stand behind it, cutting off the path between the back wall and the side window of the garage. Butch says other black birds came in front of the garage, to help too, bringing it food to coax it out. Like the cat that was not killed by Virgil's hurled flathead screwdriver stuck—*thwock*—in the base of the fence in Sacra, the bird is not murdered, either, just frightened enough to bang up its own body in the walls of the grey garage of the Red House, Virgil's dance studio!

In there, remains bird shit on the floor, signs of the black bird's alarm, and its posse trying to get in with food and directions. Virgil captures shots of his own legs, dusty brown in the light, shadows, caught from his iPad Pro. On the grey, epoxy floor, Virgil stretches near where some of the black bird's white shit is left, even after the cleaning, in faded dots, where Virgil has caused quite enough chaos, too.

The Priest has a micropenis, one that looks like an actual little boy cock, or even a baby's. However, his chest is wide and dense with white hair, hair so thick it orangutans, but still the fur is soft, fine flecks shooting out of his brick Button Down. Virgil could not believe it was The Priest all the way in NY at The Townhouse bar! And for a second, Virgil lost track of which coast he was on, so Virgil said hello, flirted quickly and held, for a sec, The Priest's face, in his mind, to link him from the west into the present.

In his flirtation, at the end of the night, or maybe at the start, he does have a conversation with The Priest. Virgil tells him of his vision of a set of performances along the McLaughlin Eastshore State Seashore to be Lucy-near-the-Bay, Mirinkai, Where. What Virgil does not tell him, is that it's something that he wants to do alone. But The Priest says something so dumb in response, that he should, "check in with the Emeryvillians."

Yeah, Right.

The Priest's eyes turn in, as though Virgil is wrong, for even thinking of such a plan, without The Priest's rando request, which is why Virgil cannot follow up on any return to attend again to the wide bay view windows in the Hilton Garden Inn rooms that overlook the San Francisco Bay from Emeryville, the quiet of that scene, how it shifts, given the tide, is so far from where Virgil needs to be, somewhere in the still of his own heart, a stillness that leads him to wonder.

The Priest says that he and his fellow Emeryvillians, "have no center," something that strikes Virgil as correct. The lack of traffic, closed doors, locked gates, and the rising and falling bay, SF in the distance underpins what Virgil needs: to articulate his field of knowing along the MacLaughlin Eastshore State Park, which surrounds the condo complex where The Priest lives.

Virgil would like to *live his best life*, between the fictive and the possible, and to have no center is precisely the only way that he can return to the project, a project of parts, and half-starts, a project of what might be known, hence the titular claim of his fictive video response: *Land Mirinkai, Where.*

Virgil, for some reason, doesn't want to face his own reality, that he's had all of the ghosts in The Townhouse, four or five, and one he isn't sure of, but whatever the case, Virgil looks into the mirror that walls the long hall of the upstairs bar, and it's too bright, showing Virgil's face has grown wider with age, and his body seems now, too dense to seduce.

Kris looks ancient, his head which was a shock of yellow-blond only a few years ago is now grey, and he's no longer someone of dramatic weight loss, the rail he temporarily was, if even from a glimpsed past, is now a figure desperate and heavy, but worse than any of this, is his need for the attention of the entire piano bar. Virgil knows Kris is a professional singer, and Kris's powerful voice bellowing from the back bar is no surprise as it reverberates, as if to say, *look at me, listen, and you'll know.*

As Kris's voice booms from the seat, un-microphoned, across from the piano, flanked by men, who surround it, and if they are singing, and if the singer who is at the microphone is singing, they all go unheard. Perhaps Virgil is talking shit about the performance, because he realizes it's a scam, but more than this, Virgil realizes that his relationship with intimacy and being with any ghost is complicated by what Virgil perceives as shared desire, a desire to be wanted, too, in any measure, but to bust out with one's professional best at a bar for attention is not what Virgil would do with his life. But would he? Who knows?

What Virgil does know is that he is now so far from the bay, and even further from the Marianas, and the new track lights above the front bar look cheap, and the light is also penetrating there too, and when Virgil, suggests this to the bartender, CrunchedNowPetiteBlondeOldjeFace, reports, "I didn't touch the lights."

Virgil, who was always pleasant with the bartender, was surprised. Though Virgil does not care that much, as he leaves a nice tip on his soda water, and checks his phone. Not bored, but certainly Virgil looks like the Asymmetrical Blacks he's seen at bars, bearing into their cellphones at the fringes, but where Virgil has his hair cut low, theirs is usually some odd mix of a black square, or tuft in the cell phone light.

Maybe Virgil thinks he's better because he can get what he wants, in most cases, his top ranked "1" or "2," at The Townhouse, but he's just not into it that night. Virgil, in other words, just can't stop working. But perhaps he wants anyone to talk to him, which is the power of the cruise, but this is precisely the feeling Virgil wants to leave behind.

Back in the piano bar, Virgil sees that Kris's face is still flat, and when Virgil waves the wave of *we know one another*, Virgil wants to understand something not of connection, but the bond, at least in Virgil's mind, in being trapped with Kris in the city in a snow storm, some long ago winter night turning morning, the grey and snow blowing against Kris's apartment's massive windows, Virgil's memory cast against a breathing, white sky.

But on this summer evening, Virgil vomited before he went out, which was unusual given that this was not often the case for Virgil in the city, which stunk as it sometimes does below Canal, but the chili oil he added to the arugula salad pizza was from the start a little sickening.

"Let me know what's goin' on...
They're here to do the lawn."

Butch's lips are not dry. They're soft when he gives Virgil a kiss; and this couplet he says to Virgil reminds Virgil that he must fight for the quiet of the story, assembling events into often passive coherence, but for what effect, and to what end?

In the room, a gun is being assembled in front of Virgil, and it's turned around in the same dream, until at some point, it faces him. Love is being fired. Her services are no longer needed says the dream, and in this expectation, her body shakes from sadness.

Love manifests as a shape, black hair cascading into Virgil's arms. The holes in his new, expensive, and highly distressed white T-shirt give Virgil a way of seeing himself, the collar torn, its white, unusual fabric, a constant indication of what's possible in Virgil's ever transformation.

All the books at the Drawing Center are uniform, and all the jeans at the AG store are too. Virgil knows that whatever he wants to get at, he can. It's a way of seeing that Virgil understands most, and for him, the view remains steady.

From the vestibule in the hall, Virgil remembers The Artist's underwear, baggy, dingy, but it was so long ago when Virgil was in The Artist's basement apartment of some Midtown East building which Virgil also remembers, his looking at a series of walls, walls that Virgil cannot quite now see, but walls connected, somehow to the brass railing he held onto as they walked to The Artist's front door.

Inside, The Artist's paintings were intricately lined, and abstract, as he leaned into, to show Virgil. He talked about which of his paintings were at the MoMA, and which artists he did not like, but Virgil cannot recall these other artists, but does recall, how, like Virgil, towards his peers, The Artist felt a tinge of hate.

"Is there anyone that you did not mess around with?"

When Stream asks this question, Virgil finds it only, for a second, offensive. For in the end, Virgil's hope is that he will learn to deal with the growing, frayed hole in his AG Jeans, the way the denim will eventually unravel then split to a giant opening, all brown skin, but for now, Virgil makes a pact. This is that he will not follow sorrow as the route to freedom, nor will he so loosely accept "exhaustion" as a demarcation of the same.

What matters, here, is the leftover recollection, the tight torso that holds The Artist's entire body in place, the way that it forms a space, too, for the memory of Virgil naked with him so many years ago, touching his soft, sunless skin, below the thick brown T-shirt The Artist slipped into for better sleep, after they were done.

But now, when Virgil sees The Artist in the red Townhouse light, looking older and more broke, here is another equivalency: The white tee that Virgil buys and off of which he cuts away the price tag, $88 USD, soft and also holey, will also grow old, and, too, remain like those he takes from his black father now Who,WantstoDriveDespiteSpineBreakingtheOFFICER.

For Virgil, a path is opening, but it is a difficult one to reckon, one in which Virgil is attempting to recall where he was, and how he was still, then hot, but he cannot understand how what he wanted to let go of then manifests as it does now. No matter—

> Virgil paints
> with gold
> glitter, water
> colors into
> a self-portrait:
> The tension
> is in the dreamt.
> Chamber—
> where form,
> seeps,
> as if this,
> could rend.

Virgil's seemingly constant return to The Townhouse—a way to move into the center beyond what's extracted from it. The act? This isn't memory. Memory is the least important thing. Memory is a way back, a device for simultaneously seeing both into the dream, and the real.

However, in this collapse, something else is looming. It is the gesture, the smallest one, where out of the blue, Butch gives Virgil a piece of hot, well buttered toast—it comes in and splits the screen open, against what he does remember, softens his need to clarify. So much of Virgil's want, this feeding from the now into the past.

Under a boat are a pod of Orcas, but before they are under a boat, they are breaching some distance away from The White Boys in their small rowboat. The water around The White Boys is an unsuspecting green, flat enough for them to go crabbing in, and their crabbing, at least in terms of their joy, in Virgil's estimation, serves as an even disruption between both Orca and Race.

Thus, The White Boys are far from civilization, yet close enough to the viewer to register their giddy fear, but they are not afraid enough to stop shooting video of the event from their vantage point, which begins with their laughter, into a site in a saltwater bay that no one, then everyone, is able to see. It is innocent. It is humble. They row away with the innocence of a row of white boys who tumble, or those who kick.

The YouTube comments section is where the surprise is blown. The reader knows what is coming, whereas the viewer does not—unless the viewer seeks to be the reader first. In a sense, what Virgil wants is to find a way to think through his own feeling of despair, a sadness he feels in the grey time. *It is sad*, Virgil thinks, *to work in black and white for a while, and to be alone*. But this is what it means to work in the body of prose. It is not poetry. It is not collage, and it is certainly not performance.

A time when what is robbed is the feeling of the mark—that is, to be marked by race, by website, by job, or to be in the emergence of the mark, the pocks bubble up in the night, awake from being bitten, or the wish that this were the case—Virgil thinks of the television series *V*, and the penultimate news conference, announcing the Aliens' takeover: the zipping off of a regular, white face to reveal the watermelon head, the monster inside the entire time. So much of performance Virgil wants to theorize around is bound by the feeling of this constant gesture, the weight of it hovering around his own release into sense, perhaps, more than voice.

Thus, Virgil consents to writing through sorrow, and in sadness, a pull he must learn to deal with, one thing becoming another, or else his life will always be ancillary to another, whomever this may be. So Virgil goes on, the feeling in his heart, the things he carries along the way, never jettisoned, always reduced to his own and hard-won selfish movement.

Virgil and Butch, by chance, make it to the two last seats in the final back row of *Notes from the Field*, they— or at least Virgil—does not anticipate the start of the play beginning with the screams of Freddie Gray, after the snap of his spine—that precise pain, the scream cast as breaking and starting point, the new body worn into the old groove of the unknown. Yes, he is dead. And yes, Virgil got tickets to see how this is worked out by ADS, playwright and actress alike.

The White Boys and the Orcas in the middle of the water are a fissure of the imagined, the mark of some impending altitude, the high measuring up into how the event is transposed, and simultaneously reached by pointing to and revealing what Virgil takes in, and what he considers.

The open court, not the pass through the tire. How easily the press is satisfied by the weird jokes and the cover up of antics, how we have seen him in his topcoat, the OrangeBLOWHOLE, the press secretary says, tosses a football through a tire, and shoots the basketball in the hole from the foul line, and then, too, can make a three-foot putt.

An equation overtakes Virgil, his heart open and raging—and he feels more or less broken, not by consequence, but by the staggering feeling of something approaching, loss of Stream, sure, letting that go, too, and him, the dependence on anyone. In the draft, it is never clear. In the podium is the lecture's anticipatory call to normalcy, so that the time in the lecture becomes the track that is marked by expectation, Virgil's heart remains so heavy.

Go on and play, Stream, because Virgil is sad behind the eyes, and heat, too, grows in his heart, but this is not new, and in the end what matters is what keeps Virgil moving forward, trudging, and ultimately alone.

Did I leave the kettle on?

Is the glass in my door smashed in?

This is the role of the art, the reality of what might happen, and what does, however in the head, however across activities, of mammal and flat green expanse, pulls from the city street onto the now of the AC quiet into the future of what might be, a future where Virgil finally sees what he has been making for so long, the need to make shapes beyond anything else, and to feel fluid in doing so.

"You are from Sacramento," is what the Sardine&Cracker says to Virgil, and it feels as though he's snatched up, but there is a collective opening, one that spreads from being from nowhere. The body, too, goes unnamed, but still Virgil feels the press of the peaked and scratched skin: the dot-heat on the wrist—in the grey time—to address the fictive is to be in the moment of what has been, to be in the moment of redress in what's precise and enough, or how hard, the start of its notice.

There are tracings that inhabit Virgil, one in the form of a memory that visits him as he inverts his spine, chest up, bowed, rendering his thinking through a curve in this language, *to trespass*. During the arc into what Virgil knows, he recalls Wobbly Arm Hater who told Virgil "You're putting it on," calling out the weight around Virgil's middle—

"Lift up onto your toes."

There's no singular recourse to shaming and such commands, which fuse so quickly, but how Virgil wants to respond is his own. Nonetheless, something inside of him, whether flow, or fluid comportment, is the act of moving between such statements, one bark after another, like these, altering his balance.

There's a hole, cut in a fence at the Vista Point off 280, towards San Francisco, by Palo Alto, that according to Virgil's sense of scale, could be the breach in a spider web. Across from this hole, the Reagan Era Republican calls Virgil his "baby boy," and Virgil plays against the plate that he feels in the Reagan Era Republican's body just above the Reagan Era Republican's groin.

And though he does not see his skin until later—patchy with eczema, red, under the hair, as if the hair wasn't attached to the paunch, as if it were laid into clay, instead, as if the clay were like the fields in Salinas covered with plastic tarps, "food sent around the world," Butch says, after which Virgil follows: "It's sent out locally, too."

This is a study of sequence, or follicles, but the fictive is the constraint as much as it is the view. These vantage points allow Virgil to soar, in every reality not always his own, in every spectacle borne from his curiosity, to touch.

The "u" drops from the word, "curious."

Virgil announces this discovery and he wants to write, *curiosity*, but he can't spell it. As he signs a book, or draws in it, or thinks about the vowel sounds, he also thinks about sadness, how loss attracts loss, how he wonders if his need to court loss is about pulling in the long line of what he was, and now is, a body no longer in fragments, but one lost and exposed across a region next to the road—should he keep on driving, or should he stop?

These choices have everything to do with the Vista Point, where the Reagan Era Republican admits, "I feel good in Khakis."

Virgil does not, but if the line is right, then the feeling of feeling well in Khakis is certainly a possibility. If the sky is there, then Virgil, no matter the clarity, will move into the atmospheric, into the angles of what he deduces to enact. There is a record of this in yellow chalk, black pen, and refuse wire, a collage rendered on a two-inch wide ribbon of off-white cotton "canvas" that Virgil calls his "Vertical Journal," pushpin tacked from the top so it hangs down, a long line flat against the dry-wall pillar, inside of which is the tiny studio's heater, its orange coils visible behind the metal vents.

Carltons are what the Reagan Era Republican smokes, and they make his lips crisp, so it makes his mouth unable in its crispness to kiss deeply, but he pecks like a white man, so Virgil, is of course satisfied by the pecking. The Reagan Era Republican's mouth is like a tea cup, a porcelain "tink," a peck—so it makes his mouth almost unnoticeable, and it makes his inner eyelids glisten, amplifying their red-pink wet.

The black bird bangs in the garage. Stream goes under for a second sleep. Butch moves from the sink.

Virgil is fed. Virgil follows. Virgil thinks of the long flight back across the country to his ride, Manitoba. Who's red, red, red. Butch believes his own eyes to be hazel, but they aren't. Nor are they crystal blue. In fact, they inhabit another color in Virgil's perception. Splinters of rust and dark seed. Butch and Virgil notice that, in the end, there's an insistence in knowing what it means to be with one another forever, a feeling that they will never release. This too is eventful, if even only as the route of sight. So that when Virgil lowers his Oliver Peoples shades in California, he sees true green, not the blue-green that he notices over his shaded eyes, looking into the expanse of the tops of trees from the Vista Point.

The broad bodies of water are eyes, too—*the truth is precious now, more than ever*—

In one's dreams, a girl's legs are not working, and a boy's whose never have, is beaten. She cannot save him. She saves herself. The legs don't manage to crack the body of the shore leastwise, as the sun coats the bridge, so far from where Virgil stands.

Virgil is traveling nowhere, even as he floats across the bridge with only his eyes, and as he does, he thinks of the opportunity to think, through the wind of the 17, in what felt like a folded hour. How removed from this time, to recall a more fleeting trick at the Vista Point, the RedWound, and more particularly, his inability to kiss, but his hard sucking like a true pig, his wanting to be fed, or how he calls Virgil "big," which is sometimes true, like "Grab them by the pussy—"

Virgil's desire to deliver his own load, untracks.

In the RedWound he sees the scar of his own want, his complicities with power, and the distance between what he has been and where it has taken him is where Virgil releases into the RedWound's mouth. The mouth as cause and effect, akin to the peck, or the zip—so that the note is constructed in the body of the Vista Point, so that the protracted rear view is the mustard seed's flying by, forward in Manitoba along the 1, along the 37, so that the seed is the yellow flower itself, and it's the reason too.

Virgil's face, at times, is almost square, lined, dimpled, jawbone a flight of birds escaping, as it was described in a letter from The Visitor. Virgil remembers her husband, B.O., back then at The Visitor's cottage. As B.O.'s life was obviously frayed, so much so, that The Visitor and her family would return back home to Belfast. Virgil is stilled by the letter, yet it feels painful to be ripped into the hole of identification where Virgil both feels the pain, but only hopes to keep up with its pace.

But Virgil doesn't want to feel intact, the needles atop his head releasing from above, through his entire body. He has not gone far, stuck at the desk, stuck in the lines between the walls of what he wants, and how he looks across the space of where he thought he would go in the writing, but his discovery is that the draft might simply be the sketch, or a line of notes tacked up in a sequence, one next to one another.

The lines across his face, in the in-motion Selfie he constructed while dancing into his iPad Pro's camera lens held up in the blue, icy air, show how far away he has gone, lost in the rocks piled up at the boat ramp's edge somewhere in the Berkshires, snow in between— Virgil stomps.

Virgil holds anger in his heart, driving the black truck with what Rafa calls *the calm*—How far has Virgil traveled in order to be broken, split? Virgil wants to reach out, but realizes that he has to settle inwards, to run to such dock ends, or onto the beach, the long wall that leads to another set.

Virgil stops the run on the beach in front of the Monterey Tides when he hears Kendrik Lamar's "DNA" and wonders about the mapping of the internal, to connect not through what is perceived, but by what pulls, the drawing of the body on the body, every day a way of looking, every second Virgil is a figure to be held by sequence, by thread, by flight.

Tallulah, the Cocker Spaniel, who wanted to say hello does, and when the PizzaDad, says "Hi," in the lobby of the hotel, it might be reconciliation, how the random-whites might not despise him, but if they do, it resounds in how Virgil remains faithful to PizzaDad and Tallulah.

Having a nice life triggers Virgil's return to the cold beach and Virgil's even colder hands. *La Niña* is what Virgil called the painting he'd worked on that morning, a painting that was completed with sushi on his mind, and on the bodies of the six to eight golf club men at the restaurant tables as far away from their wives as they are close with one another's laughter and hot morning Joe and syrup and eggs. The painting, too, was a stolen shot. Virgil recounts in time-lapse:

Pork bellies and unagi means

Virgil is rich,

beard-stained

& smoke and shit-lets,

or belly hair out of a Vista—

Sacra

The bed's sheets are cream with stains resembling the rust that's collected on the white painted steel laundry rack Virgil keeps for his dress shirts and tees out on the tiny deck of his *pied-à-terre next to the sea*, at least this is what Stream calls it, though Stream had not yet seen Virgil's Santa Cruz apartment in person.

Virgil is sick as Butch says, and in fact, it's not funny when Virgil thinks of Stream's naming his little place a *pied-à-terre next to the sea*, a naming Virgil considers next to Butch breathing through the night so far away from Santa Cruz in the cool, white bed at the Harvest Inn in Napa, the plush mattress clutching Virgil's and Butch's bodies like a clamp.

Virgil knows Stream is cruel, but perhaps only as cruel as Virgil, a cruelty based on keeping oneself safe when one has been alone on one's "own planet" for so long. Or perhaps this cruelty stems from having this kind of freedom, a freedom that inhabits and moves around the body, a freedom that seeps into one's dreams where there are consequences.

To be pulled into Stream's body, this clamp, too, is a hook, like when Harriet Beecher Stowe presents Topsy, "A freshly-caught specimen," 9 years old in a worn li'l slave singlet. Stream pulls Virgil in hard. And Virgil likes to tap Butch who sleepily turns around to spoon Virgil. Either way, Virgil is wanted. More and more. A white dwarfish dad, all wrinkle sag-face in a Notre Dame Shirt; and another tee on a sleepy faced daddy sez UNLV who thinks Virgil is hooked up, not on "a lecture circuit," but more like by the live wire falling onto the ice sheet, electrocuting the red coat kid sliding on a patch of ice to his surprise death at the end of *The Ice Storm*.

Can Virgil have it all? Love that is? For Virgil, love is not a game, nor to him is Butch and Virgil's episodic, but what they both hear in San Francisco is a sound that Butch describes as something he's never heard come from a human. The Homeless San Francisco Black barks between yelping and seal. He's even braying, but he doesn't ask for money. Another Homeless San Francisco Black wears black planks for shoes, scraping across a street, zombies the both, as Virgil catches a whiff of piss from the San Francisco "street-nest" that he and Butch pass.

Virgil recalls how, once, A Homeless San Francisco Black (a woman) hurled a beer bottle at Desiré and The CrossDraft as they drove by, all because Virgil met A Homeless San Francisco Black (a woman)'s eye. And when Virgil told The CrossDraft that they should drive around the block *to jack that hoe!* with Virgil's hot white tea, The CrossDraft thought Virgil was serious. Virgil was. Virgil wanted The CrossDraft to lean out of the passenger seat *to blast that byatch!*—Virgil laughed at that too, because the CrossDraft at the thought of the scald-bomb, slid-crouched below the window, and *"Nooooooo!"* as Virgil faked-looking where to U-turn.

Virgil is often horrified by the sounds and smells of the San Francisco Street when he's near that block, and is still cracked-up by thought of such an uneven assault, yet finds himself a few seconds later, looking up at the Dale Chihuly jellyfish chandeliers in Faralon, into a tear-ing whiteness that drops into the room above the bar in the restaurant that Stream tells him was once a Men's Social Club, all the grand columns and tile, originals.

When Stream does visit Virgil in his *Pied-à-terre next to the sea,* he drops cheese on the floor, rips into the baguette, almond butter crusts the knife, and sleeps hard, his grey head a reminder that everyone shits, and smells, and a hole is like a fresh surface amidst the fur for the tongue that is a puckering muscle too.

Virgil's love absorbs, creates murky interiors, where he draws, perhaps, from the "waste-stream" that the two young, brilliant Black Artists (Dead Thoroughbred) describe mining as a primary source the morning after their performance in Portland, one instance in which they taught him everything he needed to know about desire and pressure. DT lies on the floor, and writhes to jet blasts, and loops of no melody, as no melody serves as the waste-indicator, as in this is the palpable site of Black Matter, where the discomfort on the floor is after all, a meditation.

Virgil likes a desk, but loves the floor, too, yet the symphonic is what so old-fashioned Virgil craves, to be cemented in, a kind of whiteness, a self-locked-in constant and yet, maybe like DT, for Virgil, exploding its hold is the force of the sound that pounds his heart onwards, behind black on black earplugs stuffed in some ears, some bear the rest and go on, *werk*.

The thundering room from the jet blasts is finally triggering, the space between no windows that approx-imates natural light, reminding Virgil a bit of Vegas, the perpetual day painted on the high walls of a crappy mall. One should go nowhere but in, accept that trace, too. But in Faralon, symmetrical raw fish trays and lob-ster claws erupt from the ice and salt, small shields pass by, and the squid ink streaks on the plate of the Aussie Tuna, a fish softer than any Virgil or Butch have ever tried, like a newborn's palm would be, if sliced—And the squid ink, raked on the presentation plate is black-shiny as fresh asphalt, and the pan-seared skin on Virgil's plate, Ling Cod, is "farm to table typifying California," describes the Asian CaveWaiter.

Virgil understands his life to be this: to live outside of his means, good paycheck to paycheck, or spoil to spoil, to glimpse a pattern he's after is his idea of the fictive. To chase his heart into the pursuit of being here, and there, and chasing, still, some form of a stable dad, is, for now, Virgil's being *in love*. In this love, fantasy is hinged by way of sometimes journal, sometimes sketch—*To have it all*, Virgil looks up into an endless eclipse:

Virgil loves Butch.
     Virgil Con Butch.
Virgil Y Butch.
     Virgil c/s Butch.
VGS.
          Varrio Gardenz de Sacra

          Y Que?

Stream is excited at the prospect of his dropping in on Virgil and Butch at the Union Square Hilton where the seemingly flood-lit lobby sears even the most remote possibility of a Homeless San Francisco Black from foot-scraping into the lobby. Never.

Virgil's heart is erratic, beats at the thought that he can't reconcile the space between Butch and Stream, Stream on the phone, or in the lobby in a trench coat, and shades.

"Bye Sweety."

To the smells of the San Francisco Street, so close to the Homeless San Francisco Blacks at street level, so far from the City Scape SF panoramic view overlooking the lit city, Butch and Virgil gazed at one another and across the night sky on their first date when that Hilton featured a full restaurant on the 46th floor.

Virgil remembers a story that Stream told him, maybe more, *a scene,* one where Stream, as a child, pushed a Bic pen refill into the tip of a quill, and ran around the house planting his flair into his parent's imagination, and Virgil recounts his own seedings, curious when he held a tampon holder up to his eye, and pulled back the tiny loose cardboard cylinder forming the "telescope" his mother would not let him go to school with, but still, she laughed.

Butch is flat. Virgil is curved, his back against the headboard, and in his latest dream, he recalls a giant mattress taped down in a large bedroom, and the sheet on that mattress is crimson, beaded, and inlayed with graffiti. Virgil cannot recall the entire dream, but he does make out the patterns of desire that fix him to the surface of how the dream fragments in the narrative on the sheet.

Virgil is a young man in a bed in the back of the house where he once lived in Brooklyn, the place where he figured out how to get off, the hard ass bed upon which TheMidwesternTheaterCook shot and left "a pearl necklace," around his throat. In that back bedroom, next to the kitchen, a large lock secures the fire escape, and the key to open it hangs on a nail next to it on the wall, to the right, the key visible when the curtain's slid left.

If Virgil writes with too much weight, the wine glasses on the table at the Harvest Inn will lightly clink against one another, and then a small bug floats out in front of this motion. When Virgil loses it on a

Friday morning, and before that on a Saturday night, Butch says Virgil going off on him was like being shot in the face twice with a shot gun blast, and Virgil guesses the sensation would grow more debilitating over time, but what is Virgil to do but pursue the vectors in the spread?

On their way out of Napa, Virgil feels so compelled to pull over to the The Hess Collection Winery to see the art, but they stop at Robert Biale to try their Zinfandels instead—*Black Chicken*. Psychic timing? Virgil, like Stanley Kunitz, usually knows exactly what time it is by heart: 6:51 a.m., or 6:50 a.m., in the morning, or 3:32 p.m.—out of one nap— still in the crush of some dream sleep, Virgil says to Butch "I love and want to protect you..." while awaking next to Stream.

Stop Crying
Open your hand.
Empty? Empty. Here is a hand

Says Sylvia Plath, but then The Lawyer texts and says he's looking forward to seeing Virgil. And Virgil imagines himself lying on The Lawyer's mattress on the floor in that bedroom disaster. Tissues. Left open lotion bottles. Dust.

Wine Country bopping around with Butch in Manitoba, never mind the black bird droppings massive on Manitoba's flat, red tail, or the *Sistahs on the Reading Edge* who sued for millions after being kicked off the Napa Valley Wine Train for being themselves—Because Virgil learns on a tour and tasting at Schramsberg, deep in a wine cave, pickaxed by first the Chinese, then later, giant drills, that the champagne cage is there to steady the cork, while one twists the bottle, one quarter turn, its elegant opening. Let Freedom Be.

Virgil will never return to the apartment, save in his dream, where the ceilings are painted over pre-war thick with cream paint, so that anything art-deco is now only hinted at by the impressions deep under the surface. There is also something banging in Virgil's heart, a restlessness that he pursues and fills with Stream. This impulse he understands when he rubs one of Butch's eyes closed, and Butch responds by throwing a pillow at Virgil's face.

It's pretty basic. He loved Clean, until Clean voted for the OrangeBLOWHOLE. He loved Grey Chest Hair Patch, too, and thought of his stupid, still tongue that he stuck out and left still like pink dog dick. This is the sick part—Virgil opened his mouth to receive it, as if he was under a hamster water dropper. Until that is, when Grey Chest Hair Patch thought he owned Virgil. Fuck that. No one owns Virgil.

Virgil eddies next to Butch, but in the quiet-snores, Virgil understands, or at least hopes, that he'll figure out where he'll go with Stream. He imagines the stain on the cream sheet on the too small full bed in Santa Cruz to be the color of iron, as if the "iron" stains rust into what's real. In other words, maybe Virgil needs to get down to earth, and to stop playing, to figure out a way to clear a place in his heart where he no longer holds his breath.

For now, Virgil breathes through the Pine Sol, and Tilex, and strives to get his little bathroom as hotel-sterile as he can manage. But still, there is always the shadow of mold in some grout, and no matter how presentable, like his little pink hole should be, his place will never be forever cleaned out. Mold bleeds from the drain's rim when Virgil is away for too long.

And when Virgil is home, things drop in the middle of the morning, a pounding, Spanish radio blaring as if Santa Cruz is New York, a dumpster or a Ryder moving truck quakes the street. The Dentist's office alarm blares too often into the red twilight.

In an alternative dream, Virgil is in the head of the California Arts Council's snuggling arms. Virgil was at the head of the California Arts Council's home when GGP won the real genius award. That event was Virgil's first understanding of his, one day, wanting to be, or to acquire anything *like that*.

Somewhere embedded in Virgil's dream, black packing tape holds down sections of the mattresses stacked against the walls in the largest room of a house and the mattresses are "paintings," not hung, but held in place, their fronts half-leaning forward into the room. Maybe their suspension is the source work of Virgil's desire, the material's pitch—vectors out of which Virgil continues to figure.

Virgil finds himself attacked. The attack is mental, and it's as much a surprise as a breach, though the whale's impact is not fact, it was massive, destroying the small boat where two people on YouTube, if not CGI, died in the tonnage and splash. To be crushed at peace, before what Virgil understands as peace, a peace unknown by the watching body, the nervous body as the primary feeling, the feeling as the form of capturing the self at bay—listening, or the scribble when Virgil, at a table, is knotted in a corner, only to be met by The Rumble of The San Francisco Street.

The Rumble of The San Francisco Street is a frame of understanding—that noise, unnatural and urban, singing against his own early morning contempt, or perhaps the release is from what Virgil needs to under-gird the heft of his feelings at any given second, as in seeing the Oliver Peoples SF family unit, strolling down the Fillmore, as mockups of whiteness taken in from inside Stream's car, late model Infinity silver hatchback, Tink, Tink Drone silence.

Who knows if Virgil will ever return to The Rumble of The San Francisco Street, for its knocks into Virgil's soul are too easily absorbed, and all the while, he cannot cancel who Virgil is. In Tink, Tink Drone silence, Virgil thinks about the saliency of the poem, that the poem as a singular form was essential at a certain time for him, but now that he is forty-seven, and no longer twenty-five, the form of poetry has done something dif-ferent to Virgil, and to his body. It seems apparent that this has to do with Virgil's looking over his shoulder for what comes, looking up at Stream's assessment of him in front of a door, or the disdain down near the garage, but Stream is Virgil's creation, and what Virgil notices has less to do with the person he loves than the route of Virgil's internal mappings.

Virgil feels the sun against his face in the Santa Cruz morning, and though Virgil is settled at home, he writes in his journal early in the morning, thick with language where alternative paths encroach: Routes of drawing. Routes of dance. Routes of swallowing. Routes of licking, or touching, or unfolding, or routes of seeing the edges of something. Routes of jumping—even Cave Crickets explode!

Virgil will not move anywhere for anyone. We know this. Virgil knows this. Butch knows this, but Stream does not, yet. Stream is not dumb, but he is a star, streaking and still, burning white hot and there, and in the middle of the night, when Virgil awoke, there was a blast of light in the tiny front room, and for the first time, Virgil awoke angry at Stream for turning it on, even though Stream wasn't there, angry for making him feel unsafe and unwanted, simultaneously, in a neon blast. Stream was not responsible for turning on any light.

But Virgil understands nothing but light and breath, these days, and cleaning, and making, and moving his own self towards the wall, then the chair.

Where is the poem?

It's in the sun that bleeds in the box studio bed, how it reflects less the body than how it cubes on Stream's face. Virgil's love for Stream takes place in the gut, or the head, or up there on the moon, but still, Virgil wants to hold it, and him, and to bear it, and to move from it, expanding in any way that he might have his quiet mind back.

"Who gets to be pregnant?" Virgil asks Stream. Virgil wants a conversation, one, recognizing, in particular, why this *must* unfold as a long question in a city, in a bar, in a bed, but the question's activation as a source, his body as temperature gauge, for what's constituted around it, no matter the deduction of class, or race, the weight of being left alone hovers near Virgil's body, behind his eyes. "What's *that*?" Stream asks, as Virgil holds his grey, foggy head, his breath, the sweet stink of the night, and meat, smoke, the sticking black beard bristles.

That is Virgil's soft, fat, though small, paunch.

Virgil needs his P.E., like SNAKEface in Verve, does his *CHEST and BIKE*, before *X 5:30 Surf with Kelsey*... A Fit, White stranger's TTDs! To move into the fray of Stream's needs, or into what Virgil eats as now too hard a seed, but bit anyhow, is to choose to see an attack as only lingering smoke caught in the mountain. The fire still burns. Virgil is surrounded, now, in fact by four volcanoes in Portland, OR.

So too is the tug of Virgil's arm, and his spins on his toes, trying to spin less on his heels, to lock out of this into a shape, to pause, to say that the frozen move— *This is the letter, a shape.* In the dance, the quads alter the entire body, the body broken by a much longer pain from a slight, in a pool, touched at the foot by a punk bitch hovering over Virgil on Virgil's kick turn, another face of contempt to meet Virgil in his world of whiteness; or "Your car is open," and it shifts, and travels, nevertheless, still the surprise is in seeing a small moth on the brushed steel railing of Virgil's very own home.

Virgil wants to be able to return to Emeryville, his wishing self, looking across the silvery water and sails across from which Stream first spoke to him from San Francisco, for this speaking leads across the bay into the

Pacific, and beyond that, where MommaSpine once was and where she was born, and lived, a time she does not speak of, perhaps, because she was never asked.

The Beautiful Filipino Man at the Paramount Hotel says—"You should visit your mom's home."

Am I pulling up the carpet when I spin?—Virgil asks himself. Virgil could not have predicted any of it, the stacks of furniture as much as he could have predicted the images he deleted from his phone of the moving of things for the cleaning of things, all the texts, too, deleted because Stream's love often hurts, nor will it float easily to be recounted, unless Virgil runs, and opens up into the morning, and confronts what was there, and how. His decisions to record remain fixed to only what Virgil needs, and wants.

Malcolm asks Virgil about the sky, and how wide he can see, if they might collaborate, one day, on a series of talks on space. Virgil looks into the sky and sees only a white wall and thinks he, too, could make money at creating things as quickly as Keith Haring, but for Virgil, he is so often saddled with language that he cannot get to the pictures with as much angle or intent. After all, Virgil is, mostly, a writer.

But Virgil, the writer, wants to promise himself that he will be stilled when he visits the woods as a full-fledged interdisciplinary artist to use his time for constructing what he will need to make by looking into his heart and his books whenever, in all of the twenty-four hours, in which he feels, after the random buzzing quits.

This is my heart. Virgil wonders if he ever wrote about it. Beetle Back Boy at the Vermont Studio Center dissed the repeating flat hearts that one artist made, cutouts in various shades of pink. For Beetle Back

Boy—these flat hearts, singular or whole, were an overdetermined symbol—dead aesthetic, but still, for Virgil, the white streaks in the strawberry yogurt and granola plate suggest an embedding of how he remembered her hearts, not casual, dense with the weight of feeling, even in the artist entertaining Beetle Back Boy's confident critique.

Were it raining, Virgil would not hear the bouncing of the streets, the electricity flying along the thread of the tracks summoning a train Virgil will never ride, predicting the thread of the story of an account, the account undone by what Virgil would never do, like smash a candelabra over any lover's head but his own. The act would be a single-suicide, and his lovers, then and into the future, would be saved, so too, like this, configures the hyperbole—a self promise to never murder, but always to kill, as in to render the sense of its amplifications into what's a life?

Virgil knows this not only starts somewhere, but it leads, that the swirl of his insides in the morning doesn't begin with Stream, or his need to hold him, or to hold Butch, but to clamp both. It's simple, and neutral. Perhaps this was the sign of the repeating flat pink hearts, for Virgil, the overdetermined, that that sentiment does not for him, deride; rather, it haunts, so too does the prosciutto and arugula in the bowl that Chunk Diesel Man Boy eats, to save our lives, Virgil thinks, is the flat, flat heart, the scene of the first Valentine, *be mine*.

A first trap. In the shed, a screwdriver slid into the latch, so the latch locked from the outside keeps stupid boy Virgil inside. As the journals records do not lie, Virgil thinks, *So why hold on if only to understand the arrow that leads back—*

How is love not the pressure in the eye, or the back, or the holding of the breath, or the recognition in the coming heat, the fear of living in it with no plans, but an appearance in a condo Virgil hates, deep in a summer, now gone?

An orange stain near the inside of an eyelid.

A tear duct ripped out by the cat.

The Black White Pinch Nose says, "Here's the thing…" Virgil must learn to thin his hate for anyone Black encroaching on his turf.

In Virgil's Dance-Notes, he theorizes about the weight on one foot, how an entire universe moves around this subject out of place, the improvised, a subject less on the surface than its appeal, to turn, and to mark its infinite.

"Do you hear the fog horn?" Stream asks. His Bison-Blue bag looks so rich, faux Balenciaga, or something, a return into the structure of his own realization of what happens in the phrase: "Jews will not replace us!" When Virgil was so enraged by being locked outside naked, Virgil threw a flip-flop to break the front window of his family's first home, off base, which marked some of his depth, a low well that filled the arena of his throat, and if he wanted to sing, he would have in symmetrical waves and hard shapes—

"Tutting" he makes his way into poses where he could have been, before, just saying, he could have gone there, too, or in the paper he carries around, assemblages of a journal, the act of working across forms is to be compelled by them.

To form the document outside of the political accounts of race, which is black which is white? This is the lecture that Stream needs, this is the I.Q. that registers the resilience of the body that is not allowed, but makes his genius. The trouble is in once being owned. While Stream goes dark, and in Virgil's hands, Virgil uses the dry shaving brush to flatten down the pastel flag in the collage that also burns red in Virgil's heart.

So stupid to run, and to be adjacent to the pain as Virgil's body cannot remain, unmoved by the pulsing sirens that engulf the San Francisco Street humming under Virgil, or the whizzing of car after car breezing by in front of The Red House front's writing window. Virgil is access point and mode, denotation and point in the smudge of what is constitutive feeling. Being abandoned. Being sucked. Into a dirty hole is the dirty boy who leaves a stain, who remains open to being opened. Even if up into the air, lost, found:

> *Fox News was on in the kitchen in a house near a sky that did not care about the Angry Mouth. The Angry Mouth says that President O-Fine is a Piece of Shit and even a Monkey. Virgil, over it, but is still stunned, kneads into the clotted hate of another white home, but this one so close to the sky, had a lot of clay, a makeshift wall, money from sausage, and soup, and unhung art, and dust, where whatever else gathered against one wall, a wall bolted to an unhinging, a wall breaking open Virgil's being—a long ago used para-ramp.*

> *The Angry Mouth is racked with pain, through the night, and he screams into it, for his brother, the brother his parents had killed, intentionally overdosed that disabled baby on iron pills:*

"Just fill the prescription," is what The Angry Mouth's dad said to kill his son, and now, the Angry Mouth carries his father's actions forever.

Baby D, MommaSpine's first son, died a crib death, SIDS, so Virgil, too, lost a sibling, not by murder, but still he feels the emptiness, Baby D, missing just under an always there, in a room, and in every row and line. The hotdogs on the porch Virgil served to his new "club," a friend, then several, on the back of the porch like little puppies munching. Virgil's little soul moving, then, toward reconciliation of that good life, and his being sickened and hurt, then out of a traveling and thickening hate: "I should tattoo *Trump* on my dick and fuck you with it," says The Angry Mouth.

"This is a most serious matter," is what Virgil is thinking, the dream so frightening because it asks him to flee from his relaxed state, one in which he is only listening, and not reading, but is moved, still, by WispBlondeForearmHair who taps Virgil on the shoulder to let Virgil know it's Virgil's turn to go to the bathroom at the front of the plane.

WispBlondeForearmHair's Kindle and *natural* Sperrys on the Southwest flight only slightly move Virgil before this, but not so much movement where his feelings have left him wanting something more, because he left this behind, Virgil thinks, in the City-of-Smoke, where he was compelled by the state of his own continuously changing state.

When BigWhiteSunkEyes sees him in the café, he tells Virgil that he might do something, "maybe something great one day," but Virgil can't figure out why this total stranger might imagine what Virgil may become in the future, but Virgil and BigWhiteSunkEyes are thinking, however directly or indirectly, about fame. But Virgil is already famous. He sells books. He teaches. He travels. He performs. He receives calls to do all of these things a rather good amount of the time, and of course, his honoraria increases at a similar rate to his need for 4 to 5 star hotels.

He eats well. He looks at books and cruises on and off-line. He has Butch. He is letting Clean go to a new place in his psyche; however, Stream helps him access a past that Virgil is only now seeing in disparate parts, flat dreams, steel girders that he is willing to assemble either on drives, or while still. Virgil hangs his masks on the hooks in the studio, and on the upper ledges of the moveable wall to begin to register his movements between subjectivities, but mostly to give him some means to mark the relationship between his material, his practice, and his body.

He is thinking, of course, of Nick Cave, and the fact that Cave is an actual dancer, while Virgil is only a visitor to this (and other forms), but in each, save poetry and cultural criticism, for Virgil, training is mostly peripheral. But in any case, Virgil notes how Cave, especially, in his large-scale exhibit *Until*, fills spaces between the floor and ceiling, like Kara Walker did in her *A Subtlety* in the Domino Sugar Factory in the BK. *Our Past*, Virgil thinks, which is a constraint, prompt black jockeys (Cave) or black melting torsos (Walker), each loaded on top of another in Virgil's reach.

As Lucy, Virgil was pushing the moveable studio wall backwards. They misestimated their sense of leverage, placing too much pressure towards the top, not thinking about balance. The wall crashed backwards, hitting one of the permanent ones that would hold, soon, Virgil's drawings. It left a small yellow pock, bruising the rubber cheek of YELL-O-FACE, the injured mask marking one of the white studio walls, but just like he does to the tubs and the toilets after most every *use*, Virgil rubbed the evidence away.

But then here was the issue—the heat wouldn't cut off in the studio. It blasted and blared after the wall hit the floor, the crashing of it, still reverberating in Virgil's body, sometime after it stunned the floor. *Did I destroy the heating system?* Would MacDowell blame Virgil for destroying Cheney, the artist's studio's floorboards, or its very foundation? But Virgil wasn't even really dancing. He was simply moving backwards, his lost girl delirium unfurled in Lucy's camel suede cape and her tasseled heels grip—then, *a falling,* that was both an accident and footage caught by Virgil's gaping iPad Pro.

Virgil thinks, *I look so dumb and surprised.*

Other B and B artists have died, Virgil thinks, too early, because they did not enjoy their lives in ways Virgil does. Virgil Lives: Masks in cathedrals, streets, holds forth in classes, gets paid, or is alone; even the blind spots count as techniques—staring into the sun, or pushing over walls into who knows what, or where?

Virgil will never forget when June Jordan stood behind the lectern. For Virgil, he understood then as a beaming undergrad, that the lectern is a prop, that could be laid on its side, or it needs to be ridden like Virgil wanted the Thai Lady Boy to ride that White Beaver Dad, but this did not happen in that particular porn.

The White Beaver Dad did some pumping, but it wasn't violent; it was stiff, and still, but that passive motion made Virgil cum, for sure. And once, during a polite JO, or in the two *smiles*, and then during the close of the scene, before the camera went off when White Beaver Dad stopped the recording, Virgil thinks of what stood in the way between him and what he wants.

For June Jordan, the lectern was a shield.

"You would not talk to your White Professors this way!"

But still, June Jordan was often flanked by whites who probably thought they could talk to her however they liked. Where did they go with June Jordan, and what did they edit of hers, and how did they say her name, and, really, how were those Whites, as people, who seemed to be so attentive and close to June?

Virgil's voice was then being formed, his seeing what he understood, then, to be the "podium," as a mode through which to activate one's safety as a raft, and as a defense. For Virgil this was imperative, in the sense, that it allowed him to see an escape route, no matter how minor. But the thing is, June Jordan was taking one for the team. Perhaps, it was an important thing to do, to take one for the team, but Virgil, who is cold to his fingers, while writing on the porch, is unable to accept the reality of the cold being the sign of any future failure to one day understand *why*, but he's getting close.

Oh yeah, Virgil will soon propel from New Hampshire to California, a California that is on fire, and burning while Virgil is cozy in a cool room overlooking curled, red-punch looking leaves. Virgil thinks: *June fought*. So Virgil is invested in prose, and there was a time when he thought of "the prosaics" as something that existed *in the field of his desire*, despite the fact that he hadn't executed a form of prose he wished to create, yet. But still, Virgil has a body. And he has a body of work. He understands his calling:

"Jasmine Peals Re-steep!" "Is this for you Bud?"

Virgil sits at the brown, broad table at Verve, to recalibrate from all of the times he was patted, and tapped, but unlike some of the writers, like June Jordan, who died, he feels, of course, way too early, Virgil does not feel *some kind of way*, about this tapping, because he, after all, is a flirt.

Virgil holds no resentment towards the "touch-ers," but, no matter what, he will not forgive the "touchers" on GP. Virgil is not a waiter. His laptop is not a menu. Virgil's iPhone is not sanitary. Its "flashlight," also will not reveal the lost 100K earring in *The Big 4*, which belongs to PrettyWhiteOldLady, who is not the arbiter of what's interesting to Virgil, but she's right—Virgil *is sweet*.

The contracts are so set, like James Baldwin reminds Virgil—they form a cage, and there is, ultimately, no transcendence, but there is always tension knows Virgil, the play between characters, memories, figures, even the slightest dreams, those that flash next to one another, forming relational ideas, so that the transformative form of prose, for Virgil, emerges out of chaos, revealing a way to create thinking that ricochets between subjects and time, or maybe even, simply, in time!

In other words, Virgil's escape between his life and his dreams is the price of fame. There is a space in which the signing of a book becomes the arena for making *live art*, say a drawing as a union between symbols, multiple, and however available. There is no tie, nor anchor. Simile. Simulacrum. Line—

It doesn't matter to be so stuck in the dense field of prose Virgil thinks, because Virgil cut his teeth in New York with jennifer jazz, The Famous Artist. It was at a basement reading on the Lower East Side in which jennifer jazz, The Famous Artist performed, teaching Virgil to understand the reality of producing what matters, intuiting and remaining open to both collapse and explosion. At this reading, jennifer jazz, The Famous Artist taught Virgil that he could, at any moment, like her, come in with a giant binder, yell back at the heckler, in the corner of the room and drill out to the street without reading at all: "FUCK YOU STEVE!!!"

Pondering that night, Virgil also wants to grapple with this dream:

Butch is brown, maybe South Asian, and waiting for him at the movies, and then leaves the movies, and WalrusStache is kissing everyone in the same room before he leaves for a birthday celebration to which Virgil and Butch are invited. But the invitation is made up of a long dream of steel girders, and walkways Virgil can see while he's submerged below them. Clean is in the dream, and in the dream, he promises Virgil that he will take him to a mansion, and Virgil understands that the mansion exists. And though Virgil does not imagine the mansion, that is, what it might be like inside, or is for real, he does develop a sense of it from the long summer grasses that brush his legs as they walk with one another. There isn't a home that either of them head towards. Something else is moving them, propelling them forward together into a world of privacy, of seconds, of a shadow toggling against a wall. Virgil is so quickly ready to lie, to say he may not go, not because he would not want to actually meet with any friends, but because he could blame the calendar for the mistake, the mistake of Butch not letting Virgil know about their dinner date with their friends. In the end, Virgil will not go with Clean, but instead, goes searching for Butch, who is suddenly South Asian and waiting in a classroom that is a movie theater, too, a movie he faithfully left to find Virgil. How Sweet! Still!

The search, and the waiting—it all feels like a flood that Virgil cannot contain, his body feeding between emotion and structure, say sadness and rusted white steel plates linking Virgil's body with his vision. The vectors that Virgil pursues move between lines of feeling extend into space; they bleed outside of the bags, dripping fat and blood-grease from the lectern's base.

There's still fat in the bags, fat cut from chicken, fat cut from the meat when it was still frozen. The trimmings inside the bag soften under the stage lights. Virgil hears someone say "gross," or at least Virgil wants to hear this said, and he looks around the audience, haunting the crowd while pacing around the aisles, scanning the room, gazing at the spectacle of what was about to happen, as in what he was going to make in that room, something only Virgil knows because the position of his body is still, and quiet, yet something moves around the tip of the stage, as if plunged between forms, or seeping in the vestibule where someone like Virgil, but not Lucy, is shot.

Virgil has created an eddy in which to find his relationship to *how to love*, mostly, and on top of that, there is another diagnosis, something that draws him in, to seek more ways of understanding the dimensions of what he wants to get at through an opacity out of which he is just learning to render.

What's *under* the work, Virgil feels, is not quiet, but a flow, not anything that Virgil can control, but something else, a constant seizing of the self as it erupts out of what is both not quiet *and* in the morning rain. What would have happened if Virgil had a baby that was his own, say his only child, behind that crashing wall? What if it, or even "he" were struck by the moveable wall falling in the studio that morning in which Lucy was only starting to dance?

Virgil ponders, looking out at the field into a burst of wet-red in the gulf of trees, and the fallen gap of evergreens. There is no sound, but a fallen pine cone appears where Virgil registers, brown. Virgil, who is more interested in RedBeardGatter aka SP, who mowed down those Country Whites and Others for sport, did not predict the fires in California wine country, embers soaring into trees, houses, cars, vines, even in flat Fairfield, but he did understand the relationship between the fires, and the distant hunting shots that he would hear, and the dead, these somehow the demands of those wanting silencers still for sale to augment the assault weapons doubling by the record buys.

Vanilla.

Gambler.

Quiet.

Mystery.

In his view, Virgil hears the kinds of gunshots that he has never heard in nature, but thinks of how they echo so familiarly, and knows that even with access to the orange hunting vests, he will not walk through the deep woods, but instead, will run along the trail to sense what's trying to kill him inside, a dread that his DADWHOKNEW and MOMWHOSPIT buttressed against him. A greater power than freedom, they instilled, teaching him to continue to see far ahead, and even still, further, into his imagination. Life source, Architecture: Capacious.

Your bullets are a sign, Virgil thinks, which could be a line in a song, or a dance move, or a way of thinking, a forced thought through the rain pounding down on the pressure it takes to write, and maybe, to heal. From looking? From listening? Virgil's father, SadNowWaitingtoHeal, amidst the gun shots, understands this too—Dementia as AWOL for several years, his mind has become a retreat, captivity, a cage of lasting imprint, the body bound by fever, but a body still, never "intersectional," a hard, angular word, only cuts.

"For real...and off the hook..." PockedWhite describes the cookie in the case as such, which Virgil will not order. But he likes to think of eating the cookie as an option. The space of the wish to eat what he won't, at least not then, is caught in the site of the little brown boy, directly in front of Virgil, mouthing the edges of the Corten Steel refrigerator case at Verve. The Brown Dad notices his little brown boy after the fact of his mouthing the edge of the metal cooling ledge, and against this, he notices the slight change in temperature outside of the case and in Virgil's body, maybe warmer, which of course, is tied to a more parched memory, the transitions between building his relationship to the self and how it's marked by temperature and thought. There is simply no home, or place to where Virgil can return. Sigh. So, this little place, where the little brown boy's mouth butterfly licks, *the steel is where it's at!*

Or color: Slits in army green sweats reveal leggings, and these leggings point to natural Birkenstocks. In the echo, "Do you know what I mean?" Or "So good"—the space of the fictive relationship between the body, and the body's relationship to what's encrypted accretes in the mind, overheard—perhaps this is the writing, the choice in not dancing for a while, to check back in, in language.

BigLoveBrilliant illuminates this by providing a single gesture, the bodies attuned to the space between what is known, and that which can be constructed in what might be. Virgil must continue, he thinks, to get better, to never stop being hungry, to be fed, to desire the next point of consumption, to be altered in thinking how to not feel full.

"Try this, it's really good."—

All Virgil wants is to build his life in a panoramic relationship to his surroundings, to fly into what he hears, and to move in the feeling of a periscopic conveyance. Of every consequence, Virgil has a need to see, not to not quite "peer around corners," in the way how this vision was once described by one of his "teachers," but also how it is broken, as one can see into the truth of a lie, *I have a wide spread!*

In the office, the BlackGiant says "From Hell," when Virgil asks where the mailings are from, the feeling of the rage is configured in BlackGiant's stance, *seeing inside of the circumstance of our particular condition*, Virgil thinks.

"Yeah." "We're like in the middle of nowhere."—

"What are those??!?!"

In the edge of knowing, a black body is abducted. A fat pink black girl, who has allegedly stolen, is choked to almost death as link to one who was killed, shot in the midst of the perceived crime. The perception is the landscape that is rendered active, and in retrospect all Virgil hears is tearing in a grove that is not "ticky," a squirrel darting and a blue and brown lunch bag, *and geez, are these things free?*

BrownThick waddles in too, with Birkenstocks, hide brown, just like Virgil owns, and in this shared owner-ship, Virgil feels remorse that his body is not long. The gutting of the world as he knows it produces a set of sores in his brain from which he will never recover, or maybe he will learn to advance in this, as ever, in oh, the pulse, and the sway of an emergence in a Black Walk, peering out, to say, "...*is that you, there?*"

Skinnee and NiceNurse have returned from Aruba. In this small encounter is a possible alliance which is a composite feeling Virgil first began to render while walking down the aisle directly past first class, before he met them. Skinnee is a teacher, his wife, a Nurse. Good state schools. Big hearts. Virgil doesn't remember much more, but he recalls the walk on the plane before he met them. In this walk, Virgil receives the weight of those before, then behind him, moving forward, past where he wanted to upgrade, if only for the sake of his becoming, and if only to stare longer at one version ofThe Thin Gold Ring which grounded Virgil as he glanced, looking down and in at him as he tried not to touch anyone with his carry-on.

The encounter is contrapuntal. At the counter in the hotel breakfast, Virgil looks into the kitchen. In the line-cook's line, the black men are so close to the orange fire, and one poaches an egg, drips it onto the plate. Another, the "flesh" face-in-the-black-cap whisks the hollandaise, and he too, like the black men, wears purple polyurethane gloves. One cook tosses a burnt English muffin which hits the tile next to Virgil, meant for the steel bin, and then another version of The Thin Gold Ring shifts next to Virgil, and then too, a-powder-girl-in-a-black-merino banters with the black cooks, and with the "flesh" face-in-the-black-cap: her eyeshadow a smoky cranberry, stomach touched by another of the kitchen-men, gently, a squeeze, a tickle.

The difficulty here, for Virgil, is to render in the realm of difference, while at the same time, to be full in the field of language, to understand its marks, and to want to be, at the same time, thinking of painting. Virgil walks around race, and stumbles freely. Race is not a field. It is—Virgil notes—the work of composition. To come to this realization is the only way that Virgil can do something other than continue to draw connections between walking and being.

There are books for that, and now Virgil tries to make melodies that guide him, and still there is a buzz around his work: his image in multiple screens, iPad, iPhone, MacBook Air—Each promises a vantage point, a way to capture one self, then the next version. For Virgil, this marks an opening, his body, an internal loop. It's as if he is looking inside his own spine, as if he exists in the folding skeletal lines of the Ground Zero 911 Calatrava he winds lost around, panicked outside of the Fulton street stop, just before he decided he wanted to work, purely, but less centrally, in the quiet of language.

Virgil is puzzled, but not by his burst on the studio walls, gutted by the attempts at the erasure—News flash. President Curious is quiet because the OrangeBLOWHOLE is gutting everything in sight, to make it clear that there was never any existence in President Curious's black azz, actually, and so too the paper is fragile, and when Virgil pulls the sheet tight, it begins to tear. Virgil will not mix the oil pastels in water on the page, because this might damage the paper's surface, so he lets the paint saturate.

Virgil realizes that the draft is simply this, an opportunity to move what's left within the eddy of what's happening. He learned this a while ago, but most recently from Lucy. As Lucy, Virgil works in the mode of the fluid gesture, the expounding fragment, the radiating heat from the stage light in the mask that steams up Virgil's face, and Lucy's lips as they pucker under their top teeth. How very far desire deepens in the composite of whiteness in Lucy's pomegranate lips, that they ask themselves to unmake, and to unmoor, in the discursive space of Virgil's memory, and by extension, out of his drawing hand.

Drawing, for Virgil, is feeling, and so too is writing—and the performance is the meeting place between both, one in which to (sometimes) Harlem Shake in the many layers. But there are risks in this: Virgil is mining, not out of any obligation to discoveries, whether accidental or planned, but in his constant keeping at bay his professional relationship to the line.

Smudge—race and its equipment. Find the space where the obligation to terror has to feed itself in one more image of a black foot, crusted, African and bloated, at the bottom of the suit pant. This is not a new concern, but it has to do with Virgil's hope that he will, in the end, remain less enraged by collecting such images, and holding onto them, sites of how he wishes to return, or where he might layer them back into the only identity he knows, a self often stuck behind counters, where he pays for things, out of which alters his freedom.

Commodification as form. The infection is invisible, but it leaves a circle of marks on his calf as Virgil stares out into a patch of trees in a hot parking lot. To be lost in the prose, while four glasses of water sit on a table, and the white paper tablecloth is being wrapped up, and taken away means Virgil is a figure of resistance: a wide path cuts along a hill towards the project—now only of notes as what he theorizes as—*drafting*.

Virgil, who was once a winner, realizes that the prize is like a pill, a book that remains, also dissolves. To determine whether the art is "good," or not. What is Virgil's visibility?—to remain at the edges of the experience of who he was, or how he can make himself up? Virgil's mark in the profession is his ability to move through the edge of a discovery of the artistic self, a self, so often opened up in volatility and its ever-related conditions.

Here is the problem with Virgil's latest book. The father, in real life, does not die, the father goes on, into crazy, but also into a mixture of kindness, and sorrow, and though he is loved, and cared for, like a baby, however petulant—the father feels as though he is in a prison, and figures out a way to escape! He heals! As in, *freedom,* too, for Virgil, is ever vexed.

Virgil was so close to kissing The White, Glowing Yeti in the Red Room, and was so close to the BRNConvicted, already, and so close, too, to being attacked by both, and the attack is the assailant, is now the trial, is the refuge, and BRNConvicted's removal and its puncture—The White Brigade must hold onto what it knows, so they will always back and maintain a desire to keep everything and anything they feel they want in their shaded-in-abs, despite the criminal, however they party, however haunted they are by the obvious, and their reliance on the constant refrain of racism's clutch.

A father has died in the dream. He died in the middle of a party. The party was for his son. "At the bottom of the sea..." is what Virgil's Father says to him, when he asks where the van is: "Can I get you something to drink other than water?"

"Akbar," is the name the Drunk Tank calls the fellow cabbie when he avoids an accident as he drives Virgil closer to the Rock Bottom in the middle of the first night of Virgil's latest visit to Wisconsin. The evening is close to a dream where he is engaging with the slur, "Akbar," and then the extended memory leads itself to a ridge of knowing, to move towards sleep? Now? There are so many choices. For Virgil, the body and mind bound must web into new vocabularies, how to suspend the escaping spider under the desk into how to move within its sliding escape is how Virgil will learn to lead his own life away from such distraction.

Line

Freedom is next to nervousness in LandLock, where to some extent, he can determine how much to let in the noise of the old set of highways between CT and MA. In LandLock, Virgil feels an inconsistency folding in the hinges of an instance, so that he—as Stream suggests—still cruises. In the Fairmount, Virgil is up against a wall in a small vestibule in the tiny front theater that wasn't there when he used to have to force himself to drive past the building on his way to all the green vistas in which he once lived. But there, in the tiny vestibule, Virgil is now aware of how to capture whichever Silver Helmet he wants in his beating porno-living heart.

The WhiteArchitect in the Fairmount is discussing the trajectory of his life, which includes seven years in the U.S. Navy, and the G.I. Bill that paid for his education, so that he, today, makes buildings to withstand terrorist blasts. Virgil does not ask about what happens to the body if the world, the white one, so strong, were to explode, say as a new history, or an enduring fact. How will Virgil recount and reconstitute what's lost, here, and in this loss, is there a way to return, and in the feeling of possible return, is there, even a chance for him to find just the right amount of depth in touch and love?

This dream tethers in Virgil's reach, but Virgil thinks, as he does often, of the final scene in *Set It Off*, when Jada Pinkett's character, "Stony," drives off into the horizon one arm steering, the other secure over her duffel full of cash on the passenger seat, film cutting to a happy montage of her dead homegirls behind her not making it to where she's escaped. Some people hate this ending. Some reject it, while others hold on to it forever. For Virgil, this scene moved him into his own horizons, helping him to understand the importance of rendering sorrow, alit by choices—the root of his vision, vision as hinge, hinge as dig site, dig site as matter that carries and propels.

Virgil is alone with The Ripped Princess, who's dropped to his knees, and begging for it, grey sweats ripped off, to reveal a thong. The Fairmount, in the bathroom, no longer has the sink that sports a gaping rusted hole inside its porcelain mouth. But Virgil still remembers it, syncing the blood-rusting edges the torn open hole in how he recalls The Ripped Princess to be wide-eyed, buffed and high.

How much time is left for Virgil to understand of the landscape, the snow that cuts in front of the road, and how far is he away from all of this, inside the theater? What Virgil wants is to be shared, and to share the tongue, the spit and the spunk of strangers, while Manitoba is warm inside of his parent's garage in Sacramento—Virgil can still dream.

So many times, Virgil stops in the snow to look at the sky, to reel in the harbor of his own good fortune. It is, for instance, only the cute old white men who, Virgil realizes, tell him he thinks too much of himself and it's the beautiful ones who tell him he does not do this enough.

"Various Permutations"—This is a term that Virgil uses, because what it means is that he can stop on the side of the road to capture the image of the snow flat on the lake, some of which is frozen, and some given over to the sound of his body, too heavy, and too held onto, all of his heft bound not by abstraction, but let go into the blue, percussive line.

The phone cord is steel and it wraps around the wrist of the man who's just shook Virgil's hand. It was unexpected, both the shaking and the frayed wire at the end of a plastic antennae that simultaneously extends from the end of the phone. The line stretches as if to get a signal, the signal to reach Virgil, or that is, to connect him to the other side of the show, a concert that begins at 9:30 p.m.

Money does not grow on trees, but it doesn't matter in Virgil's estimation, something that he understands as a richness of various scales, how large arena concerts go on in his dreams, yet the concerts matter less than the figures who populate the audience. Often unreliable, and writhing in Virgil's proximity. Virgil wants to get at the question of *why*? Why are those people in the dream so fucked when it comes to race? Why has it been so hard for everyone to speak to this fact?

Madge cuts a piece of cloth in front of him, a dense grey fabric she uses to illustrate her point, a point which Virgil does not recall. But he does know Madge was *right*. Perhaps it had to do with how the man on the stage, ripped others apart, how her cutting the cloth in Virgil's sightline illuminates Virgil's own hate—A Little Glowmer playing innocently in the rows of grape vines in Napa, splitting his sight.

Could it be that it's only Virgil who wants the Little Glowmer disappeared? In Virgil's imagination, there's a field, on it, a set of figurines that he put at the field's edges, but where have they tumbled, and how has he seen his own configuration in dreams and, so often, on vacay? Virgil is so vexed when he is among the insistence-of-a-hive-of-whites, but it is so often that he finds himself there.

In *Set It Off*, the money's, at first, in a backpack, and "Stony" in a jeep, and the freedom of her going, again, is linked to a usual trail of trauma. In history. Bodies bulleted and fallen. Bodies, then, on the run. Some die. Only one lives. But this is in a pop film, and Neela thinks the movie, ultimately, is staged to mark the usual killing of bodies like hers. The usual mix—Neela's people brought in to be killed in front of an audience for everyone's eyes.

It's so exhausting, this medley, activating a feeling that propels Virgil into advantages, ways of seeing forward, but what is he holding onto if not the fraught joy of this activity? Clearly, there's some alliance: A gang of whites are at what appears to be a rally, and of course, the rally is a speech. It is not a gathering, nor a protest—the rally is a row of seats outside of the stadium, and next to the stadium is a ramp, and the ramp leads to a walk, and the walk provides a number of steps upon one of which Virgil is seated.

Virgil is the only Virgil in the audience, looking into the site of not an abyss, but into a future. One white walks out in what looks like a mask, and everyone cheers, and then he drops his pants to reveal his pink/shadowed crack. He's a football player, maybe TT, or someone equally famous, a star, someone who like Terry Bradshaw, is famous enough to show his white buttocks off to an audience, such as in *Failure to Launch*.

The effect is often the case, and the case is often the feature of what Virgil wants to get at—he needs to understand perception, both in being seen, and in seeing. This is the point of his sharing tales. It's a genre, of entertainment, one in which Virgil often guides his dreams, and as frequently, in which he is guided by them. Such dreams create encounter. There is even a "talk-back" in one dream, an exchange that Virgil understands to exist at the heart of his desire.

Stream thinks Virgil captures the White Man by the heart, and by the sex, as a way to hook them, entire. Is Virgil the mother, then—the fantasy that allows Virgil to train his White Men? *What is Virgil's Problem?*

In the mouth of the front room overlooking the San Francisco Street, tall candles are burning, illuminating Stream's black arm hair, his wide hand touching Virgil's leg, Virgil's melting. This love, its richness writhes too, as in in Virgil's rando-attack on Butch the following day, well after the candles were steel-cup-snuffed to smoke. *All so Very Wrong.* Virgil understands the power of his palm, hard bone, and as Serena wants to be surprising in play and fashion—flanked by white skinny dad host at Two Birds/ One Stone, Virgil's pitch-black Valentino shades with blonde leather accented frames—makes the composition.

The stolen Asian cuisine, the white unspun arm holds the insets, the mirrors of black and brown bodies on the walls—the corporate art (Corten Steel, including Corten Pigs)—Virgil will not be afraid, but given The Grey Time, he of course is afraid, and shakes a bit, and is not surprised by the breeze up his leg, despite his nervousness, as he reads: I LOVE MY TANKER. A long, fixed body is attached to a tendon. Stream's is soft behind a door, a dimple of flesh.

It's true. Virgil does like them wounded, or wounds them, not because Virgil is wounded, but because there is always some slow healing, often in a fissure, deep in his own little hole. He is a conduit for sense, alright, and the night sometimes finds Virgil looking at the words that come out of his others. How much has Virgil acquired? What is the aggregate Virgil, and will he understand the modes of who he might become?

For Virgil is already old, and realizes that his "spirit animal" can no longer be, but still it is, and Virgil is at ease: as the wide Manta Ray, or the African Lung Fish, wrinkled, then wet from the rains. Virgil is as alive as Octopuses, how they escape, tentacles leading them around ship rivets, over rails, or out of hull slots— Virgil as animals, as matters of consequence, consequences by which they are understood as imports, as slippery trajectories, forms however unpredictable, and however known.

The wires are low on the horizon, outside of the living room window of the Red House, and thicker, without the backdrop of old growth, as the Blacks and Browns across the street have gutted their yard of most of their trees.

Sapphire-of-the-Blacks-and-Browns came home at lunch from her phlebotomist shift to take pictures of her newly stripped yard. Virgil thinks of Sacra, and no trees, no cooling shade. On the news, Virgil sees a shark pounded by the surf against the bottom of a sea cliff.

In *Hugo*, Virgil sees his own desires in the coloring of each frame, and, too, Virgil sees his own want to chase down the boy protagonist in that city. Virgil is a Punk. Virgil likes White Dads. Virgil sacrifices his own sovereignty to be in their midst.

But Virgil, always on the run, has never had time to reflect as much as he has within the body of prose as he has now. This, according to Virgil, is plot—the plot of the life that guides him into the source of what leads him to *My 600-LB Life*.

In the two-part series, Justin and his massive twin sibling's body, like her brother's is close to a square, one sibling cannot wear shoes, while the other has black fungus on his leg, the festering patch on the calf the cameras hone in on.

On another search, *Fat Fails*, a fat, white bro trying to leap a bonfire, clips the end of a flaming log with his foot, crashing into the fire pit, and is laughed at by his friends and party-crew alike. Embers crack, an urgency cuts into Virgil's heart, and the memory—

One where he walked with fellows in the slow, humid, Vermont summer to a "tide pool," to swim, but ends up floating in an eddy, then feeling fat in the bed, as poems would come in couplets, but Virgil was still on the verge of something not verse.

Nor does Virgil need to watch a movie, because he must return to the writing, and it is imperative for him to find a way to reveal the story in which there's a deck, and on this deck is an older General, ruddy face and neat chin, who carries a voice that moves him into the intersections of all the 800 blown-apart bodies that are presupposed before the bomb is ever dropped in the cave.

There is no evidence of the war, yet, but there is the threat of war, as in the black who dropped the drones, but the pink and orange body has decided to let a bomb roll off the tip of his tongue. Virgil needs less the attention than the time to think, and to make in order to exist in the sun rays, and not the snow. Virgil no longer shovels, and in the Streets of Santa Cruz, he jokes to Butch: *"I lifted the rays with my eyes."*

What Virgil leads to has no particular opposition. In fact, his body is inert, impacted by the bomb's aftermath. There's a row of white men. The General is the only one that Virgil recognizes, and this, by the timbre of his voice. Virgil trusts sound, particularly, and how it shatters in prose, the form in which he got his start. Virgil's earliest sensations were of his moving along a chain of connections, one event connected, by tone, to the next.

Poetry, in some instances, can be a story, but for the body to write the poem, a brown body, or a black body noticing the shift in shadows—Virgil believes—comes from a different origin, an alternative sense, one that might be contained by what Virgil seems to constantly work against.

Containment is not promise. To be contained by race is not the extent to which the mask compels, particularly next to the shore, because the shore, too, is a series of movements, undone by the threat of expectation. There is, of course, the sentence; but too, there is Virgil's dream of learning to play the acoustic guitar, which, to some extent, is an intervention marked by the staging of an event before it happens.

Before the bombs were shot out of the air, the war game was replayed, every piece of it reenacted by the figure of the shooter, every trajectory refigured, the percentages broken down, the depth of madness unhinged. Arguably, art cannot be broken down like this—it can only be made into sensations, Virgil thinks, so that the feature of art's underpinnings might, at best be predictive, and at worse, just amount to things reconstituted into moves.

The self in the stack of linens.

Why does the Unknown Latina in the dream draw Virgil to look so closely at her face? It's because the Unknown Latina in the dream looks into Virgil's face, and says two things, however disconnected, that Virgil recalls. "No one here wants to tell anyone they lost weight." And, "You as well."

Virgil hates the latter phrase, as he realizes there is a disruption in what seemingly constitutes the formal. It feels to Virgil like an inexpensive nose job, pocked skin that dreams of being smooth, blood left in the close-up opening, where the amateur was all the way there with the shot.

No shame in that game.

Virgil understands that his encounter with those in the dream must be understood to be clear. The Stanford Black tells him that he cannot give up, but given Virgil's own specious class, mixed with his assuredness, Virgil feels that he understands his own self to be marked far enough by his freestyling abilities to not give a care.

For Virgil, the space of the dream is the only actual position, the position as the marked body, fused by the weight of its circumstance.

"I don't know what to say."

The Stanford Black's speech is crisp and exact—its mode, concrete, a surface that leads back to how The Stanford Black also has "a clear skin," like Virgil's. Virgil does not own the house that he encounters, slowly, but he may as well, as he walks through the gate for a swim. Virgil walks by the towels left out on the benches, folded, and stacked. They are high, and neat.

Virgil's fist on the floor in the Fairmount. *David.* How did you remember my name, or how did you know it, or did Virgil say *John*? "How did you know my name?" It is what the WhiteD's say. Below their sacks—"Lick behind them..." as one commands.

"The children are doing okay," is what Virgil learns from another. One finished at Cooper Union, another at Syracuse, or the feeling—*is your daughter beautiful?* This is what Virgil wants to ask DustyBear, but he does not.

The writing has to be kept safe in order for it not to be safe. In one moment the world could not exist. There are missiles that are launched in the dream, and since the dream is also a movie, Virgil can see that it is not going to end well, but Virgil thinks through the story, one might come to know what's possible.

Virgil wants to send Clean a note, a note that lets him know he is so far removed from the sense of Virgil's newest feelings about Clean. Because there isn't radar in the dream, Virgil simply walks out onto the deck and selects a suit, a blue bathing one, and he compliments The Unknown Latina as Virgil looks into her face, and tells her how clear her skin is, too.

The Unknown Latina wears only some makeup. Virgil will keep this private, his sense of where to work, and how to wander in the writing. "It's not my problem," is what Butch tells Virgil, so that this is why he has run so far, and now not running, but walking so slowly through another open gate. In Virgil's walk, he finds himself secured with little effort.

Virgil pulls out one of the bathing suits from the bag, and he slides it on. Even though he has bought a suit at Dick's—three in fact—Virgil stomps down the stairs, mouth guard in, for he has a revelation. There is just something in his looking at the Stanford Black that helps him understand his own place in the encounter.

He awakes from the dream, because in the dream, he looks into the face of the Stanford Black and recognizes a softness in him as he describes that he was going to be sued, that he had a scholarship, that he was going to be removed, the priceless reward taken away. To be shot up into the atmosphere, to long for the moon, and mars, to move where who waits calmly to be captured?

The General's voice echoes above the sea's surface, because he, too, knows he'll be caught. Virgil sees the moment build towards the moment of capture. Though he does not watch a movie before bed, he creates one by morning in his dream. Now, Virgil is waking, calmly, to understand that it does not makes sense, any longer, to run—to be at large—in this configuration. Instead, Virgil will try to see, as clearly, again.

Between sleep and waking, Virgil is trying to find a way to talk back to the dream, perhaps its urgency, and its relationship to the line, a way to speak, mostly directly to the characters that emerge. Virgil, in some sense, would like to pluck the figures out, or at least to query them—this is what he feels to be his most important writerly intervention.

The space between what is dreamed, and what is ultimately articulated helps Virgil to understand his relationship between what he wants to recall, and that which he can barely hold onto. The line of the story is so different from the line of the poem; in fact, there is a hole in his heart where the body cannot bring itself to hold itself up against the urgency *to tell*, because Virgil is now experimenting with rest.

Sleep is the New Future is what he read, and for Virgil, it is the next vista of class. Go to sleep while your world blows up, and the very dumbest, perhaps, will take over the earth. Virgil once thought that his first book (a collection of poems) would be called *Song of the Dark Heart*, and perhaps this was something that Virgil thought through, but the song did not have, in it, the urgency of clarity in the melody, nor the insistent pull to that which would guide Virgil to understand what would become a much more difficult, and an even darker practice, still.

In *Locked Up Abroad*, a woman next to the sleeping black bay is raped by her captors, and as this goes on, she meditates, while her free husband says, "this was our darkest time." Of course, a woman emerges in the end, married, and in a pretty dress, but it is not before Virgil is all kinds of titillated at the masked guards who hold a knife at the husband's neck, get high, and, the husband and wife recount the tale: "...we thought that it would only happen once."

For Virgil, there is a gap that he wants to move through, a sensation that is more instructive than compelling, or compels him to wander through the final days of his Radical Sabbatical, the space where he for the first time, has slowed down, and in this slowing, what is produced is a shift. Stream comes and goes. Old Stream is an anchor, dying but elegant in the chair, and Stream touches the face of a giant horse, only to ask, "Is this real?"

Virgil knows that all of his life is interrupted by the permanent specter of violence, some his own, some not, but it is this structure of violence that leads him to lines, one that opens up into a series of waves skirting across the surface of the televisual and the remembered black bay. This "Blues" for Virgil is, perhaps, the line: each of the scenes in which he has become grows out of the space of what he's recalled, running up these hills, running around this water, the body not as wandering, which he first considered as "melody," recoils as transit across race and around desire.

It seems that, in this sense, the mark of what he has become is tied to what it might reveal between the dimensions of what race, what class, and what form and impulse Virgil wishes to convey: a book of chance? A life of excitement? The source of the titillation, the sadness of what the captor might become as Virgil sees the hostage-husband bang his head against the wall at his own inability to defend his hostage-wife.

Virgil recalls being stuck between two men. Virgil, a *he*, a *what*, an *it*, could not control his hard-on. He wanted, somehow, to share it with his seatmates, but he could not. And though he flashed the outline beneath his AG Dylan's—he would never wear shorts on a flight—it felt right for him to try in Slim Skinny jeans, then, a sharing tied to his reckoning, or maybe Virgil was just attempting.

Virgil looks out into the icy morning, the peaks of the trees serrated by the snow mist, waves, this time, towards perception. Virgil wants to get back to these interactions where he should be angered, however measured, but also lets them go.

A rushing worker almost knocks Virgil down at Shin, another customer who phone-talks real estate, opens the door to move around Virgil, does not say "sorry," or" mah bad," or "'scuse me—" Against this jacked behavior, Virgil wants to "read," but shakes Butch awake from the middle of his nap, and in the center of a long flight. Intrusion is Intrusion. It's a small "read" that Virgil wants to unleash, but still one all the same.

"Your Tricycle" is the phrase that Butch shares with this rude little girl. The provocation is the point between what is stable and what isn't, between the limit of the body, and the register of its sign. What Virgil means to say is what he cannot think.

That both are in the unconscious and "out of it," attempts to derail Virgil from his own stability, whether class, race, or balance, each reveals a pull for Virgil, a pull that allows, first, Butch a way of seeing; but for Virgil, it promises a way of sorting through the muck of his own circumstances, a feeling—movements in veils that circle around the airplane, the corridor, the bridge.

The Small Girl (Who is Actually a Woman) has hair of straw, matte grey blended in, and with Butch, she shares a memory. The memory is of doing something that was private—nothing sexual—something else, something like playing in a white park, a set of landings left in the grey gravel, covered in snow.

What are the reactions to any prize?—this isn't about light, or power. It's about something else, not the state of work, for the sake of finishing it—it's a plea. Virgil is, at this stage, moving from the site of prose to the water-soluble oil pastels soaking in water— to become paint—and maybe this is the effect of his dream, to shift towards freedom which liquid holds, and succumb to the medium.

A fat cat, grey and white, struts by a ledge, carrying a mouse, and it's the mouse that understands his relationship to death is to dangle. The squirrel knows too, as it bounces around in the cut grass, what it means to barely hold on, and in the tether of an evenly mown surface, its grip is always ready to slip. Virgil can hear the laughter, coming out of a mouth, the laughter of a faraway song also bound by its protraction.

There is something proud in the cat's triumph, because it isn't dead on the street. Not a sack of guts, nor as quickly rendered into someone else's memory, driven by—

Blown Plexiglass shards crowd the edges of the tub. They fill the bottom of the "adult" latrine. Virgil holds the lock secure, because where a pilot is on the other side, Virgil knows the pilot wants to get in. The pilot warns the man behind him that there is someone in there, and he's taking forever. To alert the men behind outside the door—the pilot, and the White Top, behind him (and anyone else)—that it's Virgil, Virgil shakes the door latch and its lock loud.

The floor of the latrine is a dim yellow, and it's painted with stains, and Virgil is barefoot, looks down at the bottom of the tile with his feet touching the bottom, and he wants to leap out of it, to fly above the matter of the pools of yellow piss, and clots of brown mucus, for these are the things that are inside Virgil, too—so why would he not recall them coming out on the other side into the real?

This is the form of the line, but whether or not Virgil would like to paint its sight is up to him. Desire is long, and its mirrored. About an hour from the dream, Butch stands in the shower on damaged knees, one, soon to be filled with metal.

Virgil, who is unsure (and unlocked), is now close to Butch's age when they first met, and hears the rain and the thunder station on Pandora. This is heaven: the time to create, and this is the time in which Virgil will transition between forms, to move away from the body of the poem or the essay or, maybe run directly into the line of that which endures, whatever skill, in whatever vision or dream.

Virgil is only sure of this, for now—

The Small Girl (Who is Actually a Woman) can pop up at any time: like Skeletor, like that DishDrawer who popped up at the retreat, like them all, those that understand "place," too, but Virgil moves into where they make room for a quotidian freedom, takes them in, marks, marks, and holds on.

There are always other Whites near Virgil. *Buttery* is how Virgil wanted to describe the performance. *I was there.* This is what the Brown Boy wanted to say plainly, but ultimately this plainness was an impossibility when Virgil tried to figure out what "the lecture" could promise.

The lecture, a series of organizations, which move around examples, facts, sounds, and even footnotes, is the mode through which this new body of work will be realized. *I think it makes sense.* This is something Virgil would like to say, in all honesty, to himself, but it seems that this is too often complicated by his experiences, layers of which sit *atop* one another.

Across the sky there is a plane Manitoba sees, and through Manitoba's eyes Virgil, too, sees. A filter, opening into a sky, a way of seeing the line the plane leaves, and then another, a broken trail, dissipated into a cloud: this is the path of seeing which Virgil understands to be a reminder, the click Virgil makes his phone sound when he sees an image he might need for another time, an artificial signifier, variants, of course, between melody and mark.

Virgil looks at a broad, grey set of ripples in the bay he doesn't capture in any lens. He just wants to take it all in, free. Virgil understands nothing most of the time. He doesn't understand, in particular, the anger that holds his body together, a body held amidst the orange and yellow leaves out of the window by Clean, the only one to hold him in Virgil's first interdisciplinary studio life. When he's called *baby*, Virgil returns to understanding a thing he is told:

You can go back now.

At the edge, a fictive landscape is wedded to the real mud that builds below the intertidal shore. Between high and low, the mud creates a rhythm, too. Rhythm is a word he remembers from inside of Stream's car, Tink, Tink Drone, silence. Stream tells him about "the snap," Johnny Cash heard from the shoe shine boy, the snap, *I / got rhythm*, but it is this snap that helps Virgil to recall— "Yeah, but he's a Nigger," *Nigger* is how Stream described the pretty Black man with dreads, looking across at Stream, and maybe at Virgil, too, in the 440 Bar.

Nigger is the name Virgil wants to suppress, but he will never be able to do so, because it is a condition that lingers. It was the name that, after Hilton Als, in his intervening essay...catalogue (Dead N), and after Gary Simmons installation "play" space and exhibit (Black A), Virgil will hold fully and as fragments, closely, in his thinking forever, turning the epithet around, and wondering why he remained there through the night to take care of Stream. Virgil is perhaps weak, but his body in need of being used is not, marked through a track already well tilled through his being in knowing what kind of work is possible in these exchanges.

In the 440, Virgil tells The Browns he and Stream were talking (they were also pretty, but with sheening hair) that this is what Stream said, and how Virgil's eyes grew wide in their faces as they looked at Stream, then Virgil, who remained at Stream's side, with contempt. Virgil's eyes might have been thinking discovery, The Browns's, repulsion. Perhaps they were right?

"Buy us drinks!"

Virgil recalls Stream's face when Virgil reminds Stream of what he said— *"That's rough"*—but rough for whom? Is it something that Virgil accepts, and cannot forget? Is it a wedge issue? Is it, somehow, a pattern? Is it a contract? Is it the only way back into the relationship

Virgil does not yet, nor perhaps will ever understand?

In Stream's grey eyes, contempt emits at the point of "the deliverable," how Virgil's body will forever be recalled and recoiled, something so blankly hateful—might be the only thing tugging at whatever he loves about Stream, whatever pulls him back into where he thinks he is, or what he wants, the ebbing: "Yeah, but he's a Nigger."

So Virgil, too, is the recoil. His want is a plan to see Stream over and over, not to figure this out, but to accept some position from which Virgil will learn to maneuver in relation to what Stream may turn out to be. If Virgil feels that he is the one that can enter into Stream-as-habituation, as rhythm, then perhaps, Virgil can truly be *sick-with-it*.

Perhaps this might be why Virgil thinks, too often, the worst of Stream, that this seed as the first moment, is a kind of rejection, removed, or maybe even triangulated, that Virgil carries in him, still through every moment they are magic together, and no matter how connected they have become—Language beats, in that moment. It pulls and indicates place for Virgil, a place in which Stream, in that sense, is a constant.

What option does Virgil have but to know that the well behind Stream's eyes, and Virgil's feelings from staring into it, has nothing to do with Virgil's own worth? But it is, rather, how this worth is perceived by The Browns, *in their eyes*, after Virgil reports to them Stream's sick, racist spit. "Whaddahyoucare," is what DadWhoKnows always says to Virgil, to all his kids, whenever they care what others think. So Virgil toggles between expected and unknown distances from Stream, moving between whom he loves, and what he knows to be right.

For Virgil, this reveals an impossible penetrability for logic. Virgil, instead, learns to build something around his heart, with a density perhaps like the black, bay mud, or perhaps simply akin to the density of a thickening life.

It made sense—

The law of conservation of mass or principle of mass conservation states that for any system closed to all transfers of matter and energy, the mass of the system must remain constant over time, as system mass cannot change quantity if it is not added or removed. Hence, the quantity of mass is "conserved" over time.

Virgil looks, these days, more impulsively to the dictionary on his Macbook Air. Virgil wants to understand something the Brown Boy could not. The Brown Boy's subjectivity was anchored to the site of what he theorized as his own, supposed, white love. And not much, it seems, changes for Virgil, but, still, it dissipates, and happens, and builds almost blindingly so, these days, behind his own eyes, now, thickening too.

It's impossible to be attentive to every dream, and part of the feeling of his fear is that Virgil understands he is bound by dream as much as he is by expanse. In the open ocean air, Virgil is allowed to wonder beyond the television not on.

But nothing is optimal. There isn't a single way that one can begin to describe the experience of the racialized body, because the feeling is marked by the circumstances of a constant shift between the hurt, and the epiphanic. Often, dead exhaustion inhabits the interaction. Often these interactions come from the smallest moments, once called MA's, and those, too, are often invisible to the touch.

There is a package in the case at Safeway filled with blue cheese, and because of what happened at The Oasis, Virgil says *sorry* to no particular person, maybe even to the food, but ultimately, he does not feel the need to direct his apology to any person, and Virgil does not even recall touching the blue cheese.

It is *exhaust*. Exhaust is the mode of release that Virgil finds himself engaged with, handling the relationship that he's forced to be in conjunction with, the reel of power that pulls him back into the scene. Pulling back, breathing, or sitting there breathing, and creating something, mostly as a kind of fiction, around him.

Innocent in off-white: This is how Virgil must have looked, walking into that room, wearing brand new clothes from Urban Outfitters. He rocked an oversized tunic, in the Beiber style, untucked, jutting out of an inexpensive, nylon "Mod" Bomber jacket. Virgil, therefore, did not feel entirely elegant, but did feel sexy, somehow, or at least, *above the crowd*.

Stream's cousin, he says, is Phil Donahue, so Stream is as beautiful, and likes to party, or drink, a lot, and that's fine, because he is a happy drinker, drunk, who knows, and who cares? But Virgil, the night he is assaulted at the Oasis Bar in S.F. needs a friend, when he is attacked. Stream, however, connects their being kicked out, to being lost on the freeway in the Uber, but what does Virgil want? No one tells him no.

Affinities, and alliance, Ally ship, or Ailment— when Virgil's grandfather, DaddyJoliet, said *Pride* was what to beware of, and "...*to not be afraid to seek a trade*..." perhaps talking about himself, and not Virgil. Virgil does not recall his grandfather having a job, but does recall his face, smooth and light-brown, his glasses like Virgil's *(He looks like daddy!)* and the time he came out of the shower, black and grey pubic hair, and how much Virgil was turned on by his grandfather's drying off in front of his mother and him, and the trophies.

The house in TN, where Virgil grew up, some, was flooded with trophies, tennis and bowling, and white doilies, and furniture heavy from Japan, etched out wood, bars not built in but stacked in the corners. It is because Virgil, as a boy, picked up things with his feet that he was also able to see the world from on his back, the arc of power as not horizontal, but vertical as his toes played in the grooves of the cabinet, or the bar.

Virgil could, in fact, outline the carved wood—of tropical forests, of the villages, huts maybe, or a language, raised. White and black marble was set in wood in squares, and then the hovering of the paintings on velvet, wet, black roads around a bend with a light source, though it wasn't discernible from where.

In the thick painting, Virgil would stare, and follow the road into what he would never know, what MommaSpine would never show him, or what she always did, a nowhere, wet, and turning around the black corner. Like the miniaturized copies of weapons of the Philippines in a plaque, the edges of the swords, featuring upturned hooks at their ends, serrations, wavy along the lengths, swords that once stabbed in, or pulled out, would tear and unroot, disembowel, rip in, to clearly, kill.

Was the house violent? Sure. It had to be, because it was a scene of recovery, because Virgil's mother left Leon, Iloilo behind, so far behind, far beyond the specter of leaving so that Virgil, full of pride, could bounce into the bar with Stream who is beautiful and grey, and likes to sing *"Birds Do It!...Bees Do It!..."* and in conversation, well at least once, fades into a language that Virgil thinks of as "The Blur."

"Tell the actors they need to grow up." Virgil says this next to Stream to the hostess who has complaints that they are talking back too loudly at the drag show. In the show, Jack Tripper, Chrissy Snow, Mr. Roper, Mrs. Roper, and Janet, who was strung out on coke, are mimicked perfectly through excess. The show, in fact, is brilliant.

What staff manages an audience at a drag show? Enough to kick out guests for call and response.

Virgil goes off as he is leaving. He calls S.F. a "two horse town," but does not forget the brilliance of the play. Mrs. Roper is excited by her old husband, who looks like dust: Mrs. Roper is an expert of the MuMu. The Piglet bartender says that Virgil called someone on his staff "a cunt." Stupid, Lie.

For Virgil, instead, it is a tale of two Fernandos: One Fernando is an Uber Driver who is being yelled at by Stream, far away from the lie. The other is at the Twin

Peaks Bar where Stream and Virgil settle in long after the Oasis. The second Fernando is from Peru, Lima, and is a trainer, or was one, and the expanse of knowing, the body realized by the sun, broken and Virgil, instead, is held in that memory.

The water in the river is brown, and it does not have a name that Virgil can recall, though the river is connected to his exact anger, something that sits on the surface of his every interaction with Butch. So why does Virgil continue to see Stream when he has enough? Even when MommaSpine could have died on the couch the night when Virgil left Stream at Old Stream's house for The Lawyer. Virgil even visits The Lawyer for an afternoon of Nacho Tots, all then still a game—a brief ride on The Lawyer's fat cock during the hours MommaSpine's arterial flap whirred, arteries closing, to incapacitate her by that morning, but at least Virgil found her in time to race her to the ER.

Some of this should have served as a respite, like the river, and like the moon carved up in the blue sky, but Virgil, who cannot read more than a word, more than a sentence, more than a second, is so often taut in his anger, an anger that gets caught in his neck, which he can barely turn. He is so busy. MommaSpine, even without breath, cares, and loves, like Butch, like Stream: *"If you have time, can you drop me off at the hospital?"*

The name of the river that he cannot recall is also, and all too often what is so clear in his love for Butch. It is love on the back end of pain, and it is not rotten, but it is activated by a feeling, however extended by Virgil's ever-selfish behavior.

> *I suppose that when I was Candy, the girl, or the woman, my body was still forming, so in one way, the formation of my desire in the realm of seduction— "Hi, can I suck your cock?"— was the first instance of the shock; that is, it was the primary mode of the feeling that*

compelled the men on the other line to relent to the wishes of what was, after all, a boy's call. This Virgil realizes was his earliest performance that maybe mattered, through the imagination (his) and (theirs), which revealed his insistence.

Virgil recalls that, in the water below the Carquinez Bridge, his Uncle Joe's friend died in the Strait, fishing, and for Virgil, he recalls the death, even though he does not know, or remember the event or the drowner's name with any particularity. It was even the grey, and the brown, and the smallness of the boat that he wonders about, the tiny lunch box imagined on the deck, and the feeling of loss that captured Virgil's memory.

MommaSpine in her hospital bed recalls her Galaxie 500, and the clear water of Navy Lake, even though Virgil remembers the lake green, and filled with "turtles," he learned later were cottonmouths. In any case, MommaSpine recalls shining her car next to the sheening water. It is a memory which cannot translate to the present other than by way of anticipation, something Virgil recounts as he rides The Lawyer in the middle of the day, the act echoing porn star Swiney, the insertion of the artificial into the real.

This is one act in which Virgil anticipates the mode through which he understands his body to be temporary, even in the morning, in a morning in which he has barely eaten.

Virgil does recall the shock in the curve around the mountains, a curve that Virgil recalls, at the end of the train, whipping around the flat tables, the moves to somewhere far from the zone of feeling, swaying within him, a precision he held onto.

Is it love that tethers Virgil to a single tube of ash in the sink? Is it love that expands Virgil across the entire country, his anger whipping out into Butch's face for an assault that Virgil himself has made on his own stupid terms, an internal love that equally pulses in the throes of Virgil's stomach, a vibration, then, that also rushes just under the surface of his entire body.

Around the bend appears more water, but more than this, what Virgil sees is a ledge of dust, and from this promontory, a sense of the impenetrability of his desire to be loved; or maybe it is the case that through others he can see the love that is his own, something that he cradled as fantasy, but still, it is the desire to be wanted as not the person he is, but the self's projection, a hole, a mouth, a movement, a ride.

For this, there is no equivalent, only the sky that is pink in the morning, too, which is the surprise: in which there is often a "girlfriend," no "fiancé," no "married," but what is penetrated, is also that which becomes equally soft and wet, and the movement, like the one who Virgil does not know, is the drowning into the disappearance, where he registers.

> *When I was a boy, I pretended to be a woman. This was a fixed site, the site in which I would extoll the value of my pussy, a pussy I did not have. It was soft and always wet for the Colonel, or for Mike, and in this exchange was a pressure in the imagination to be what I wasn't. This, I believe, was the source of my wetness, something that hovered at the edge of risk, and at the end of the phone line.*

"You don't have a pool?" It's a reality Stream believes in. However, the saturation of chlorine that suspends in Virgil's body into a state of not breathing, so clear, is something that Virgil understands to be formative. Virgil chokes on it. Virgil is the one with the tears. Virgil is the one who cannot sleep. Virgil is the one that thinks through his own life. Virgil is the one, who at rest, is working to figure out a way to look into the sun forever. Stream is not that large, but still, it makes Virgil weep. Virgil weeps at his own acceptance of the failures of those he takes in.

> *I think Candy offered both a respite and distraction. Here he was, a boy, who would jump a fence, excited to use a microwave, to have lunch, to have whatever he wanted, chips, or a hot-dog, and his going home for lunch, chased (once) by Mr. Timmony, fat and black, his small black, crisp nose and ear hair representing a freedom from all possible vanity. At lunch, Virgil could jack off, and have as much fun as he wanted, yet it was so brief. Virgil had only 30 minutes to figure out what to eat, and then seduce his lovers, to change into Candy!*

The raccoons appear in multiple places: one appears in the cool light of Old Stream's house, just under the sign of the tree, or the fence that Virgil closes behind him. Another appears next to Butch, there near his tub. Another appears in Angel Face's garage, there up in the corner. The first is gone before Virgil enters the property to say goodbye. The second escapes into the night, while Butch remains naked and wet in the hot tub. And the last is startled away by constable, but Virgil does recommend, by phone, to Butch, that Angel Face should shotgun the animal in the face.

Virgil understands the insistence of his anger, or at least he attempts to, tries to feel like he can exact his desire for so much hate into, say, a found penny, but this is entirely exhausting. Virgil buys the three roses for his mother, and in his purchase he feels such anger for what is known, that he can get them much cheaper at Costco, but he will not, for MommaSpine now has four new stents in her arteries, arteries that were clogged by candy and fat, and surely the garlic fries that Virgil shared with her.

Virgil, too, enjoys the packs of Men+Care Dial soap MommaSpine always makes sure to leave for him on the shelf in the garage to take home to Santa Cruz.

This, Virgil, believes is what writing is, the chance and expected encounter between one scene, tricks, and the night in which, out of the tricks, in the early AM, emerges the luck of being able to save his mother's life. This he unpacks with Stream on their drive back to the bay, Virgil leaving the passenger seat all the way back, for Stream as he did for his mom, enabling the space that Manitoba allows for the wounded, or at least some rest for a future in which Virgil, nor anyone else, can ever predict.

I was not running along the beach, which is unusual. I wondered about the feeling, or the decision, when, in fact, I came across a series of flat stones that someone painted over in red, and then wrote, in black, words, I can't recall. I thought of this, then, as poetry, of the sea and

the waves. Were they my lovers? Candy's? Sure,
as much as I was performing a fiction, fictive
desire, the feeling of thinking through and liv-
ing through my body, however much it was not
mine. Did I love them? Sure. I learned, from the
Colonel, how to hold anger and sadness, not my
own. And from Big Mike, the role of fantasy in
desire, the way he imagined me in a tree with
him, where he was waiting to crossbow his prey.
From up there, the cord of the phone was thick,
and twirled around me, and the weight of the
phone, I still recall its heavy click on the two
prongs, silver, and depressed after I was done.

The mark that Stream leaves on Virgil's neck will be left at some point, left forever, and it will be held, and too, the bite on the neck will burn on the beard back there, a burning that cuts into him as reminder, held in abeyance. Butch sends flowers by pic on the phone, and the colors explode against Virgil's before then, black screen, his body like a drum skin taking a quick tap— and the site of the flowers don't match the lavender walls of The Lawyer's bedroom.

I suppose, if I think about it, I was courting these
men who needed something that only the fictional
could provide, a feeling of the deepest desire that
came from the nascent body. The other day,
TeTe, my nephew, hugged me, and asked "Do
you need my Energy?" It was, after all a concep-
tual question, but it really may have meant, do
you actually need my love? And how much so?
I loved those men, or at least, I learned to love

through Candy, and now that I have a suitable income, I can enact most desires that I want to experience; and I realize, too, what I learned to care about then what was not me, but what, in many cases, wanted me eradicated, so I hid, or I hid my sense of wanting to be eradicated, even as I wanted to get them off, or me, off—it was exciting, and new, and looking back, I realize that the mining of the self then, and now, through Candy, is a direct route through the prosaics.

For Virgil, who did not swim, who did not run, who did sleep, and who did attack, and who did look at the blue and smiled, who did look at the site of the sky, who did understand the body and its formation, who did turn on only his heel, but shifting over time between his heel and toe, dropped intention, who did write through the pain of desire, who did sleep until one of the old yellow earplugs fell to the bedroom floor, who did understand the feeling of falling, who did pull his body weight up, and push it down, and then did not rest, wants to construct something, somehow, symmetrical between these movements over time, space, and to maintain its energy.

It seemed like a week or so, before I left New York, I was interested in porn featuring black bois and white dads (later with CD's) and facsimiles of relational desires that might or might not sync up with what I wanted. Roads until a black stole something, or when "nigger" came casually out of a mouth, the source-work of contempt, or the stare of "...are you sure you're saying that... or this is confusing..."—at the bar, when the IdiotLady, in town for a conference, reading the large text book, challenged me, I thought, "silly," is what she was, as if I wasn't clear in my clear line of two direct questions:

What is the language of emotion?

What are its terms?

The IdiotLady reading the Large Font book—It looked self-published, pulp, not from any university, affiliate, or even related outfit—is after all, after The Lawyer. How quickly Virgil shut that shit down. How quickly the tempo changed, the exchange, and how quickly Virgil would return to the site of what he was, and what she would never have, what he already had, many men, and lots of time, lol.

Stream pissed in front of Old Stream's house. They are rich from heat and air, and I am damaged from war and erasure. I will move like the hummingbird to feed from the release of my past. The taste is bitter, and I will remove the poison from the tip, and I will learn from the feeding, a kind of ingestion that I think I understand to be necessary in order to unveil my feeling beyond the density and the sensation of love and the line that leads back to the longer query of where I am from. When will I heal? When will they? How might my family, and how will I help to move MommaSpine closer to the world, in which we can finally speak?

In the Napa November morning in the Harvest Inn, Butch's breath sounds like a whisper, but Virgil decides not to carry around what's tied to this sound; instead, Virgil lets the notes build, the finger deep into a pocket of the mouth, the hard turn towards the jaw, entering the throat, into the future—

> *I am in love*
> *with them*
> *or me leaving*
> *them, or him,*
> *but not,*
> *ever, you,*
> *which*
> *enables me*
> *to enact*
> *in the catch,*
> *as the form*
> *spirals.*

Chest Hair Baby has no real hold on reality. His tears came out thick, and where Virgil would've laughed at Chest Hair Baby, readying to take a guilty plea for another stolen vehicle, his "need for speed"—Virgil's taken by Chest Hair Baby's never satisfying his mother,

"...my only love."

When Chest Hair Baby confesses, "Yeah," to the crime, his mother darts out of the courtroom, Virgil looks up into the small screen, where he is both grossed out and moved by the juxtaposition: mom fuming, gone, then the black nappy chest hair on a boy of 18.

Is Chest Hair Baby a menace to society? The court must decide.

And the sweet brown girl explains how she's depressed, and a dropout, how she has to watch her brothers and sisters during her mother's swing shifts at the factory. Her mother wants her home, all the time. Forget school.

Jailed for fighting and cursing out the cops for not letting her return to the homecoming game to her two brothers—her face is round, and sad—she'll be released to the custody of her mom.

Never mind the white-runaway-girl—

Who wishes to see her father, whom she feels, "... is nice," and likes to think that one day she will meet him; and reveals, too, that her mother died when she was only one.

Does Virgil need his mother, too?

for Virgil has stolen every car.
Chest Hair Baby—his mother thinks
will be a child forever. And the streets
will not save him,
she knows. He was already stabbed
multiple times.

So, on television, the mothers cannot take care of their sons, or their daughters on *Lock Up*, near a Lake. Nor is there any other way to hold onto the quiet of the morning that Virgil stares into, with Butch in the wide white bed in the Harvest Inn.

Virgil cannot be anyone else but who he was in Cheney, an art studio, an event, in which Virgil holds onto nothing, dancing all the while, painting, and really, only stopping once at the small fiberglass needle, left behind from another interdisciplinary artist, the almost invisible stinger that found its way into Virgil's hand after his groundwork B-boy power move.

In the Studio, Virgil will find a corner, whether in or out of a bed, and in this corner, he will anguish, self-evolve, posed on the floor to look into the past, a past that contains a park at the far end of the school where Virgil walked as a little boy.

The walk did not seem far, and on the walk, there was a wide fence that separated one school field from another's playground, near where Naldo was nearly jumped, dropped his bag, and went into an open fighting stance, knees bent low:

"He knows the arts!"

Where's the multipurpose room?

It was where Virgil wanted to learn to tap-dance. It was a place Virgil and CeSis could not find, near where they opened the door to the boiler room, and asked, "Is this the multipurpose room?" The boiler room was near where Virgil rode around in a circle, pants and underwear down, exposed as a boy, with the Sacramento Union delivery bag over his boy head and shoulders, arms wanting to be taken by some man he would never meet.

The playground is within a perimeter where Virgil has not ever returned, yet it is where he remains, looking back, still, somehow longing—

At Goethe, his old Junior High, Virgil, in the 7th grade, Virgil left his own boy cock outline in a thick folded love note on the health teacher's windshield, clipped under the wiper-blade during lunch, and then went back, snatched it off the car before lunch ended.

Without opening it again, Virgil wanted to rip the love note apart, but it was too thick. And the note was crude. Virgil, now, would kill for the note. He ponders reconstructing the note, against a fast sketch of Stream's naked cell pic. The note was full of boy-heat—Virgil, in a future beyond the note and the sketch, in the studio, forms into its shape.

Stream will not ask about this movement.

Butch will not ask about this movement.

But others will, for in Virgil is a row of many selves, or a single-self anchored to such early unrequited love.

Virgil, in Sacra, looks at the rows of bushes along Florin Road, and thinks: *This is where I learned to French-kiss, there, and this is where I learned to think about what I wanted.*

Outside, the Harvest Inn pool he wants to swim in is impossibly cold, though Virgil doesn't approach it, but he knows the outside temp, too, is too cool and the morning too bare, and brown so instead, he's led back to school, recalling the Physical Science class, Virgil recalling a solid's transformation to vapor, then liquid, to be measured—

After Bunsen heat,
the brown fluid,
once wood,
courses through
tubes, dripping
into a beaker,
and to where?

What Virgil wants is to drive by the fence, again, and again, and to climb the roof of the school, above the perimeter, to scatter on the roof near a brick wall, tick, and wave, where his knees first buckled, and one collapsed, while doing the "ET."

Eee—
lectriciteee…..

The milk falls and explodes on the café concrete floor, but does not splash Virgil's "Cons." Who Virgil is, is looking for however far this accident might propel him.

It is, in fact, the fan, and not the rain. And so too, Virgil, will go back to his life. It is Butch's soft breath, the sound of it blowing back, then, and he'll call, now.

On the phone, what matters is not the floor, or the killing, or the student evaluations, or DadTheDriver's twisted intestines, or MommaSpine's seeping heart.

Virgil's body is sprinkled and shot on by an anon, who whispers—*don't bite, just pull at them, hard.*

The small soaking into the black hoodie on Virgil's run along the bay is sweat.

It lines the puffed suede headphone strap against the top of his head, the faux leather surrounding his ears softens, noise cancelling, wireless, holding Virgil further in.

With the long wooden ruler, Virgil smacks to death the brown ugly spider, the death delivered as in similar killings, but this one is energized by its form, a whoopin' that packs, immediately, the brown ugly spider's crouching body into itself. Pliable wood, bending in the air, snapping lightning-fast, the bug flattened between the painted white drawing table and the semi-translucent paper.

Virgil ponders the differences between the whoopin' and the spanking, which are vast in that while the whoopin' banks on the event of total surprise, the spanking leaves room for quiet retreat; while the latter though perhaps not completely ceremonial—some lessons might be learned—the former abandons logic, and is *all lesson*.

In *Dead Men Talking: Eternal Neighbors*, the surgical saw cutting into JawPainDeathDrop's head is amplified, a screeching pulse, her deceased body on the steel autopsy table out of view. BrunetteBoyAutopsyBoaterDoctor sawing close to the jaw hopes to reveal the point from where death arose. It's not the jaw. Instead, the head to toe search concludes that JawPainDeathDrop's end has nothing to do with her visit to the dentist four days before, but from a heart attack caused by severe coronary artery disease of which she had no idea. Revealing the "elusive answer," to the question of JawPainDeathDrop's sudden death, BrunetteBoyAutopsyBoaterDoctor presses the edge of his scalpel against the fat surrounding her dissected heart, the scalpel's tip, exposing the yellow plaque, the tiny artery's almost entirely occluded lumen.

Zeroing in on the brown ugly spider, Virgil hits the drawing table with an exact force, and in this force

Virgil attempts to figure his work, if not through the spider's immediate death, then animated in Virgil's protracted life—for who does cartwheels in a field—and films it—next to the Pilgrim Memorial monument after discussing, by cell, a group performance and show he'll join on Black Composition and Molecular Form, curated by TDSpider, but Virgil?

On the beach, when Virgil's tripod later crashed to the sand and the screen fractured, the event cracked Virgil open, who now worries that the glass shards and powdery bits could spread from the tips of his fingers to the corners of his eyes as he edits, "Mueller and the Others." For the short movie, he set a shed horse shoe crab's shell against a silver-glittery pump's heel, both atop a strip of mustard-yellow muslin, placing the iPad's camera lens in line with the shell's spiny tail and the pump's curved back. But this is before the wind blew the iPad Pro down near the same spot on the beach, where Virgil, twenty years earlier, stared into an icy, cold almost black winter bay, thinking: *What more do I need to understand about form?*

Virgil meditates on performance as he folds his clothes between glances in the Crowne Point hotel room's closet door mirror. He pops, listening by AirPods to "Electric Kingdom," then "Egyptian Lover"—in the ticking and bass, he hears the pre-figurations of Aretha's gospel beats slowed down, and Funk, too, and recalls a time before Virgil grew, and shaved his head, when Virgil would pop, his black Afro-Sheened curls eliciting joy, dimples leading to the blood-trail.

Something survives, he thinks. It emerges in the wide studio, Virgil drawing in solid graphite pencil on paper, grey flecks disintegrating into the middle scale images he constructed, before slipping out, into the rainy night for a run. At the edge of escape, all Virgil wants to do is not to let hate go, but to meditate on *why* in the path from the filmic to the drawn.

Every mistake counts, each gesture, too, of which Virgil becomes more and more aware. A spider drops down from a single web. TDSpider holds her hand out, wrist and palm in an L, to let it land there, then raises it back up to a safer height. Virgil's stilled arms, then they're slowly opening, waving into tight ticking, more folding. One could call these overlaps *ritual*, his insistent movement between memory and discipline. TheNightRootOracle helps Virgil to further understand what lessons might help in such a threshold when she asked: "What happens when too much of the process is given away—the artfulness, its spine too revealed?"

These become the movements of Virgil's body that is both seen as thief and star, threat and lover, healer and damage control. Often it's the case that the freedom that one finds is less in the construction of what's found, but in their effects. This is the self in which Virgil, character, place, being, begins to form, and is undone, all the while moving in the course of suffering and healing.

In The Condo, the floors look like real oak, but they are, in fact, luxury vinyl plank; and the sky is bright fire purple and hi-pink in the morning, and it's 60 degrees. Virgil is with Butch on the East, and Stream on the West who will soon, again, have his other ankle fixed, this time a socket replacement; and where the other did not properly fuse after the bone was shaved, such will be a gift when the new socket helps to hold up Stream's body in the San Francisco Street.

How much does one need to let go of to enact freedom? To move from color to grey scale, and still produce depth of longing and care? The pencil sharpener's solid graphite shavings are a fine powder, and other pieces, too, longer, curled and black which Virgil empties on a paper catch. Virgil rubs the graphite excess up with his forefinger, and uses it to shade in MommaSpine's hair, or to begin to capture the fluid contours of her body in motion, mid-Aerobics, in masks and full body costumes, in or out of Florin Convalescent.

TheBlackFatherWhoDrivesandCrashed is restless and curious, even when relaxing. Virgil inherits some of this, and each sunset during his residency on the Cape, asks himself in front of the receding tide, how to expand the limits between forms, the body of prose, the body dancing, nexus of reddening light and cooling blue air that fills what is being made to be recorded as much as it is rendered. However intuitive Virgil's sense, however fraught, weight builds as he pushes against this tension.

Virgil comes to realize that he hates, often at first sight, which is indeed nothing that MommaSpinethe-Aerobic or DaddyDancer taught Virgil; however, it's something Virgil lets course through his body as a learns source text, line of feeling that guides him into the path of the sentence, the mark, the image, the move. But why is Virgil so quick to smash the brown, ugly spider, yet lets the sun-orange monarch butterfly thrive in the iPhone portrait pic?

As much as Virgil is outside of the dream, he exists somewhere between sleep and morning's opening, the black bodies he sees destroying and being destroyed. Even in dreams, Virgil's endless tricky enmity—for who knows how long the fight lasted, there in the small kitchen of the dreamed restaurant? All Virgil under-stood about the fight was that it was important, for him, to write it down.

The kitchen is small and cramped, and it is a room in which all the decisions made express only violence, blacks on blacks, but here the blacks on blacks are entrepreneurs, the beatings, in this context, are as easy as the breeze blowing across the leaves in the Crowne Point's quiet, tucked in courtyard. Virgil knows that the dream is both visitation and call, out of which emerges a set of specific questions that ground his process with its intractable queries:

"What are your sources?"

"How do you read?"

When did the bat emerge? is another question that arises when Virgil thinks, *Why was the victim who came in to steal the first pieces of dark, fried chicken on the black on blacks's restaurant kitchen counter an Indian?* The Indian's being almost killed, or simply the attack, residing in Virgil's unconscious, in every sense, is Virgil's problem, which, perhaps, stems from the vector of hate that drives into his heart—but to resist hate is also something that courses equally in him, especially as he stares into the jetty, in Provincetown, MA.

Butch tells Virgil that ThePriestClone came to the US "with nothing," from Ireland, and when ThePriestClone's dark eyes dart across the room to meet Virgil's at Victor's, Virgil looks at ThePriestClone's hus-band MCTM, but the fried chicken, in the dream, was thick and crisped to almost black, and in the pan stirred itself before the Indian stole it. For this, Virgil won-ders *why was the Indian beaten so immediately, and viciously, by the blacks on blacks*?

A line of people extended out of the blacks on blacks's festive door that day, as this was, after all, the morning of the blacks on blacks's restaurant opening, and the customers grew hungrier by the second. But suddenly everyone in the kitchen—in here, somehow, who are also Virgil's friends—is on the attack, to kill the Indian stealing, and the Indian turns, as he is somehow, not brown, but black too, most of his teeth missing, and those there are broken after his being beaten, but like in the terror-point of all horror movies, the Indian, though bloody-faced, does not die.

Fire alarms go off and sprinklers soak the entire restaurant, because, as the Indian's being hit in the mouth by the bat, he pulls the fire alarm and, by extension, somehow also tugs out the eyes of those blacks on blacks who try to kill him, and the blacks on blacks's tugged-out eyes, simultaneously set off the sprinklers, water spraying everywhere, the confusion enough to wake Virgil into his writing.

As much as he is led by the chaos, Virgil is also led to the death of F_GutL on *Dead Men Talking: Eternal Neighbors*, where after a risky hernia operation, she came home from her elected surgery only to lose control of her bowels. The day she died, her now ghost white husband held up her 300-lb body, before she squatted, then fell to the floor shaking her head "no...to her last breath" after he begged, *"Can you make it baby?"*

In a teaser before F_GutL's autopsy, BrownHaired-SemiCurlyBoborFlybacks BrunetteBoyAutopsyBoater-Doctor'sAssistant says, "I mean, obviously, it doesn't smell like roses in there..." Later, her masked face and camera is trained over F_GutL's body, snapping evidence from atop a platform—"Yeah that's pus, smells like pus, or poop, I don't know which..." The episode's final medical mystery is solved at BrunetteBoyAutopsy-BoaterDoctor's first incision: perforated abdomen, Septic Shock—"We're back at the heart,"—blood poisoned by her own waste.

At what point was the blacks on blacks's fried chicken stolen? Was it when the wooden bat hits the Indian's head, his face turning to reveal his decimated mouth? Virgil realizes, at this moment, the automatic hot water machine's spout is too complicated for him to figure out. The chef at Crowne Point, SweetShamarCookWhoLooksLikeaBoy, makes certain Virgil has boiled water for his tea, poured into his cup from a hot steel pot, all while Virgil's in a state between waking, and writing. Dead bodies congeal in Virgil's memory.

But in the dream, those beating and being beaten, pulling Virgil from sleep into the day, are irrepressibly present and alive. They reveal their desire to be rendered as they breach SweetShamarCookWhoLooksLikeaBoy's mouth, where many of his teeth are gone—however absent, they are reparative as the work bench's saw, its muffled buzzing in the basement down the stairs just off the porch outside of Virgil and Butch's room. Virgil listens to that sound too, then the stone fountain's rush, its white water spouting out, its whipping, flicking fall.

ACKNOWLEDGEMENTS

I am grateful for the following publications for sharing earlier versions of these stories, in which they first appeared, as follows:

"Station," "Crypt," "Coast," "Fantastic," and "Dream," *Manifold: Experimental Criticism*, Volume 1, January 2021.

"Dream Collaged with Reality," and "Dream Vision in Blue and Black," (text and synthesized audio excerpts), *Journal of Black Mountain College Studies*, Volume 11: The Practice and Pedagogy of Writing at Black Mountain College, Fall 2020.

"The Fairmount," *Furious Flower: Seeding the Future of African American Poetry.* (Chicago: Northwestern University Press, 2019).

"Structure," *Oversound,* Issue 5, 2019.

"Consequence," and "Only," *Gulf Coast*, 2019.

"Staring," "The Oasis," and "Virgil," *Bæst: A Journal of Queer Forms & Affects*, October 18, 2018.

"Eyed, Virgil," *Interim*, Volume 35, Issue 3, July 22, 2018.

"Dream Vision in Blue and Black," *Nepantla: An Anthology Dedicated to Queer Writers of Color*, ed. Christopher Soto. (Nightboat Books, 2018).

"Virgil Returns to Manhattan," "The Dance," "The Vent," The Conservation of Mass," "Party, Party," "The Wounded," "Virgil Kills," "The Operation," "The After

Party," "Dream Vision in Blue and Black," and "Silent Incantations," *Virgil Kills: Stories from the Conservation of Mass,* Chapbook: EP 101 (Essay Press, 2018).

"Pod," and "Competition," *BOMB Magazine*, Issue 144/ Summer 2018.

"Basement," *FENCE Magazine*, Spring 2018.

"Lost and Found," *Cusp2*, ed. Jared Levine, (City Lights Books, 2017).

"Party Party," "The Wounded," and "Virgil Kills," *Evening Will Come*, *The Volta*, Heir Apparent Issue 45, April 2017.

"The Operation," and "Silent Incantations," *The Elephants,* July 9, 2017.

"Virgil's Findings," "The Pieces," and "Virgil Discovers Waste," *Elderly,* Issue 23, August/September 2017.

"Virgil is a Conceptual Artist," "Into the Future," and "The Greatest," *Paperbag Magazine,* Issue 10, 2017.

"Virgil Returns to Manhattan," "The Dance," "The Vent," and "The Conservation of Mass," *Mission at Tenth Journal,* Volume 6, Spring 2016.

"The After Party," *Evening Will Come, The Volta*, NSFW Issue 45, ed. Lara Glenum, September 2014.

I would like to thank the following institutions for allowing me to share these stories in readings, performances, and conversations, including universities: Amherst College, California Institute of the Arts, California Institute of Integral Studies, CUNY Graduate Center, Harvard University, Jack Kerouac School of Disembodied Poetics at Naropa University, Mount Holyoke College, San Francisco State University, Stetson University, University of California Berkeley, University of California Santa Cruz, University of Houston, University of Pittsburgh, and Reed College; professional conferences: Associated Writers & Writing Programs in Portland, San Antonio, Tampa, Washington DC, and AWP Virtual, 2021; &Now Festival of Innovative Writing at California Institute of the Arts, and University of Notre Dame; Thinking Its Presence: The Racial Imaginary at University of Montana; and galleries, readings and theater venues: Casa Victoria Ocampo, Buenos Aires; de Young Museum, San Francisco; Moe's Books, Berkeley; Mole End, New York; Poetics Research Bureau, Los Angeles; Portland Institute for Contemporary Art, Portland; Rio Theater, Santa Cruz; Segue Reading Series, New York; Southern Exposure Gallery, San Francisco; The Brooklyn Rail Radical Poetry Reading Series, Virtual; Tube Factory Artspace, Indianapolis; Woodberry Poetry Room, Cambridge; and CCA Wattis Institute for Contemporary Arts, San Francisco.

Residencies and grant support from Center for Art and Thought, Fine Arts Work Center in Provincetown, Headlands Center for the Arts, MacDowell, Millay Colony for the Arts, and University of California Santa Cruz were critical in providing precious meditative time and space in which to imagine and develop these stories. And as crucial, many friends and colleagues helped me to envision and realize this book through readerly insight, support and conversation:

Nigel Alderman, Meena Alexander, Kazim Ali, Lauren K. Alleyne, Alexis Almeida, Sam Amadon, Randall Babtkis, Samiya Bashir, Jan Christian Bernabe, Bob Boemer, Andrew Bourne, Tisa Bryant, Carolyn Cooke, Jenny Cookson, Vilashini Cooppan, Liz Countryman, Caroline Crumpacker, Iyko Day, Ben and Sandra Doller, Angel Dominguez, r. erica doyle, Torkwase Dyson, Andy Fitch, Devereaux Fortuna, Tonya M. Foster, Thomas E. Frank, Joanne V. Gabbin, Renee Gladman, Lara Glenum, Emma Gomis, Jennifer A. González, Johannes Göransson, Duriel E. Harris, Erica Hunt, Bhanu Kapil, Douglas Kearney, Claudia Keelan, Ruth Ellen Kocher, Jared Levine, R. Zamora Linmark, cyriaco lopes, Anthony MacLaurin, Dawn Lundy Martin, Joyelle McSweeney, Paul Moreau, Fred Moten, Petro Moysaenko, Laura Mullen, Rachel Nelson, Urayoán Noel, Akilah Oliver, Soham Patel, Micah Perks, Jeffrey Pethybridge, M. NourbeSe Philip, Khary O. Polk, Carl Pope, Claudia Rankine, Frances Richard, Noah Ross, Broc Rossell, Sarita Echavez See, Anne Lesley Selcer, Danzy Senna, Christopher Soto, Samson Stilwell, Jennifer Tamayo, Roberto Tejada, Jamie Townsend, Anne Waldman, Joshua Marie Wilkinson, Terri Witek, Rebecca Wolff, Karen Tei Yamashita, and Wesley Yu.

Forever gratitude to Nightboat Books: to the amazing Stephen Motika for believing in this book, as well as Nightboat's keen and generous editors, designers, and publicity team: Lina Bergamini, Lindsey Boldt, Jaye

Elizabeth Elijah, Gia Gonzales, Rissa Hochberger, and Caelan Nardone, all for providing such insight, expertise and guidance.

Finally, I would like to thank my husband Dallas W. Bauman III., my parents Carmelina C. Wilson and Donald L. Wilson; my sister Ceonita C. Wilson Dockery, and brother Donaldo T. Wilson, each gifted human beings, helping me to embrace the importance of stories as they compel and guide across time, space, and love, precious material, life.

RONALDO V. WILSON, PhD, is the author of: *Virgil Kills: Stories* (Nightboat Books), and *Narrative of the Life of the Brown Boy and the White Man* (2008), winner of the Cave Canem Prize; *Poems of the Black Object* (2009), winner of the Thom Gunn Award for Gay Poetry and the Asian American Literary Award in Poetry. His latest books are *Farther Traveler: Poetry, Prose, Other* (2014), finalist for a Thom Gunn Award for Gay Poetry, *Lucy 72* (2018); and *Carmelina: Figures* (2021). Co-founder of the Black Took Collective, Wilson is also an interdisciplinary artist. He has presented his work in multiple venues, including the Atlantic Center for the Arts, The Center for African American Poetry and Poetics, The Emily Harvey Foundation, Georgetown's Lannan Center, Louisiana State University's Digital Media Center Theater, Pulitzer Arts Foundation, The Studio Museum in Harlem, and UC Riverside's Artsblock. The recipient of fellowships from the Anderson Center for the Arts, Cave Canem, the Djerassi Resident Artists Program, the Ford Foundation, Headlands Center for the Arts, Kundiman, the National Research Council, The Robert Rauschenberg Foundation, and Yaddo, Wilson is Professor of Creative Writing and Literature at the University of California, Santa Cruz, serving on the core faculty of the Creative Critical PhD Program; principal faculty member of CRES (Critical Race and Ethnic Studies); and affiliate faculty member of DANM (Digital Arts and New Media).

NIGHTBOAT BOOKS

Nightboat Books, a nonprofit organization, seeks to develop audiences for writers whose work resists convention and transcends boundaries. We publish books rich with poignancy, intelligence, and risk. Please visit nightboat.org to learn about our titles and how you can support our future publications.

The following individuals have supported the publication of this book. We thank them for their generosity and commitment to the mission of Nightboat Books:

Kazim Ali
Anonymous (4)
Abraham Avnisan
Jean C. Ballantyne
The Robert C. Brooks Revocable Trust
Amanda Greenberger
Rachel Lithgow
Anne Marie Macari
Elizabeth Madans
Elizabeth Motika
Thomas Shardlow
Benjamin Taylor
Jerrie Whitfield & Richard Motika

Please change to: This book is made possible, in part, by grants from the New York City Department of Cultural Affairs in partnership with the City Council, the New York State Council on the Arts Literature Program, and the Topanga Fund, which is dedicated to promoting the arts and literature of California.